Nigel Power was born a year before the outbreak of WW2, within 20 miles of central London. He studied mathematics and music at university before following a career in education based in the West Midlands. Retiring in 2005, he relocated to a village in Dorset, where he continues to play the organ in the village church. In March 2020, his wife, for whom he had been her full-time carer for nearly ten years, was admitted to a care home. When the national Covid lockdown began eight days later, Nigel began writing short stories. This book contains the second collection of his stories to be published.

I dedicate this book to my son and daughter, their spouses and children. Also, to good friends in the village of Winterborne St Martin who have supported me in the last three years of living alone and encouraged me to continue writing.

Nigel Power

SURVIVORS OF WAR

...And Other Stories

AUSTIN MACAULEY PUBLISHERS™

LONDON * CAMBRIDGE * NEW YORK * SHARJAH

A CIP catalogue record for this title is available from the British Library.

ISBN 9781035836000 (Paperback)
ISBN 9781035836024 (ePub e-book)
ISBN 9781035836017 (Audiobook)

www.austinmacauley.co.uk

First Published 2024
Austin Macauley Publishers Ltd®
1 Canada Square
Canary Wharf
London
E14 5AA

I am indebted to John Nichol, author of '*Spitfire*', from whom I learned much about the development and performance of the WW2 fighter plane.

I wish also to record my own appreciation of the song 'Silent Noon' with words by Dante Gabriel Rossetti and music by Ralph Vaughan Williams, part of which I have quoted in the text. Unlike Hugh, I never had the opportunity of singing it to a beautiful girl, as she lay with her hand open in the 'long fresh grass'.

Table of Content

Survivors of War
Chapter 1

1 May 1931

For Richard Bailey, 1 May 1931 was a day that had a formative influence on his future life. He didn't know at the time how his life's journey would be moulded by what happened in the evening of that day. His father, Dr George Bailey, the village doctor, and friend of the local vicar, had suggested that he might like to become a choirboy in the village church choir. Richard was a month short of his eighth birthday. He had always enjoyed singing with his mother at home and at school where they sang at some point on most days. There were just 22 in his class in the village school, of which, exceptionally, 16 were boys. He could read quite well and, for more than a year, had been learning to play the piano with instruction from his father, who also sang in the choir. Dr Bailey considered that his son displayed both interest and ability in music.

The village where the Baileys lived, on the outskirts of Southampton, was quite large. In addition to a pub, known as The Farmers' Arms, there were several shops, including grocers, greengrocers, a co-op butcher, a bakery, a chemist with a post office counter at the rear, ironmonger and a shop, in the front room of one of the houses, that sold wool and haberdashery items. It would be at least two decades before a small supermarket was opened at the end of the village. There was a primary school for children aged four to eleven after which pupils transferred either to the elementary school in the village where they stayed until they were 14, or, if they passed the entrance exam, to one of the grammar schools in the city.

Although less than ten miles from the centre of Southampton, the village enjoyed a rural position with good access to the countryside and several well-husbanded farms within easy reach of the village centre. There was good grazing land and the climate encouraged the growing of soft fruit. The rural economy also benefited from a popular riding stables that attracted visitors who could hire mounts and ride along several bridle-ways in the surrounding area. From two of the hills near the village, one of which sported a stand of conifers, it was possible to look across to the Isle of Wight.

Dr Bailey's surgery was attached to his house, a large imposing residence on Church Street, at the opposite end of the road to the church of St Mary. At the rear of the house was a self-contained two bedroomed annex, which may have originally been accommodation for servants. In addition to most of the population of the village, Dr Bailey's practice extended to several families who lived in adjacent hamlets and farm cottages. He had qualified as a doctor just in time to serve during the last two years of the Great War in field hospitals in France. After the end of the war, he had married Grace, but their wedding had been delayed by the Spanish Flu epidemic. George had been kept so busy caring for those taken ill that he hardly had time to sleep and had no time to prepare for a wedding.

Now 42, George was six feet tall and slim, with searching blue eyes always ready to twinkle when he smiled. His reddish-brown hair inherited from his mother was now turning grey and receding in places. As a teenager, he discovered that girls found him attractive and he never lacked female companions for any local event or dance. When opportunity allowed, he enjoyed a game of tennis and he otherwise kept himself fit by gardening, maintaining a productive vegetable patch and attending passionately to his roses and chrysanthemums. Of the latter, he always tried to provide a fine display to decorate the church at Harvest Festival. His other form of relaxation was playing the piano and encouraging both his sons to develop a skill on the instrument.

George and Grace had two sons: Richard born in June 1923 and Stephen born in August 1925. Having arrived in the village in 1924, when the previous village doctor had retired after 40 years in the post, George was regarded as having much more relevant knowledge for post-Great War living and was now accepted as one of the key members of the community. His patients appreciated the time he allowed them in consultations and the way he gave considered thought to their ailments rather than make snap decisions about the most appropriate way to treat them. They liked his sympathetic manner, particularly when he needed to visit them in their homes. When villagers talked about their doctor, they agreed that he was a very caring man. They felt that his fee structure was fair and they knew that he would never refuse to treat a sick person if they were unable to pay.

Grace, three years younger than her husband, was a five foot six, neat brunette with hazel-coloured eyes who had maintained her youthful body shape. With her cultured voice, energy and organisational abilities, she retained the manner reminiscent of her imperious Victorian grandmother who had been the Lady of the Manor of a large Hampshire estate.

The parish church was built of Portland Stone in the reign of William IV, when the village was much smaller and, as the village had grown around it, was in a good central position. The congregation appreciated that all the pews were 'free' and they could sit anywhere that suited them. The box pews seen in older churches had not been included in the original specifications. The ceiling was quite lofty with beautiful timbers and the windows were large enough to admit sufficient light to make the interior feel spacious. The east window above the altar had stained glass that depicted the four evangelists either side of Mary, the mother of Jesus. Unlike many churches built around the same time, there was no gallery at the west end, for an organ had been installed in the chancel behind the choir stalls when the church was built. The pulpit and lectern were beautifully assembled and carved in stone and timber. The font was medieval and had come from another church. That church in Dorset had fallen into ruin when the village was abandoned during the fourteenth century as the plague spread from Weymouth where, it was thought, it had entered the country by ship. Much of the stone from the church had been robbed for use in other buildings many years later and the font had been discovered upturned under a hedge when a new gateway into a field was constructed in about 1800.

The vicar, Revd Peter Adams spent his early years in Great Shelford near Cambridge. His singing voice was recognised early and after a recommendation by a local clergyman he was admitted to the choir of King's College, Cambridge. Later, as a theology student, he continued to sing in the choir, before training for holy orders and subsequently being ordained in the Church of England. He came to the village in 1929, with his wife Mary and one-year-old daughter Angela, after serving for three years as a curate in a town church in Portsmouth. His duties as curate included chaplaincy work in the naval base for which he was well suited having spent five years in the Navy before ordination. He worked industriously in the village and was well liked by his parishioners who recognised that he brought about change with tact, subtlety and diplomacy. Standing nearly six foot tall with a back as straight as a ramrod and wavy brown hair, his most remarkable feature was his beautiful speaking voice, a rich baritone that compelled attention from his listeners. Even those of his congregation who did not understand every word of his sermons enjoyed listening to his voice, especially when he sang the versicles and collects at Matins and Evensong. There had been friction between his predecessor and the church choir, but because he was both musical and had a wide knowledge and experience of church music he had been able to establish a choir which was much admired for the way it led worship. In this respect, he was much assisted by the talented Doctor Helen James, who played the organ and trained the choir. She had relinquished her post at The Royal Academy of Music in London to live in the village so that she could look after her ageing and infirm mother. She also taught piano to an increasing number of young pupils.

Soon after Peter Adams took up the post of navy chaplain, he came into contact with the daughter of one of the senior naval officers. Although there was guidance on how the offspring of officers were expected to behave, Mary was something of a rebel and was happy to fraternise with lower ranks. Peter discovered that Mary was very happy to assist him in his work with young ratings who were sometimes disorientated, confused or homesick. Her cheeky smile, dimpled cheeks, often unruly fair hair provided sailors and shore staff with the confidence to share their concerns. It was not long before Peter was also captivated by her charm. It was completely in character that when Mary Adams became the wife of the vicar, she worked tirelessly in supporting her husband in his ministry. Even though she had a young daughter, she nevertheless found time to tend the vicarage garden with some local help when it came to the time to host the Summer Church Fayre. The church was blessed with a very active Mothers' Union, which Mary supported in the background, being happy to leave the leadership to one of the experienced ladies who had led it successfully for a decade. In 1933, the church would celebrate its centenary and Mary had already established planning groups, with the encouragement of the Parochial Church Council, in readiness for the events to mark the celebration.

The choir practice at St Mary's Church began for the boys of the all-male choir at 7.00 p.m. and they were joined by the men three quarters of an hour later. At 6.30, Dr Bailey took Richard to meet Helen James for a voice test. She invited Richard to sing, for her, a hymn of his choice and, although it was three weeks since Easter, he chose the Easter Hymn 'Jesus Christ is risen today'. Dr James soon realised that he loved singing the Alleluias, which he mastered without difficulty. After she had checked his ability to pitch notes accurately, she talked to him about his piano playing and his ability to read music. He was very happy to tell her what piano pieces he was learning and she noted his enthusiasm for music. She had no hesitation in inviting him to join the choir as a probationer. This was the start of his career in church music: beginning, as a probationer, by standing next to one of the senior boys, he soon progressed and by the age of 11, he was often invited to sing solos. He loved the music at Matins and Evensong and particularly the anthems which the choir of about 16 boy trebles and the seven men performed in most services. Two years after Richard's introduction to the choir, his brother Stephen joined.

6 September 1934

An auspicious day for Richard Bailey was his first day at the boys' grammar school in Southampton where he would be educated until he completed his Higher School Certificate in June 1941. He travelled to school on the green and yellow Southdown double-decker bus that ran through his village: it was a twenty-five-minute journey and he was a member of the group of boys travelling to the same school. There were two other boys in his year and a few senior boys, who travelled on the same bus. Also on the bus were girls who attended the neighbouring girls' grammar school. There was a degree of discussion and banter between the older boys and girls, but Richard, as a first year student, paid no attention to the female passengers on the top deck. His discussions with other boys in his year included school-related matters such as knowing which teachers to steer clear of, which ones taught good lessons and school sports. He enjoyed his years at the school where he did particularly well in science, mathematics and history. He participated fully in football and cricket, getting into the house teams for both sports. He also sang in the school choir: when his voice broke he first sang alto before progressing, when his voice settled, to join the tenor section. He continued to sing in the church choir and at the prompting and instruction of the organist, Helen James, he joined two other older boys who had already started playing the organ for the Sunday afternoon Sunday School.

One of Richard's hobbies was model making, particularly aeroplanes. The interest in aviation was prompted by the activities of the Vickers Supermarine factory within five miles of his home. Test flights over his village were a fairly frequent occurrence. He was pleased with the models he had made of a Gloster Gladiator and a Supermarine Nighthawk, although the latter had never been very successful in flight, being slow and cumbersome. His father was also impressed with the models and suggested he show them to one of the choirmen who was employed as a foreman at the Supermarine factory. So, one Sunday evening in May 1936, Richard took his very carefully boxed models to Evensong and put them beside his mother in her pew with strict instructions to make sure that no harm came to them. After the service Jack Forbes, who sang bass alongside Dr Bailey, was invited to examine the models. He examined them minutely asking questions about various features and pronounced them very faithful and beautifully executed. He then asked Richard more questions and discovered that this 13-year-old had seen a plane a couple of months earlier that he did not recognise. He had noticed the unusual shape of the wings. Jack Forbes, himself a very knowledgeable aircraft enthusiast, realised that Richard had obviously spotted the first flight of a prototype fighter about which the bosses at Supermarine were very excited. He had also spotted the K5054 identification number on the tailplane. Before they went home that evening, Mr Forbes asked Richard if he would like to visit the factory to see this new plane. When Richard responded that he couldn't think of anything better than being able to see planes in construction, Mr Forbes said he would try to arrange a visit for him. Mr Forbes was as good as his word and a date was fixed for about six weeks later.

A few days before the scheduled visit, Richard heard his father and the vicar talking in rather sombre tones about Germany becoming aggressive and the possibility of another war. Both having military experience, they wondered whether they would be expected or required to offer their services. This conversation was occasioned by the fact that Dr Bailey had recently taken on an assistant, Dr Josef Wronski, who with his wife Golda and two young children had emigrated, or more truthfully fled, from Czechoslovakia. Dr Wronski's English was not perfect, but he was a very knowledgeable doctor. Several times, Richard heard his mother explaining and instructing both Josef and Golda in aspects of the English language and gently correcting pronunciation. The children had also learned some basic words and would make good progress when they joined the local school. The Baileys had offered the Wronskis the use of the self-contained flat at the rear of their own house until they were in a position to buy or rent a place of their own.

Chapter 2

13 June 1936

When Richard was taken to the factory, he discovered that the new plane had been named 'Spitfire' and the factory had just received an order from the government to make 310 of them. The tour of the factory enabled Richard to see the ways the different components of an aeroplane were assembled and then combined. Looking at the assembly line, he could see planes in different stages of construction. In another part of the complex of buildings, Richard spotted some wall displays with photographs of some of the models that Supermarine had designed and built. There were also plans and sectional drawings of some of the planes, including the Nighthawk. He spent several minutes studying the diagrams, mentally comparing them with the way he had constructed his own model.

At one point while walking around the factory, Mr Forbes and Richard came upon three men standing beside the new plane, the Spitfire, and pointing to some of its features. One of them turned, saw Mr Forbes and Richard and came over to them. Speaking first to Mr Forbes and pointing to the Spitfire he said, "Good afternoon, Jack. I think we could have the makings of something special here, it could be in a class of its own. It needs a few more tweaks and some minor modifications, but it's definitely exciting. Now is this the young man who built those models you were telling me about?"

"Yes, sir. This is Richard Bailey; he has a rare skill and is very observant about detail."

Turning to Richard, he continued, "Are you enjoying your tour of the factory?"

"Yes, sir, very much. I think it's fascinating to see how the parts are brought together and assembled to make something that can fly. I think the new plane looks beautiful with its sleek lines."

"Did you learn anything about design when you made your models?"

"Oh yes, I think I know why the Nighthawk didn't perform very well in the air. I think the triple wing would have caused too much wind resistance and it lacked streamlining to help it cut through the air."

"It's a pity you weren't around when the plane was designed, but we have learned a lot about flight since those days as Mr Mitchell would tell you. It was Mr Mitchell who was mainly responsible for the design of the Spitfire. He could also tell you how he discovered the elliptical wings."

"Yes, I noticed those wings when I saw it flying and wondered what difference it made to the flight."

"How old are you, lad? Still at school?"

"Fourteen, sir, I'm at Grammar School."

"I suppose you are actually old enough to leave school." Turning back to Mr Forbes he said, "You know, we shall need to recruit people to build these planes if we are to fulfil this new order. There could be jobs here for people like Richard. I don't expect his parents would allow him to leave school yet."

"I'm pretty sure they wouldn't. He should be aiming at university."

This was when Richard had an idea and spoke up, "If you need extra workers, I could maybe help out in the school holidays and on Saturdays."

"Now that might be a possibility. We'll think about it. If we want to pursue the idea, I'll ask Mr Forbes to have a chat with your parents."

As they continued their tour of the factory, Mr Forbes told Richard that the man who had spoken to them was one of the test pilots and he had flown K5054. It was his experience of flying the Spitfire, especially its speed and the way it responded, that made him so excited.

When he got home, Richard's parents didn't need to ask him if had had a good time for they could see the excitement still in his eyes. However, when he told them the factory might need to recruit people to build the new planes and that he might be able to work there during school holidays, they said that they felt he was still too young, but they might consider letting him go in a year's time if there was still an opportunity and he didn't let it interfere with his school work.

By the time he reached his fifteenth birthday, Richard's voice had deepened, he could no longer sing treble and had joined the two male altos in the church choir. He was now nearly as tall as his father and his mother sometimes complained humorously that he was blocking her light. He had also inherited his father's clear blue eyes, but not the red tinge in his hair. However, he had not escaped the teenager's tendency to acne, but he had been assured that his skin would eventually be clear of spots. When an appropriate opportunity arose after Evensong one Sunday, he informed Jack Forbes that he was now 15 and the school summer holidays were only a few weeks away. Jack perceived the request behind Richard's words, and while giving nothing away at the time, he went away, made some enquiries at work and at the next choir practice asked Richard if he would like to come to the factory to meet the Personnel Manager the following Saturday. The outcome of the meeting was employment during the school holidays and Saturdays as a temporary trainee mechanical engineer. Richard's dreams of getting experience of hands-on aircraft production were about to be realised. The end of term could not come quickly enough. His parents knew that there was no point in trying to persuade him to focus his attention on other matters and accepted that mixing in a 'working man's world' could be valuable experience for him. They considered that he would learn the importance of taking responsibility for his actions. They did try one test on him, pointing out that if he worked at Supermarine on Saturdays in the cricket season he would not be able to play with the village team. His reply demonstrated his commitment. He said that it would be a pity not to play with the team, but if a war with Germany came, England would need as many Spitfires as the factory could make.

3 September 1939

The first day of the Second World War was followed three days later by Richard's first day in the sixth form and the start of his study for Higher School Certificate (HSC). He had worked throughout the school holiday at the Supermarine factory until the day the school term started. After more than two years working on Saturdays and school holidays, he had gained experience on virtually every component that made up a Spitfire. In fact, he quite often found himself instructing new employees and explaining features to pilots and aviation ministry boffins when they visited. If the war looked likely to last for more than two years, he could be called up shortly after completing his HSC and even if he qualified for university he didn't know whether he would have to wait until the war was over before he could start his course.

Meanwhile, he needed to concentrate as best he could on his school studies. In addition to studying mathematics, physics and chemistry, he kept his interest in music alive. He was fortunate in finding three other boys in his year who were as keen as he was in singing early English church music and madrigals. They spent many happy lunch hours in one of the music rooms practising anthems and madrigals by composers such as Byrd, Gibbons, Tomkins, Weelkes and Wilby that Charlie, one of the boys, researched. They also tried pieces by Palestrina and Orlande de Lassus. Occasionally, they would meet in the evenings at Charlie's home. While Charlie would sing either tenor or bass, depending on how many parts there were in the piece, Joe would sing bass and Brian was a very competent alto: Richard provided the tenor line. When they met at Charlie's house, his twin sister Pat sang soprano with them. He discovered that the intricacies of some of the pieces, both in notes and timing, quickly improved his sight singing.

Richard was still singing with the church choir, although the number of men in the choir had reduced as three had departed to join up, two in the Navy and one in the RAF. However, the arrival of a new curate, Simon Lane, who could also sing tenor, provided vocal support for Richard and pastoral support for the vicar in an expanding village. In the previous year, when the Bishop of Winchester visited the parish, both Richard and Stephen had been confirmed along with ten others.

At the end of September, Grace Bailey answered a knock on the front door to find a lady who said she was a billeting officer seeking accommodation for possible evacuees. Grace explained that the flat at the rear was already occupied by the family of her husband's assistant in his medical practice. They had one guest room but that would not be suitable for a family. The officer informed her that they were only identifying possible locations at present, but there may be a need in the future to find temporary homes for single children or perhaps two siblings. Grace agreed that her room might be suitable if needed.

The first few months of the war turned out to be a quiet calm before the storm that engulfed the Bailey and Adams families and brought them closer together.

Early December 1939

After three months of war, the country's fighting forces had accumulated several casualties, both fatalities and injuries. Just over two weeks before Christmas, Dr Bailey received an official communication asking him if he would like to resume the role he had performed so well towards the end of the last war. He suggested that he may not have the skills to deal with the sort of combat injuries that the style of warfare now being waged might produce. He was assured that his previous experience meant that he was better equipped than doctors and surgeons that had not met battle injuries before. The ministry men had clearly done their homework because they knew that he now had a competent assistant who could carry on his practice in his absence.

George and Grace discussed the 'invitation' and came to the conclusion that it was the sort of invitation that could only be turned down on grounds of physical or mental disability of either of them. Before replying, they consulted their sons and informed Peter Adams. Peter visited the family and prayed with them all that their faith would carry them through the period of separation that would follow. Richard and Stephen assured their father that they would look after their mother while he was away from home. Therefore, on the second day of 1940, Dr George Bailey joined the staff of a hospital that had been established in a stately home in the Surrey countryside. He would be dealing with a wide range of injuries and illnesses, including bullet wounds, broken limbs, gangrene and a host of other conditions. He became doctor, surgeon, physiotherapist and counsellor to those suffering mental anguish.

Chapter 3

May 1940

By the beginning of May, the effects of the German harassment of British shipping were having an impact on the morale of some of the naval recruits. It was then that Revd Adams was informed of the need for a chaplain in the Portsmouth dockyard. As his parish was not a million miles from Portsmouth, he was asked if he could combine the roles of parish priest and naval chaplain, especially as he had a curate to share parish duties. He discussed this request firstly with his wife, then talked to his churchwardens and his curate. He had to consider whether the services and pastoral care could be maintained when he was absent. While both churchwardens had served in the First World War, they were now too advanced in years to be called up this time, although the younger subsequently joined the Home Guard as it became known. Simon Lane, the curate, however, was young enough to be drafted into service, but his poor eyesight and one leg an inch shorter than the other as a result of a childhood illness, determined that he was considered unfit for service. In spite of his disabilities, his features in earlier centuries would have been described as comely. He was not short of female admirers and if a task needed volunteers, he never had difficulty in finding them. He was full of energy, was frequently seen cycling around the parish and his pastoral visiting was kind and supportive. Bereaved families said that they felt comforted after his visits. He was particularly assiduous in visiting the families of war casualties, whether they were church members or not.

When Peter was assured that the parish could call on sufficient resources, particularly with the occasional help of two retired clergy living in the parish, he requested an interview with his Bishop. With his Bishop's agreement and blessing, he began the combined role just in time to provide support to those who worked so hard to bring back members of the British Expeditionary Force from the beaches of Dunkirk at the end of May.

His support and counselling were called upon to help ships' personnel who had witnessed harrowing scenes. They had seen ships sunk with the members of the crew and members of the BEF who had just escaped from the beaches drowned or maimed. They had also taken on board soldiers with injuries and they had witnessed German Stuka dive bombers strafing the beach where men were waiting to board ships of all sizes. Many of those who came to him for support were only 18, or in some cases younger, and this had been the first exercise on which they had been engaged.

As Peter established himself in his new role, he found that he could manage about one week in four to return home to keep in touch with parish matters and to spend some time with his wife and daughter.

September 1940

On 7 September 1940, the German Luftwaffe began its blitz bombing on London. On Tuesday and Thursday 24 and 26 September, attention was turned on Southampton and the Supermarine factory was badly damaged. However, production of the Spitfire was able to continue. Spitfires along with Hurricanes, hassled the German bombers in their nightly flights of destruction bringing down or damaging many of them. The German bomber pilots feared the presence of the British fighter planes for their speed and manoeuvrability made them formidable foes.

With their husbands away, Grace Bailey and Mary Adams sought to support each other and gave much of their time to helping around the village and encouraging other wives and mothers whose husbands and sons had been called up. Many of those who had been conscripted to join one of the forces were either at sea or fighting overseas. On Monday, 4 November, George Bailey was granted a 48-hour pass to visit his family when there was much news to exchange. He was sorry that he could not meet up with his friend Peter Adams as Peter, three days earlier as naval chaplain, had joined the crew of a destroyer on convoy protection duty for two weeks.

George and Grace were pleased to have some time together and George was particularly keen to have information about activities at home after several months focussing on injured and sick service personnel, too many of whom were so badly maimed that he was unable to save them. He asked how Dr Josef Wronski was coping with the practice and was pleased to hear that his English speaking skill had much improved and there were times when Grace was conversing with him that she forgot he wasn't speaking in his native language.

George asked, "How about the boys? Are they progressing with their studies?"

"They both seem to be applying themselves to their studies," replied Grace. "Richard has been getting some good grades in his HSC subjects and has mock exams immediately after Christmas. He still finds time to sing with his small group of madrigal singers and also spends his Saturdays helping with Spitfire production."

"So, his enthusiasm for aircraft remains as strong as ever. Does he talk about learning to fly or does his interest lean towards the maintenance and improvement of the plane?"

"I think that is right. He comes home saying that he has been discussing some possible modification with some of the design team and it seems they listen to him. He sometimes has an opportunity to talk to one of the pilots who has been on operations as most of them are not much older than him. He thinks that the designers listen to him because he provides feedback from the lads that fly the aircraft. He was very excited one day when one of the visitors was a composer who was in the process of writing the music for a film. Apparently, he spent several minutes asking Richard about the Spitfire and what he knew of Mr Mitchell, who designed the plane. Richard said they talked about the instruments that the composer might feature for different aspects of the film music. The composer's name was William Walton."

[I must interpose here to say the film Sir William was working on was 'The first of the few' and the music was first performed in a concert version with full orchestra as 'The Spitfire Prelude and Fugue' in Liverpool on 2 January 1943]

"What about girls?" George inquired. "Does he have a girlfriend; I think I must have been on about my third when I was his age?"

"Only three by then?" laughed his wife, "I seem to remember that you were a modern-day Don Juan. George either isn't interested in the fairer sex, or more likely, he is too wrapped up in his own pursuits. The only girl I have heard him talk about is his friend Charlie's sister, but I think he only notices her singing voice. I doubt if he could describe her or even knows how to."

"Amazing that," said George, "when you consider that composers often give the most seductive melodies to tenors which Richard as a tenor could sing, but he would need some knowledge of girls to do the music justice. What about Stephen?"

"Oh, he notices the girls, alright. I think he must have inherited your genes in that department," teased Grace. "I think, or rather I hope, that most of his conversations with girls are about his schoolwork and although they don't attend the same school, they seem to be following some of the same syllabuses. I guess that a fair amount of comparing their studies happens on the bus on the way to school. I'm glad he is applying himself as he is due to sit his School Certificate examinations next June."

"Thank you for that update," said George, "I think it must be time for supper drinks. I'll go and make them." When he came back with the drinks, he said with a grin, "You must realise, my dear, that me having several girlfriends is only the same as when you visit a shop to buy a new dress. You try several before you are satisfied that you have found the best."

"So, you are comparing courting me to buying a dress," she teased in return.

"Oh no, I was talking about selecting the best, which is what I achieved. Shall we go up?"

Chapter 4

Wednesday, 6 November 1940

Early on Wednesday, Mary Adams phoned to invite Grace to join her as she planned to go into Southampton's Civic Centre to find out more about voluntary support for the war effort so that she could report to the Mothers' Union at the meeting the following afternoon. Grace would willingly have accompanied Mary, but she felt that as it was George's last morning (he had to leave at noon) she should decline as she had no idea when she would next have any time with her husband. However, she agreed to visit the vicarage at 3.00 in the afternoon to hear what Mary had discovered. Towards the end of the morning, the sirens sounded as German bombers approached on a daytime bombing raid, probably intent on destroying more harbour installations. When George left to catch his train from Eastleigh station, the 'all clear' had just sounded, but when he reached the station, he learned that there were delays to the trains as there had been heavy bombing in the city centre with many casualties. He hoped that Mary Adams had not been caught up in it and thankful that his own wife was safe at home. He was also hopeful, that as the boys' school was on the outskirts of the city, both Richard and Stephen would be safe.

After George had departed, Grace warmed up the portion of stew, left over from the previous day, for her lunch and then busied herself with domestic tasks before making her way to see Mary. As she approached the vicarage, she met a worried parishioner who told her that she had heard that the Civic Centre had been bombed and that there were casualties. She didn't know any details, but a neighbour had heard the news from a bus driver. Grace said that she was on her way to a meeting with the vicar's wife who had gone into the city in the morning. There was no response when she rang the bell at the vicarage. Fearing the worst, she decided to wait in the porch hoping that Mary's absence was because her bus had been delayed or cancelled. She hadn't been waiting many minutes when

Simon Lane, the curate, arrived. He had heard that there had been several fatalities of the daytime bombing raid, some at the Civic Centre.

"Where did you hear that news, Simon?" Grace asked. "I didn't catch any lunch time news bulletin."

"I didn't hear any radio news either, but I called on a parishioner just after 1.00 p.m. She had just listened to the news and told me what she had heard, but there were not many details. I think the authorities were still assessing the damage and there may have been people buried under debris."

"Mary intended to go the Civic Centre, but I'm not sure what time she was going. If she caught the 9.30 bus, she would have got there soon after 10.00. Can you remember what time the sirens sounded?"

"I didn't really notice the time, but I think it must have been just before 11.00. Do you think Mary would have been in the Civic Centre by then?"

They chatted for a few minutes more speculating whether Mary had been delayed or injured, or terrible thought, killed. As Simon had a key to the vicarage, they decided to wait inside as a cool breeze had sprung up although it would be light until after 6.00 p.m. now that they had the 'summer-time' extra hour of daylight even in November. Simon had only just opened the door when PC Williams arrived on his bicycle.

"I am afraid I come with bad news," said the policeman. "You may have heard about the bombing of the Civic Centre. It appears that Mrs Adams is one of the fatalities although I don't know all the details. I believe she was trying to rescue some of the children who were caught up in the mayhem when a wall collapsed. I wanted to get here before the lass gets home from school and I had to go and see Farmer Strangelove as his wife was another who lost her life and she usually helps him with the milking. I hate having to be the bearer of sad news, but someone has to do it. It's not just bringing the news, but it's about seeing if there is any help I can give before I report back to the station."

He wasn't sure how much Grace and Simon had taken in of what he said, but he rattled on a bit as he was wise enough to know they needed a couple of minutes to absorb the news before saying anything. In this endeavour, he was successful, for although Grace had half prepared herself for bad news, it wasn't until the policeman had mentioned the lass that she woke up to the situation that twelve-year-old Angela would be arriving home soon and with her mother dead and her father at sea, she had better come up with some practical help.

Grace took charge of the situation. She turned first to PC Williams, "Thank you, John, for coming as quickly as you could. I think we have about 30 minutes before Angela arrives home. Do you think you could see if you can get a message to Revd Adams? He is at sea in his navy chaplain capacity, but someone at the Portsmouth base may know how to contact him. When you have more details of Mrs Adams' death and her personal belongings, please let me know."

"Certainly, Mrs Bailey. I'm glad you were here—I was going to call on you first, but one of your neighbours saw you go out. I'll get on to matters right away."

Grace then turned to the curate, "Simon, could you cycle round to each of the churchwardens to tell them the awful news; then go to Mrs Bennett and tell her that we had better cancel tomorrow's Mothers' Union meeting. I think you are going to be quite busy in the next few days, but try to get some quiet time to think about next Sunday's services. I'll look after Angela until we hear from her father."

"Yes, Grace, I'll contact the people you mentioned. I expect news will spread rapidly. I've already realised that I shall need some time for preparation before Sunday, especially as it is Remembrance Sunday. I'll phone you later. Oh, I don't know if Angela has a key to the vicarage, but you and she may need to get in. Good-bye." And he went off to inform the key members of the parish.

Grace Bailey then sat down in the vicarage to think what else she needed to do while she waited for Angela. After a few minutes, there was a knock at the door. It was Florrie Shaw, wife of the Vicar's Warden, wanting to know if there was anything she could do to help. Grace knew that Angela regarded Florrie almost as a substitute grandmother, so she asked her to stay until Angela came home and then to help her pack what she would need to go and stay with the Baileys. While they packed, Grace planned to go home and get the spare room ready and alert her two sons of the situation.

When Angela arrived, she ran up to Grace and said, "Auntie Grace, is it true? My friend Barbara heard some mothers of other girls telling them that the Civic Centre had been bombed and that a lot of people had been killed including several children and a vicar's wife. I know Mummy was going into the city this morning. It wasn't her, was it?"

Grace put her arm round the girl's shoulder and replied, "Yes, Angela dear, I'm afraid it is true, although we don't know many details yet. The police are trying to get a message to your father. We are all terribly upset—war is such a horrible thing." She paused with her arms round her while the girl wept. When Angela quietened for a moment, Grace continued gently, "Now, we would like you to come and stay with us until your father decides whether he wants to make other arrangements. You know Mrs Shaw here. While I go home to get a room ready for you and to tell Richard and Stephen what has happened, Mrs Shaw will help you pack everything you might need to stay with us for the next few days."

Mrs Shaw was a grey-haired lady of ample proportions, with a constant smile always waiting to light up her face. With her infectious laugh, she was adept at putting people at ease. She had had four daughters of her own and she was the ideal person to comfort the heart-stricken girl. While she worked her magic with Angela, Mrs Bailey went to her own home. She was making the spare room ready for their unexpected guest when her sons arrived home.

"Where are you, Mum?" Richard called.

"Upstairs in the spare room."

Richard on the way upstairs started to impart his news. "Charlie's done it again! He's found another old composer—Josquin des Prés—and a piece called El Grillo which means The Cricket. We all have to make sounds imitating… Hey, what are doing, Mum?" Richard cried. "Are we expecting a visitor?"

Their mother told the boys the tragic news and that she had offered Angela hospitality. Both boys said they had heard that the Civic Centre had been bombed and that Supermarine had been targeted again, but they did not have any details. They were appalled to learn that the vicar's wife was one of those who had died.

As she finished telling the boys of Mary's death, Grace clasped her hand to her mouth and stood shaking.

"What's the matter, Mum?" Richard exclaimed.

"I've only just realised. Had your father not still been here this morning, I would have gone with Mary and then what would have happened? Oh dear, I hadn't thought of that until now."

"Sit down, Mum. Have you had a cup of tea since you heard?"

Seeing her shake her head, the boys took her downstairs and made her some tea. As he handed the cup to her, Richard quoted, more to himself than to his mother, "One will be taken and the other left."

"What are you talking about, Richard?"

"I was just reminded of the text that Simon preached on last Sunday. I think it was from Matthew chapter 24 about the end times."

Richard and Stephen realised that their mother had done the right thing, but they weren't sure what it would be like having a girl in the house. Richard reflected that although he was now seventeen, he didn't know much about girls, as there had been so few in his primary school class and a male choir and a boys' grammar school hadn't prepared him for this eventuality. Charlie's sister was alright, but then she could sing. He couldn't remember having ever spoken to the bespectacled, pig-tailed vicar's daughter, who would be sharing their home for a few days or perhaps longer. Perhaps he wouldn't need to have much to do with her.

It took a week to contact Peter Adams and another six days before he arrived home. In the meantime, Grace and Simon had made what arrangements they could for Mary's funeral and Angela had been able to tell them about relatives that needed to be contacted. Peter had a few days compassionate leave, but while the war continued to rage, there was little time for bereaved relatives to grieve. People had to pick up the remnants of their lives out of the tragedy that had engulfed them and continue to battle for survival. Many were in similar situations. Peter and Angela were somewhat comforted when they learned that Mary had managed to get some children out of the bombed building and it was when she went back for more, that a wall and part of the ceiling had collapsed trapping her and the remaining children inside. They had died of suffocation by a mixture of dust, smoke and gas fumes from a severed gas pipe, before they could be rescued. Mary had been found with her arms round two of the children.

Peter asked Grace if Angela could stay longer with the Baileys, rather than send her to a different part of the country to stay with relatives she hardly knew. He would also like her to continue at the girls' grammar school where she had settled well. The boys initially gave a somewhat half-hearted approval to the arrangement, but when they discovered that Angela was very willing to help with laying the table for meals and washing up, they realised that there were some benefits in having her in the house. Before long, Stephen found himself helping Angela with her science and maths homework and as they both liked geography, they spent several hours studying maps together and identifying countries affected by the war. Richard was taken by surprise when he discovered that Angela had taken to slipping stealthily into the room to listen to him playing the piano as he prepared for his Grade VII exam. He had no idea if she could play the piano, but he seemed to think he had noticed a piano in the vicarage when he had visited on one occasion.

In the middle of January with the London Blitz continuing, Grace received another visit from the evacuation billeting officer. She was seeking placements for several children from London, but Grace had to tell her that the spare room was no longer spare as she had already taken in a refugee from the war. She explained the situation and the officer, clearly disappointed that she had drawn another blank, nevertheless thanked her for helping someone to cope with the bereavement that resulted from the evil of war.

Chapter 5

Late June 1941

Shortly after completing his HSC exams and celebrating his eighteenth birthday, Richard received his call-up papers. He opted for the Royal Air Force and explained that he had spent many hours working on all aspects of the Mark 1 and Mark 2 Spitfires. He passed his medical without difficulty, but he was advised to put any desires he may have had of flying Spitfires out of his mind as his eyesight, although good, was not good enough to be a pilot. After his initial training and being assigned to two Spitfire squadrons in East Anglia to work on the maintenance and repair of the aircraft, he was posted to Malta in March 1942.

He arrived in the middle of a sustained barrage by German bombers worse than the blitz on London in 1940 and 1941. The number of Spitfires was inadequate to keep the Germans at bay and even when new ones were flown in, they were likely to be bombed on the ground as soon as they landed. Richard and the small team of maintenance staff had to work flat out, sometimes without the correct spares to keep the planes serviceable. His experience in the Spitfire factory enabled Richard to use parts from crashed or badly damaged aircraft to repair those that could be made to fly again. It was soon recognised that he possessed vital knowledge and skills and many of the ground crew and some of the pilots would seek him out for advice and instruction. The pressure on pilots and ground crew was intense and a significant proportion of the civilian population lost their lives while a great many homes were destroyed. From arriving in Malta not long after being a schoolboy, within weeks, Richard felt he had aged ten years.

The tide only began to turn when the latest mark of Spitfire arrived, flown in from an aircraft carrier in the Mediterranean that had manage to elude U-boats and their torpedoes. This new plane was faster and more manoeuvrable than anything that the Luftwaffe had. The enemy aircraft persisted, but no longer were they in the ascendency. The air battle was being won, but the island was still seriously short of food and other vital supplies as shipping was still being torpedoed and bombed. By October, however, the island was close to being saved, as a convoy bringing vital supplies had managed to get through the blockade that the German forces had imposed on shipping. As the Germans needed aircraft for other areas of conflict they reduced their siege on Malta. As a result, the need for further Spitfires was lessened and supplies of the fighter could be diverted to other war zones.

After more than six months of working long hours every day under intense pressure in often very high temperatures, with shortage of food and witnessing injury and death of comrades and civilians it was recognised that the state of Richard's mental health was becoming fragile. Accordingly, when there was an opportunity to return to England on a transport flight, he was given a place. He returned at the end of November and was given two week's leave before being posted to a Spitfire squadron in the south of the country.

Richard spent his leave at home and found the pace of life much slower than the frenetic rate at which he had been working. He also appreciated the quieter atmosphere with Stephen and Angela both at school during the day and disciplining themselves to pursue their studies in the evenings. The house was often silent during the days as his mother had found a niche in helping with church and parish matters that might otherwise have been neglected following the death of her friend Mary Adams. With time at his disposal, Richard filled it with walking, playing the piano, reading and sitting quietly in church, but discovered that he could not settle to any one activity for very long. When his mother was at home, he talked to her about several different subjects. Only after he left for his new posting did Grace realise that he avoided talking about his war experiences.

Richard's knowledge and skill were quickly recognised when he joined his new squadron and he was soon being 'loaned' to other squadrons to help keep their aircraft air-worthy. He was pleased to find this movement between bases allowed him to have another five days at home during the Christmas period.

Christmas 1942

The two days before and the two days after Christmas Day of 1942 turned out to be an oasis of calm and celebration in the desert and trials of war for both the Bailey and Adams families. Both fathers and Richard enjoyed the 'luxury' of five days leave. However, it was noticed by Grace that although George and Peter often talked about some of their experiences of the last two years and debated the progress of the war, Richard sat for long periods without saying anything and he did not show his usual enthusiasm for the carols and Christmas music. She also noticed that Angela often sat near him, quiet and wearing a worried frown ready to offer him anything she thought he might need.

Richard was aware of the discussions taking place between his father and the vicar and he wondered if he should share his experiences with them. Could they help him to live with the traumas that had touched his life? Between them, they cared for both the physical and spiritual effects of war. He recognised that he probably needed some help, but he didn't think he had the strength to describe what he had witnessed without breaking down. He also reasoned that although they had experience of helping military casualties they had not actually witnessed the scenes that produced the injuries. He decided that he would try to fight his own battle with his memories and hope that time would bring improvement in his mental health. So, he resolved to try to focus on other matters and found it helpful that Angela sat near him as he could ask her to tell him about her studies and hopes for the future. He stopped himself just in time from asking her how she had coped since the loss of her own mother, as he realised that might take him into dangerous territory if he was asked how he coped with the horrors of war.

In 1943, Richard remained based in England with Spitfire squadrons, but was given time to familiarise himself with all the different marks of that plane that had been developed, the reasons for the changes and specific features, such as the ability of a particular mark to operate in hot climates or in jungle environments. Following discussions he had with Air Ministry officials, he was also given a few weeks assignment to examine the construction, strengths and weaknesses of other British aircraft, including Wellington Bombers.

Significant dates for the families included Stephen's completion of his HSC courses, his eighteenth birthday in August and his call-up at the beginning of September. He also opted for the RAF and after training, he was posted to a bomber squadron as a navigator to utilise his geographical and map reading skills. Angela meanwhile completed her School Certificate and began HSC courses. She had already determined that she wanted to train as a primary school teacher after helping with that age group at Sunday School.

In November, Peter Adams was taken seriously ill. Having caught a cold just before Remembrance Day, he had stood outside for the parade on a wet and very cold day, which led to pneumonia and an extended stay in hospital where he needed round-the-clock nursing. He returned home in early December for further convalescence, but his war service was at an end as he was invalided out of the Navy. While he still needed care and support, Grace took him into her home so that she and Angela could help his recovery.

While preparations were well advanced on the south coast of England for 'Operation Overlord' in June, war continued to rage in the east and the Japanese were making preparations in Burma to invade India. It was decided that Spitfires should be sent to Burma to support the Chindits, highly trained jungle fighters. So, early in March 1944, Richard travelled to Burma by Dakota for another spell of Spitfire maintenance and repair in a different theatre of the war. The enemy this time were Japanese and they had their own aircraft suited to the conditions.

27 June 1944

Peter Adams took many weeks to regain his full strength following his illness. Grace and Angela encouraged his recovery aided by doses of one of the first antibiotics prescribed by Josef Wronski, who was, by now, as much liked and respected as George Bailey as the village doctor. By May, Peter had resumed many of his clerical duties and was taking a full part in church services. He was considering moving back into the vicarage where Simon Lane had been living since Mary Adams' death. It was also high time that Simon looked for his own parish after the noble way in which he had covered so much of the work in the vicar's absence.

These plans were halted on Tuesday 27 June. Peter was downstairs by 6.00 a.m. with a view to making an early start. At 6.30, Grace was on her way downstairs when the phone rang. As parishioners had become used to ringing the Bailey's house if they wished to speak to the vicar, Peter picked up the phone. Grace heard him speak.

"Revd Peter Adams, can I help you?"

The voice that answered Peter said, "I need to speak to Mrs Bailey, but perhaps it is good that you are there Reverend. You may be needed."

Then Grace heard, "She is just coming. Did you say The Ministry of Defence?"

Passing the phone to Grace and pulling a chair out for her to sit down, Peter heard her say: "Oh no! When and how?" And then she stopped talking and listened, before handing the phone back to Peter with the words, "George is dead, will you speak to them, Peter?"

Peter discovered that George had been operating well into the night on young soldiers, some only eighteen, who had been injured during the Normandy landings and had been repatriated by hospital ship. He was just about to remove bullets from a soldier's leg when a flying bomb landed on the stately home that housed the hospital and penetrated the operating theatre. It seemed that George must have heard it coming down and threw himself on top of the soldier to shield him, but he was hit on the back of his head and probably died almost instantly. The soldier survived, saved by George's prompt action. There must have been some malfunction in the doodlebug because it came down well short of its target area.

When Peter finished the call and put the phone down, he saw that Grace was sitting on the chair, leaning forward, shaking, with her face in her hands and moaning, "No, no, not that, it can't be true, I can't believe it." Peter went to her and put his arms round her and tried to comfort her. Gradually, she began to stop shaking and to sit up.

Then a voice behind them said, "What's happened? Was there a phone call? Why so early in the morning?"

Peter turned to his daughter and replied, "I'm afraid it was bad news."

"It's not Richard, is it?"

"No, my dear, it's Uncle George. He's been killed by one of the flying bombs early this morning. He was about to perform an operation when the bomb landed on the building containing the operating theatre."

With a mixture of relief and sadness, Angela went to Grace and said quietly, "Four years ago, you had to comfort me and look after me, making practical arrangements. It's my turn now. I am not going to school today. I'm going to stay here and look after you. Daddy can go to church as he planned and pray for you and Uncle George. And then we will work out how we tell Richard and Stephen."

Grace turned to her and said weakly, "Thank you, I shall be glad of your company. Are you sure you can miss school? You're right, we do need to get this terrible news to the boys. I thought George would be safe, not being overseas and the bombing much less than it used to be. But no one will be really safe while Hitler's madness continues."

"You need not worry about me missing school," replied Angela. "My school exams have finished and the teachers are busy marking and writing reports so they are giving us reading assignments which I could do at home. I will phone school and explain the circumstances. In the meantime, I shall concentrate on supporting you and anything that needs to be done we will do together. I will also speak to Dr Wronski and see what help he can give."

Peter and Angela put their return to the vicarage on hold while arrangements were made for another funeral, which Grace wanted Peter to conduct. They had received a brief letter from Richard in Burma a few days earlier, so Angela offered to write to him, knowing that he would be unable to attend his father's funeral. Peter managed to send a message to Stephen's bomber squadron and he was given leave so that he could be present to support his mother. It was not surprising that the church was packed to bid farewell to the parish's long serving and popular doctor.

Sometime in the middle of July (he had lost track of the date), Richard received a letter with an envelope written in a hand he did not recognise and with three Xs on the back. He soon discovered the handwriting belonged to Angela and she had written as sympathetically as she could to tell him of the death of his father. She mentioned the date set for the funeral, but that had already passed by the time the letter arrived. Angela also gave him other news from home, especially how his mother was coping, and that they hoped Stephen would be able to attend the funeral. At the end, she included her own little message, stating that she prayed every day for his safety and protection. She ended with a simple 'love from Angela'. He found a quiet place to sit and think about his father and reflect on all that he had learned from him. The envelope was on his lap face down when one of the mechanics came up to him. Seeing the kisses on the envelope and Richard's withdrawn expression, he teased, "Letter from home, Rich, has your girlfriend sent bad news?"

Richard came out of his daze and replied, "Girlfriend? No," and then thought how to explain the kisses. "No, it's from my sister telling me that my father has been killed by a flying bomb."

The mechanic offered a solicitous, "Sorry to hear that, I'll leave you in peace." When he was alone again, Richard wondered why he had described Angela as his sister: *was that how he thought of her?* And why had she put those kisses on the envelope? She had said that she had been supporting his mother, perhaps she was feeling tender towards the whole family, and although he had had very few days at home since her own mother had died, he had noticed how she had become part of the family.

Chapter 6

3 August 1944

The war hadn't finished with causing heartache to the Bailey family. A Lancaster bomber in which Stephen was the navigator was returning from a night raid over Germany when two of the engines failed and one of the others was misfiring badly. Although the pilot tried to get them home 'on a wing and a prayer', they didn't quite make it and the plane came down in the English Channel a mile from the home shore. Fortunately, the sea state was calm and the plane sat on the water before slowly sinking. All seven airmen managed to get out alive, but not without injury. Stephen suffered a nasty injury to a foot and broke both legs and his left arm, but he had been able to give their position accurately before they clambered out. Although there was an early sea mist, they were located by a minesweeper that had been in the area and had received the message on their radio: some of the crew also heard the plane come down.

The crew of the minesweeper took them all on board, but they were still posted initially as 'overdue' and later as 'missing' before the good news of their survival came through.

Stephen was taken to a military medical facility in Oxfordshire where he spent the next three months recovering and learning to walk again. Once his injuries had been attended to, he was well looked after by the nursing staff and his recovery was aided by the attention afforded to him by one young nurse in particular. When he began to start walking, it was Nurse Jean who managed always to be the one to escort him round the grounds. Her long, naturally fair hair and vivacious smile motivated Stephen to work hard on his recovery and with her encouragement he made very good progress. While practising his walking, they talked about many subjects, including themselves and found they had much in common, including village doctors as fathers. He was delighted to have her company, especially when she supported him physically to ensure that he didn't fall. Jean suspected that he didn't always need the support he welcomed, but she was happy to give it. Thus it was not long before a strong bond developed between them. This bond held when he was able to return to light duties at his squadron and they corresponded as often as they could. At the beginning of December, he was granted a weekend leave and he chose to spend it in Oxfordshire where he met Jean's parents and had several conversations with Jean's father about his role as the village doctor.

When Christmas came, Jean was introduced to Stephen's mother and Grace was delighted to welcome her as it helped her to get though her first Christmas since the death of her husband. It was a busy time for Peter with several services and home visits to bereaved families, but he made sure that he and Angela found time to enjoy the celebrations with the family by whom they had been virtually 'adopted'. Grace and Peter observed how happy Stephen and Jean were in each other's company and wondered how long it would be before they were given news of an engagement.

In Burma, Richard worked hard to keep Spitfires in the air as they battled with the Japanese aircraft. One incident, in particular, raised the Spitfire even higher in his admiration. When six Spitfires had flown 200 miles to an airstrip cut out of the jungle, they had just landed when Japanese fighters surprised them. Two of the Spitfires managed to get airborne, but the remainder were damaged or destroyed on the ground. Of the two that were airborne, the leader was shot down before he could attain any height. The second pilot, a New Zealander, found himself pursued by twenty of the enemy and was unable to find space to get above two thousand feet. He managed to shoot one down, but he often had three of the enemy on his tail trying to shoot him down. As he twisted and turned for forty minutes, making split second decisions and putting the aircraft through manoeuvres it was not built for, he somehow managed to make himself a target his assailants were unable to get in their sights. When the enemy aircraft called off the attack, possibly because they were low on fuel, he was able to land on the jungle airstrip. Having inspected the plane, he decided it would fly, just, so he set off on the 200 miles back to base. When Richard saw the Spitfire, he found that both wings were bent, scores of rivets had sprung free from the sheer G forces the pilot had been forced to pull. The engine was damaged by the power demanded of it and a cannon shell had entered the cockpit but not damaged anything vital. Richard was amazed that after the pounding it had received it would still fly: and yet the pilot had nursed it for 200 miles. His reaction and admiration was expressed in a few simple words: "Some aeroplane, some pilot!"

While Richard remained in the east where the Japanese war continued, the war with Germany was moving towards conclusion, but it would take more than four months of 1945, before Germany finally capitulated. In the Bailey and Adams families, conclusions of a different kind were approaching. After so many months of supporting each other, Peter and Grace decided that they wished to continue to support each other for the rest of their lives. It was no surprise, when in July, Stephen and Jean also became engaged. The main question on the minds of the two couples and one other member of the family group was whether Richard would be home before the weddings. Angela was also concerned to know what state of mind Richard would be in when he did return. She was very worried that the war may have inflicted damage to his mental stability.

After her first letter to Richard telling him of his father's death, she wrote three more times with news of Stephen's accident and recovery and the two engagements in the family. She didn't know whether he would receive them, but he noticed that they seemed to be a little tenderer each time. In particular, he wondered about the unfinished sentence in the last letter that said: 'that's one brother hooked, but there's still one left (and then there was a space).' He then considered that after his mother married Angela's father, he really could regard her as his sister, so the tenderness in the letters must be an expression of sisterly love. As he had limited opportunities to write letters and had to be careful what he wrote, he kept his comments brief and addressed his letters to his mother for the whole family. It was from his mother that he learned that Angela had completed her Higher School Certificate and had obtained a place at a teacher training college in Exeter, which she began in September.

Richard did not return to England immediately after the Japanese surrendered, as there was still work for him to do ensuring the serviceable aircraft, spare parts and other paraphernalia were ready for transport back to England or other locations. The conclusion of hostilities provided Richard with opportunities to visit parts of Burma he had not seen, including the Shwedagon Pagoda in Rangoon, the holy Buddhist shrine. While he was in Rangoon, he wandered round the market stalls. One stall fascinated him and he met an English soldier of the Royal Corps of Signals who was also drawn to the stall. This soldier, from Birmingham, had just purchased some rubies and sapphires that he intended to take back to England with him. He hoped that someone in the

Birmingham Jewellery Quarter would be able to incorporate them into jewellery items for his wife and sister. He told Richard that an officer, who in 'Civvy Street' was a gemmologist had told him that they were genuine gemstones. Richard decided to make a purchase as well thinking that, if he ever found someone with whom to share his future, they would look good in an engagement ring.

He arrived in England on 8 November 1945. Although his military career was not concluded at that time, he was given immediate leave and arrived home two days later, the day before Remembrance Sunday. His family was delighted to welcome him, but Grace and Angela, who had come home for the weekend, soon perceived that he would need time to leave the war behind. Stephen, who had been demobbed earlier in the year and had started training in hospital administration also realised that Richard would not find it easy to adjust to civilian life. His mental state was somewhat fragile, but when asked if he would give his mother away at the forthcoming wedding, he accepted willingly and was glad to have something pleasurable on which to focus his mind.

8 December 1945

It had seemed appropriate to Peter and Grace that they should be married in Advent, a new beginning for them both. At the reception, modest so soon after the cessation of hostilities, Peter announced that they were looking forward to another new beginning as he would shortly be conducting his last Christmas services in the parish he had served for nearly 16 years. He would be taking up the post of rector in a village parish in Devon at the beginning of March 1946. He also announced that one of the last services he would be involved in before they moved would be another wedding, that of his son Stephen. He had been invited to assist when Stephen married Jean in her village church in Oxfordshire in February, before the beginning of Lent.

When Richard had asked Peter about his new post, he explained that he had attended a two-day clergy conference in April after Easter. One of the aims of the conference was to help them prepare for the celebration services for the end of the war that it was anticipated would occur fairly soon. On the first day of that conference, he found himself talking to the Archdeacon of Exeter, who was adept at eliciting information about Peter's background and experience. The Archdeacon then probed with further questions to see if Peter had given any thought about a change of parish and whether the time might be right to make a move. The next day the Archdeacon, who must have made some enquiries overnight, asked Peter if he would be interested in the post of rector in a village in his diocese. After prayerful consideration and a visit, with Grace, to the parish to meet the churchwardens and view both church and rectory Peter accepted the post and it was arranged that he would move to Devon at the end of February the next year. This would leave the churchwardens of the Devon parish to manage an interregnum of nine months, but a retired priest living in the parish and a lay reader had offered to help with some of the services.

Chapter 7

1946

With the first wedding completed, Richard returned to military life, being posted to RAF Duxford in Cambridgeshire to help with the task of collecting serviceable fighter aircraft from other airfields in preparation for any future conflict, and by recovering as many of the different marks of Spitfire as possible to chart the development of the plane that had played such an important part in winning the war. He spent six months at Duxford before he was demobbed at the end of May. During this time, he turned his attention to what he was going to do in civilian life. He discovered that his days followed a normal pattern that he had not experienced for years and he was able to join a choir for a few months. There he met with other singers and enjoyed evenings singing four and five part harmony with a small a cappella group. He also thought he should try to continue his education, so applied and was accepted to pursue a degree in physics at the University of Birmingham starting in September. He was allowed a week's leave in early February to perform the duties of best man for his brother when Stephen married Jean on 10 February, with Angela as the bridesmaid for the second time in two months.

When Richard completed his work in Cambridgeshire, he spent a couple of weeks at the Devon rectory for rest, recuperation and adjustment. He used the time to do some preparatory reading for his degree course. His mother soon noticed that, although he had books open in front of him and a notepad, he wasn't reading but rather just gazing into the distance. She realised that although his body might be resting and recuperating, his mind certainly was not. It worried her that he must have witnessed some dreadful sights and he could not forget them; rather they were very much in the forefront of his mind.

Towards the end of the two weeks in the rectory, Richard received a letter that had been re-directed from his previous home address. It was from Charlie, his old school friend. After a general enquiry about health and activity since they last saw each other at school, Charlie asked if Richard was still singing, and if he was, did he have any uncommitted weeks in the summer. He went on to explain that with his sister Pat and two other singers he had accepted an invitation from a hotel in Bournemouth to provide some after dinner musical entertainment during the summer. He wondered if Richard would like to join them for a week or longer.

As Richard had been wondering how he was to spend the time until he started his university course, he decided to phone Charlie and find out more. Charlie had information about Joe and Brian who were the other members of the singing group at school. Joe was now living in France having married a French girl after the war. Joe had always excelled at French and it seems he met his wife when he was somehow involved with some sort of 'undercover' Resistance activities. Brian had died from his injuries sustained in the attack on Pegasus Bridge following his arrival in France by glider at the commencement of the Normandy landings. Richard expressed his sadness at the news of Brian's demise, but wondered how Brian, at 6 foot 5 had managed to get his frame into a glider. Brian's uncle owned the hotel where they were to perform. Charlie himself had remained in England using his mathematical skills in some secret location in the south Midlands. He was also married to Margaret who was another singer. The fourth singer was Margaret's brother Hugh. They had been engaged for July and August and Richard was welcome to join them for as much of that period as he wished. There would plenty of rehearsal time during the day, but they planned to meet for the weekend at the beginning of July.

Richard decided that five weeks starting towards the end of July and the whole of August would help to fill the gap before he went to Birmingham. He could use the last two weeks of June for walking, discovering how much of the coast path in Devon was accessible and then giving most of July to helping his mother bring order to the rather neglected rectory garden. He hoped that these activities would help to rid him of his war demons and enable him to sleep nightmare free at night.

During the weeks when he helped with the rectory garden, at Peter's invitation, he spent a few hours playing the organ in St Lawrence's Church. He found this task quite therapeutic, but was surprised on three separate occasions to find that he had an audience. On the first occasion, Peter and Grace slipped into the church to listen: his second visitor was Hubert the regular church organist. Hubert was over 80 and had agreed to 'help out' for a couple of weeks twenty years earlier when the resident organist had to go into hospital for an operation. Unfortunately, the organist hadn't recovered from the operation and Hubert was still 'helping out'. He was quite disappointed when he learned that Richard would be away at university for much of the next three years. The third listener took him by surprise. He was unaware of anyone's presence until he heard a movement and turned to see a beautiful young woman who was looking at his feet while he practised a pedal passage in one of Bach's eight short preludes and fugues which he hadn't played for several years. It was a few seconds before he realised that it was Angela. He was unaware that she would not be at college in Exeter, and he did not know she had sat quietly in the church for ten minutes, enthralled at the music he played.

When Richard had finished his practice, he and Angela walked back to the rectory together.

"I didn't know you were coming home today," said Richard.

"I only decided this morning and rang Mum to warn her. I've only just arrived and I came over here almost straight away. The end of term is in three weeks' time and as I still have two assignments to finish I thought I might have less distraction at home. Are you going to play the organ for some services?"

"Possibly, Old Hubert; I'm sorry, Mr Simms, asked whether I would and I told him that I might be able to help out occasionally. We had quite a laugh about the idea of me helping out someone who himself was helping out."

Richard had noticed that Angela called his mother 'mum'. Initially it struck him as strange, but not unnatural considering she had been a mother to the girl for seven years. It confirmed his perception that he should regard Angela as his sister. But when had she changed from the bespectacled girl with pigtails to this beautiful woman? He must have been blind when he last saw her, which could have been when she was a bridesmaid at Stephen's wedding.

After the evening meal, Angela went to her bedroom to work on her assignment, while Richard thought he might go back to church to the choir practice to give his voice some practice before he joined Charlie's company. However, Peter said he would like to discuss a matter with him, so they went into Peter's study. Peter explained that the PCC had decided that they wished to make a record of those service personnel from the village who had lost their lives in the recent war and he would be meeting with the churchwardens and PCC secretary the next day. He had received a number of suggestions and he would like Richard's opinion as one who had survived, but seen colleagues killed or maimed. The first question was whether they should add to the Great War memorial or have a separate plaque for the recent conflict.

During the night, Angela woke with a dry throat, so she went downstairs to fetch a glass of water. As she passed Richard's door she heard his voice, calling in distress, "No, no, not the bus, they're all only islanders." She realised that he was having a nightmare flashback of something he had witnessed. When she returned to her room, she did the only thing she could think of which was to kneel and pray urgently that Richard should be healed of whatever was causing his mental anguish and that if she had an opportunity to help him she would know how to act.

At the end of Angela's term in late July, she returned home to find that Richard had already gone to sing in Bournemouth. He returned early in September as Angela was preparing to start the final year of her course. Richard didn't need to go to Birmingham for another two weeks after Angela returned to Exeter. They had a couple of days to compare notes about their studies and Angela wanted to know where Richard would be living, so they exchanged addresses. Angela lived in Hall in her college, but Richard had found accommodation in one of the Selly Oak colleges supported by different Christian foundations.

Angela asked, "How did you get on singing in Bournemouth? Was it enjoyable and did it help to focus on something pleasurable?"

"It was good to meet up with my old school friend Charlie and his twin sister Pat. They haven't altered much. Charlie's wife Margaret seems very pleasant. She and her brother Hugh both have good voices. It was good that I had had a sing with the church choir here, so that I wasn't too rusty when we started. Most of the music Charlie had selected was fairly straightforward and easy on the ear for the listeners. We didn't all sing in every piece and when we sang pieces that required an accompaniment there were three of us who took turns at the piano."

"Will you join them again, if they are invited to do another season and do they sing anywhere else?"

"I don't know about another season. It depends how much demand my degree course makes on me—it's a long time since I studied seriously. Charlie did ask me if our rector would like his singers to perform a concert in the church here sometime."

"Oh, yes. That would be a splendid idea. I'll get Dad to arrange it. I'm sure, like most clergy, he will be able to think of some good cause for which to raise money and, of course, he loves music especially with good voices."

"But you won't be around during term time to make sure it all happens, will you? How much longer is your course and are you up-to-date on all your assignments?"

"I have another year in Exeter which will include another teaching practice in a school somewhere. I have done some studying and reading while you were away and I also carried on with work in the garden from where you left off."

When Richard started his course, he didn't find studying easy. He had to re-adjust to becoming a student again after so many years since he completed his HSC and he found the style of teaching alien to that he last experienced in the school environment. He was a little behind when the end of term arrived, so he decided to stay in Birmingham, using the university library during the holiday and just returning home for a three-day Christmas break.

Chapter 8

1947

The year 1947 became notorious for its bad winter with exceptional heavy snowfalls in January. Richard was glad he returned to Birmingham before the first bad snowfalls and he found that by the time term began he was up-to-date with his studies and began to enjoy them. *If only,* he thought, *he could banish the nightmares that still haunted him.* Whenever he had a particularly bad night he found it difficult to concentrate in lectures the following morning.

In the evening of Wednesday, 9 April, in the week following Easter Sunday, Charlie and his group of singers, including Richard, gave a concert in the village church. They all arrived before lunch and spent an hour or so in the afternoon rehearsing in the church and refining the programme Charlie had devised. As it was a lovely afternoon they decided to go for a walk. Before long, there seemed to be three distinct pairs in conversation. Charlie was walking with his wife Margaret, Richard and Pat were discussing the duet they were to sing in the evening and considering other soprano and tenor duets they could try and Hugh accompanied Angela, who had been invited to join them.

Hugh asked Angela, "How do you like living in Devon after being in Hampshire?"

"I am enjoying it. We haven't been here very long and much of that time I have been living in Exeter, a city with a lovely cathedral set behind a fairly extensive green. I am looking forward to the end of my course and am starting to look for my first teaching post. But I also want to explore more of this county. It is so large that there are many different aspects to it ranging from coastal areas to moorland on Dartmoor. Do you know the county at all?"

"No, my home is in Derbyshire, where we have the Peak District. I wonder how that compares with Dartmoor. Perhaps I can make a longer visit sometime soon and improve my knowledge of the West Country."

"I'm sure we should be pleased to see you if you came this way again."

Overhearing this last statement as Pat and he caught up with them, Richard wondered what might have led up to it. Hugh was certainly very good looking and had an easy personable manner.

Pat interrupted his thinking by saying, "I haven't had a chance to talk to your sister yet, Richard, so you two boys can leave us girls to have a girly chat."

When the men had moved away, Pat said to Angela, "I called you Richard's sister, but you are not really his sister, are you?"

"No, I'm not his sibling, but now that his mother has married my father, I suppose I'm his stepsister. I'm not sure how he thinks of me. I was twelve when my mother was killed and Richard's mother took me into their home as my father was away on war service. Richard was 17, studying for his HSC and working at the Spitfire factory on Saturdays so we didn't come into contact much. I don't think he took much notice of me. He was called up soon after his eighteenth birthday and he has been missing from home nearly all the time since. It's only in the last six months that we have had any conversations."

"You said he hardly noticed you. Did you notice him?"

"Oh yes, and I have seen how the war has changed him. I think he needs a bit of stability and love in his life."

"Do you love him?"

Angela thought for a moment before replying, wondering how important her reply would be to Pat, then she said, "Yes, I do love him, but I have never got close enough to him to say that I am in love with him. I don't know if anyone has got close to him. How do you find him, Pat, especially when you sing duets with him?"

"He has changed since I first met him when Charlie brought him to our house with the other two boys to sing madrigals. We had such fun in those days, particularly when we got in a muddle with a new piece we were learning, which often ended up with us all giggling. When we sang in Bournemouth, his singing was correct and competent, but you couldn't call it lively. In our duets, I tried to inject some passion into our performance and he would respond briefly, but then he would sort of 'switch off': he would sing his part beautifully, but there was no sense of theatre in his performance."

"That is much as I have found him. There are times when his mind is somewhere else as if he is in a place where we are not."

"Exactly," said Pat. "I think he must have had some traumatic times during his war service. I used to be able to flirt with him and he would meet me halfway.

When I try occasionally now, his response is quite reserved. He doesn't rebuff me, but neither does he encourage me. I used to think he would be my man; now I am not so sure."

In the evening, the concert was well received by a good-sized audience. The programme was varied with solo items, duets and a cappella items sung by all five. Both Richard and Charlie played solo organ pieces and both acted as accompanist on piano or organ for vocal solos and duets. Angela watched Richard and Pat as they sang their duet from Mozart's Marriage of Figaro. Pat's performance as Susanna included a range of emotions, including coquettishness while displaying her wedding hat and annoyance when she realised the nature of the Count's scheming. Richard's portrayal of Figaro was very well executed musically, but Angela wasn't fully convinced that this Figaro was absolutely delighted with the prospect of marrying Susanna. When Hugh stood up to sing a solo, he looked at Angela and smiled and then sang the Vaughan-Williams setting of the love song 'Silent Noon' gazing in her direction and she felt he was singing directly for her. At the end as he acknowledged the applause, he smiled at her again and she felt her face redden. She wondered if Richard noticed, but then realised, thankfully, that she was probably not in his line of sight.

Richard may not have noticed, but Grace certainly had and it gave her cause for thought. She was fairly sure she knew that Angela had strong feelings for Richard, but how would she respond to Hugh's attention. She thought that if either of the two men were to sweep Angela off her feet it was Hugh who seemed to have the necessary attributes to be able to do so. Was he just flirting with her as a passing pastime or was he more serious?

When the singers left the following morning having been billeted in the rectory, they thanked Peter and Grace for their hospitality and responded positively to a suggestion to perform again in the church or to visit if they were in the vicinity. Hugh said that he was looking forward to an opportunity to explore Devon at some stage in the future when perhaps he could accept the kind invitation to call.

In April 1947, Angela was nearing the end of her teacher training when a post became vacant for the following September at the church primary school in her father's parish. She applied and was called for interview. As rector, Peter was a member of the governing body, but he had to declare an interest and withdrew from the interviewing panel. The diocese was represented at the interviews by the Archdeacon. Angela was given a searching interview and she felt exhausted at the end of it, but she was appointed thus securing her first teaching post. It was the first teaching appointment made at the school since the 1944 Education Act appeared on the statute book.

In June, Richard received a letter from Stephen and Jean asking him to be godfather to their newly born daughter, Rachel Anne. Angela and Dorothy, Jean's friend from nursing days, were chosen as godmothers. The Christening was conducted by Peter Adams in Devon at the end of July. Richard had stayed in Birmingham for two weeks after the end of term, but was home in time to accept the invitation to attend Angela's certification ceremony when she had completed her teacher training, which took place two days before the Christening.

A fortnight before the end of term, Angela was invited by a college friend to stay with her at her home in Cornwall for a few days after they had been given their teaching certificates. So, when all the celebrations were over, she caught a train from Exeter to Penzance for a holiday prior to planning for her first teaching post. When she returned home, Richard had left to spend another season with Charlie and company in Bournemouth. Thus, again Angela saw very little of Richard, but she did hear him shout out in the night again. This time she heard him call, "There's fire, get the pilot out." It worried her that he was still suffering and she resolved to try to find a cure for him, but she suspected that it would mean that she would have to confront him about his problem.

At the end of August, Richard came home and seemed more relaxed after his singing holiday and especially when he had been over to church to practise the organ. Angela and Grace began to hope that his demons were less active and time would bring about a complete healing. Mother and stepsister watched and discussed Richard's progress, sharing their observations. Grace became more aware of Angela's feelings for Richard, but was not sure how much they were reciprocated, if at all. Angela wondered if his better mood had anything to do with spending a few weeks in Pat's company. She couldn't help remembering Pat's remarks about Richard 'being her man'. Had Pat mounted a charm offensive, she wondered, and if so, how had Richard reacted to it? She might have to use every opportunity she had to persuade him to take notice of her and not think of her just as a sister. Perhaps regular letters to him might help to make him more aware of her?

On his third day home, Richard returned from a walk to find his mother and Angela looking at some photographs.

"What have you got there?" He inquired.

"They have just arrived from my friend Penny in Cornwall. They are some snaps her father, who is a professional photographer, took while I was on holiday. They show the countryside and good views of the beach. He also took some of Penny and me in the sea."

"May I see?" Angela passed them to him, wondering how he would react to those of her on the beach. Richard soon realised that the photographer clearly knew what he was doing: the pictures of the landscape were clear and well composed. Then he came to the ones showing Angela and Penny in their swimwear. Looking at Angela, he received a shock. The swimsuit accentuated her figure and he realised that she was certainly no longer a girl, but a beautifully proportioned young woman. As he looked, he felt himself getting warm and wondered if this warmth was a manifestation of a desire he had not experienced before. He was certainly seeing Angela in a new light. This ugly duckling of a sister had been transformed into a most attractive swan. He noticed, in particular, her firm, well-rounded breasts, her slim waist and long slender legs.

As he gazed at one revealing picture, Angela, who had been watching him covertly, had an idea. "Richard, would you like to keep that particular photo you are holding?"

Coming out of his trance, Richard made to hand the picture back, then thought, *I would like to be able to look at this again*, so replied, "If you can spare it, I would like to keep it to remind me what you look like when I read letters from you."

Bingo, thought Angela, *just the ticket to keep him thinking about me.*

In September, Angela started teaching the seven and eight year-olds at the village school and was able to live in the rectory. Later in the month, Richard returned to Birmingham for the second year of his three-year course. Having felt more relaxed after his spell in Bournemouth, he decided to join the University Choral Society where, as an experienced tenor singer, he was warmly welcomed. After his second practice session, one of the other tenors invited him to join a group of them that went for some refreshment when they had finished singing. In this way, he gradually got to know students from other years and different faculties. Shortly before the end of term Julia Turnbull, one of the first-year female students who sang soprano, approached him with an invitation to sing in the Christmas concert to be performed by the Birmingham School of Music. As a local girl at a Grammar School in Bromsgrove, she had travelled into

Birmingham by bus on Saturday mornings to study at the School of Music prior to going to university. The concert was scheduled for Saturday 20 December in St Paul's church at the end of Ludgate Hill near the city centre. He decided to accept as they were short of tenors, but it meant that he did not return home until a few days before Christmas. Nevertheless, he arrived before Angela's first term was completed and was just in time to see the school's Nativity Play.

The Nativity was well supported by parents and grandparents. Some of the children were confident and knew their parts well; others were inclined to slip out of the characters they were portraying. The innkeeper received a sympathetic response from the audience when Joseph asked if there was room in the inn. "Yes, how nice to see you, come in," the innkeeper replied and then suddenly realised that was the wrong response so added aggressively, "No, you can't, there's no room for you here, get out!" and pushed Joseph away.

The next few days were busy, especially for Peter, but when they sat down for their Christmas dinner, they could look forward to some family time together. Angela told Richard about her first term and some of the amusing incidents that had occurred and some of the sayings her children had regaled her with. Peter, Grace and Angela all wanted to know about Richard's progress and asked him what Birmingham was like. They also enquired whether he had any ideas what he would do when he came to the end of his studies. He replied that he had been giving some thought to the question and had identified a few possible options, although he wanted more time to consider them carefully as his course progressed. It was clear that they all hoped, that whatever he decided, he would return to Devon or Dorset so that they would see more of him. He did let slip that one of the options under consideration was teaching as he felt he understood the environment, which was why he was interested to hear about his sister's experience. He wasn't sure whether working in an industrial setting appealed to him, but he had been offered an opportunity to find out. A fellow student was hoping, after graduation, to gain employment with Metro-Cammell in Saltley on the eastern side of Birmingham. This firm developed and constructed trains for London's underground system and his friend had secured a vacation job with them. There was another vacation opportunity in the summer for which Richard could apply. He was thinking of pursuing the offer, rather than sing with Charlie's group, even if they were engaged for another season.

He was also quizzed about singing with the University Choral Society and they were pleased to hear that he had been able to enjoy some social contact with other students. When asked how he had been recruited to sing in the Christmas concert, he informed them that the invitation had come from one the female students whose home was a few miles outside the city. He didn't notice the look that passed between Grace and Angela, particularly the raised eyebrows of his mother or the slight frown on the face of his stepsister.

Chapter 9

1948

At the beginning of the year, there was no indication that its end would be momentous. Richard returned to Birmingham early in January, hoping that the winter would not be as horrendous as 1947. Angela started her second term of teaching, feeling less of a novice than in the previous term. Richard continued to make good progress with his course and began accumulating good grades. He continued to sing with the University Choral Society and meet with the other students after practices. One day, Julia asked him if he could be persuaded to sing tenor in the choir of the church she attended in Bromsgrove. As he had not become a regular in any church while he had been in Birmingham, he thought it might be a pleasant experience as it also meant getting out of the city for a few hours. So, the next Sunday morning, he caught the bus from Selly Oak to a bus stop near All Saints church which was on the northern side of Bromsgrove. Julia was waiting outside the church, looking for him and she took him to meet the organist and choirmaster Terry Johns.

With his knowledge of church music, he found singing with a new choir reasonably straightforward and the only other tenor, who lacked experience and confidence, was pleased to have Richard beside him. After the service, when he had been thanked by Terry Johns and some of the choir members and invited to come again, he was wondering what times the buses returned to Birmingham or whether he should walk on into Bromsgrove and have a look around. He had not come to any resolution when Julia found him and introduced him to her mother, who immediately invited him, if he had not made any other arrangements, to come back to their house for Sunday lunch. Having come to no conclusion about his next move Richard accepted the invitation.

After a short walk with Julia and her mother, they arrived at a pleasant semi-detached house on the road leading to the cottage hospital where they were greeted by Julia's father who had stayed at home to cook the lunch. Also waiting for them was Julia's brother Raymond who Richard recognised as the young man with whom he had sung tenor that morning. Julia's parents asked him what subjects he was reading at university and her father was interested to learn that he was a physicist as he worked in the design department of the local motor car factory. Richard also learned that Julia's specialisms were English and history. During the course of conversation, the family discovered that Richard had worked with Spitfires for several years, but Raymond, in particular, was disappointed to learn that he had not been a pilot so didn't have any tales to tell about 'dogfights' with German fighters.

Coffee was served after lunch in the sitting room where there was a piano, so Richard asked which members played it. Julia and her mother confessed to playing a little, mainly to help them to learn songs that they sang. Julia's mother asked if he played and he admitted that he did, but quickly informed them that he played as an accompanist and not as a soloist. Even that confession, he soon realised was a mistake as he was asked if he would accompany a song Julia had learned during her lessons at the Birmingham School of Music. After one song, which he played without much difficulty, and before another was suggested, he said that he would need to catch his bus as he still had some reading to do before the next day. As he was preparing to leave and having thanked his hosts for an excellent meal, he was asked if he could join them the next Sunday. He had an inkling that that question might be asked and had his answer ready. He said that perhaps he should join them for Evensong next time, a service that he preferred, and that would allow him to spend time on his books in the morning.

On the bus home, he reflected on the 'inquisition' he had faced from Julia's parents and wondered how Julia had represented him to them and, indeed, how she viewed him. She was a very pleasant and open young lady, but he did not feel ready to view her as anything more than a fellow student who liked music. He would need to be careful not to raise expectations. He tried to remember how he had described Angela when he told them he had a sister.

Next Sunday, he alighted from the bus at ten past six for the 6.30 Evensong just as the Turnbull family was walking past the bus stop. He then remembered that Julia had asked him what time his bus was due to arrive. Julia asked what bus he planned to catch after the service. When he said he would aim for The 8.00 p.m. bus, he was asked if he could delay his departure for an hour and join them for a supper drink before leaving. Before they entered the church, it started to rain and there were white flecks in the rain. The world looked different when they came out an hour and a half later, as the rain had turned to snow and it was already settling. Richard decided that while the roads were still passable he would catch the first bus that came, before the snow settled too deeply on the Lickey Hills. He told Julia that he would not be visiting Bromsgrove the next Sunday, but he went to one more Evensong before the end of term.

Meanwhile, Angela was proving popular with her pupils and attracted commendations from their parents. She received a positive report from the county inspector who was monitoring her probationary year when he visited her class to observe her teaching. This report was sufficient to enable the governors of the school to feel they could congratulate themselves on making an excellent appointment.

In the middle of March, Hugh Latimer phoned the rectory to say that he would be in Devon the following weekend and asked if he could visit them. As Peter and Grace had several engagements on the Saturday, they asked Angela if she could entertain Hugh. She said she would be pleased to do so, about which arrangement Hugh was highly delighted.

Hugh arrived in his car, recently acquired, an Austin Seven Ruby. It looked very smart and when Angela admired it Hugh explained, "It will enable us to explore places that are not really accessible by bus."

Angela wanted to know, "Have you anywhere specific in mind?"

"Not really. You tell me which compass direction we should face and we can find out where it takes us—a mystery tour."

They set off in a direction which was vaguely westerly. It was one of those exceptional March days which show that spring wishes to announce itself. It had not rained for several days and the month seemed to have packed its winds away. The sun shone strongly in Hugh's rear mirror to help them keep facing west. They passed through two villages and when they came to the next they stopped at the village shop, bought sandwiches, cake, fruit and drinks and continued their journey as the ground began to rise appreciably. Rounding a bend they could see swathes of heathland and shortly after they were on Dartmoor.

Finding a convenient place to pull off the road, they left the car and taking their picnic with them walked onto the moor. Having walked up hill for several minutes they discovered a little hollow beside some standing rocks that provided an ideal sheltered spot to rest and enjoy their refreshment. Hugh had had the foresight to bring a rug from the car and they were soon sitting comfortably looking back to the way they had come. Noticing some early spring grass and

Angela's hand resting on it, Hugh sang, 'Your hands lie open in the long fresh grass, the finger-points look through like rosy blooms. Your eyes smile peace'.

Angela looked at him and smiled recognition, "That's what you sang at the concert, isn't it?"

Hugh smiled back and sang the last words of 'Silent Noon'. 'Oh, clasp we to our hearts, for deathless dower, this close-companioned inarticulate hour, when two-fold silence was the song of love'.

"That was lovely, Hugh, and beautiful words. Who wrote them?"

"I'm glad you liked the words. I wish I had written them, because they seemed so right for this moment. They were written by Dante Gabriel Rossetti. Now, let us just sit and listen to the silence."

They sat for a while looking at each other and feeling at peace with the world. The spell was broken by the sound of munching behind the rocks. Jumping up and looking round, they discovered they had been joined by two Dartmoor ponies who were grazing on the first new tender grass shoots.

They enjoyed their picnic and looked again for the ponies to offer them their apple cores. It was then, looking west that they felt a strong breeze and noticed a dark cloud coming their way. Hastily gathering all their litter and the rug, they decided to run back down the hill to the car. Laughing as they ran and frequently looking behind to check on the progress of the impending storm, they had nearly reached the car when Angela caught her foot on a tussock and before she knew what was happening she found herself on the ground with pain in her ankle. Hugh stopped, checked that she was not hurt anywhere else and having assessed the situation, handed rug and rubbish bag to Angela and then picked her up and carried her to the car. With her still in his arms, he took the opportunity presented to him and kissed her before carefully helping her into the car. He was excited that she responded to his kiss.

Grace had returned home a few minutes before Angela and Hugh arrived. As Angela limped in assisted by Hugh, Grace sprang into action. She felt round the ankle and bathed it, then bandaged it believing there were no bones broken, but rather that it was a slight sprain. While she received first aid, Angela turned to Hugh and lamented, "Sorry, Hugh, to spoil such a lovely day."

Hugh reached out to hold her hand, thinking about the kiss and replied, "Dear girl, you didn't spoil the day. It was a great outing. I thoroughly enjoyed it and found the part of Devon we saw entrancing."

Angela's ankle soon became more comfortable and by Monday, after Hugh had left, she was able to hobble into school, where she enjoyed the sympathy of staff and pupils, who chorused, "What did you do, Miss? Does it still hurt?"

Chapter 10

During the Easter holiday, Richard returned on the Wednesday of Holy Week, and at the request of Hubert Simms, sang with the church choir on Good Friday and Easter Day. He and Angela exchanged progress reports and he again asked her about the different techniques she would use with pupils of different abilities and aptitudes. Richard felt he was learning some very useful information and appreciated the quality of Angela's pedagogy. He also realised how comfortable he felt in talking with her. Without taking her for granted, he felt he had no need to try to impress her with his contributions to their conversations. His awareness of her as a person and her beauty increased. He was able to observe her in a way he had never done before. He noticed that she was now about three inches shorter than he, her clear complexion, her silky auburn hair, and her beautiful green-brown eyes. He loved the way she smiled when she spoke and imagined that her pupils would just love being in her presence. In spite of these observations, he felt detached from her, still thinking of her as a sister and considering that the man she fell in love with and married would be a very lucky man indeed to have such a beautiful and considerate and clever wife.

When the subject of the summer holidays came up in conversation, Richard explained to all the family that he would be staying in Birmingham during the summer recess to work at Metro-Cammell so that he could gain experience of industry and an insight into industrial practices. Angela observed him closely during the week in an attempt to gauge his mental state and was distressed when she again heard him talking in his sleep. On this occasion, she heard him say with a note of despair in his voice, "How can I tell his family that he was blown to pieces?"

Towards the end of May, Hugh phoned to say he was planning to visit Devon the next weekend and hoped Angela might be able to help with a project on which he was engaged. He had spoken to her twice since the trip to Dartmoor; first, understandably, to ask about her ankle and then on a subsequent occasion.

When he arrived for the weekend before Whitsun, he explained to Angela that his father had asked him to write a piece for his local newspaper. His father owned the paper and he wished to include an article comparing Dartmoor to the Peak District in Derbyshire. When Angela asked him if he was a journalist, he said that he did some freelance work, but that was not a career he wished to pursue. Otherwise he was rather evasive about his career plans. Angela wondered whether the initiative for the article came from Hugh or his father, but she enjoyed their motoring tours around parts of Dartmoor. However, she didn't feel that they had been able to recapture the magic of the first excursion when she sprained her ankle, even though Hugh had kissed her again.

One evening about a week later, returning from church after meeting a couple who planned to marry later in the year, Peter found Grace sitting alone, apparently deep in thought. "A penny for them," suggested Peter.

"I'm sorry," apologised Grace, "I was thinking about Angela and Richard and Hugh and that girl in Birmingham and how it might all turn out."

"Turn out! What do you mean?"

"I think Angela has had strong feelings for Richard for a long time and I think she might hope for a relationship that is more than just brother and sister. For a long time, I thought Richard was quite ambivalent about any relationship, but on his last visit, at Easter, I thought I detected a small spark of interest and there were more conversations between them. I know Richard needs time to sort himself out, both regarding career and his mental state, but I fear that he might take too long, especially as Hugh seems rather keen on Angela. I'm not sure how interested she is in him or whether there is any relationship in its infancy developing between Richard and his friend Julia. I just hope neither of our children gets hurt."

"I see what you mean. You may not have realised it, but I have not been unobservant. I can perceive that there is more than one line of development and those lines are not all progressing at the same pace. I am not sure we can intervene, but as Angela sometimes confides her concern for Richard's health to you perhaps you can advise her to exercise patience. I think I might talk to Stephen and see if he has any access to his brother's thinking."

"Thank you, dear; two wise thoughts, I'm glad we see things the same way."

"I try never to compare you with Mary, but on this matter, I think you and Mary would have reacted in exactly the same way. Which is why I feel so blessed to have enjoyed relationships with both of you."

He left the room immediately to answer the phone. When he came back ten minutes later, he announced, "Phase one under way. That was Stephen. He is going to work on Richard; his phrase, not mine."

"Oh good. That was good timing on Stephen's part."

"Indeed. He won't mince his words, and if necessary, he will be quite direct in his questioning and observations. But I haven't told you about the phone call I took just before I went over to church. It was from Canon Simon Lane…"

"Canon!"

"That's right, but that wasn't his only piece of news. He is getting married and he wants us at the wedding and has asked me to participate in the ceremony. I don't know any details yet, but I think it will be in July. I had to be brief as I had that lovely couple waiting for me. I'll go and ring him back and get some more details, including information about his bride."

"Oh yes, do. It will be lovely to see him again."

Chapter 11

September saw Angela start her second year of teaching with some changes in her class as some went up to the top class and new pupils arrived in hers. Richard began the final year of his degree course, seeking some clarity in his thinking about his future career pathway. In the middle of October, his thinking was shifted up a gear or two. He was invited to spend a weekend with Stephen and Jean at their house a few miles outside Oxford. He arrived on Saturday morning and after a pleasant day getting to know his granddaughter, Jean ushered the boys out of her way and suggested they spend an hour or so at the local public house.

They were lucky to find a quiet table in a corner where they could talk without interruption. Initially, they talked about their mother and how she had adapted to being a rector's wife in a new parish. Stephen wanted to know about Richard's studies and university life. Similarly, Richard asked about Stephen's career. After responding positively to Richard's questions as to how he was enjoying married life, Stephen looked at Richard and asked, "Well, Brother, when are going to find yourself a wife and settle down?" And followed up with, "Have you met any likely girls while you have been in Birmingham?"

Richard was taken by surprise by such a direct question and, whereas he would normally have thought to prevaricate, responded with the answer he had become accustomed to give himself.

"No, there is no one and I don't think it would be fair to marry in my present state. I had better correct myself. I have spent some time with a young lady who I think quite likes me. She is quite musical and it is through music and the University Choral Society that we met, but I have been careful not to encourage her to think there is any readiness on my part to develop a deeper relationship. I doubt if anybody would want me at present."

"The nightmares are still persisting, are they?"

"What do you know about my nightmares? I haven't told anyone."

"Look, Richard, we all know you had some terrible times. Your expression and your body language give you away. We recognise that you can't talk about it, but you need help. And as for there being no one who would want you, that's rubbish. There is a lovely girl you know who with a little encouragement would be yours immediately."

"Who? I don't know anybody. Unless…" And he went silent.

"Perhaps the penny's beginning to drop. Yes! Angela; she almost worships you and has done so almost from the time she came to live with us. She is so worried about you."

"But she's our sister, especially as Mum has married her father."

"She is not our sister; she is our stepsister. There is no blood relationship. You might need to establish with her father whether there would be any bar to a relationship between you. Whatever else, she is the ideal person for you to talk to about your demons. She has inherited all the right genes from her parents. She has the faith and sincerity of her father and the care and approachability of her mother. Take more notice of her and don't go around at home with blinkers on. Please think about it, for your sake and Angela's. Now, drink up; we'd better be getting back."

The following morning, Richard accompanied Jean to Matins in their local church while Stephen looked after Rachel and prepared Sunday dinner. During dinner, Richard was asked if he had decided what he would do when his course finished. He replied that he was still undecided, but that the options he had been considering were reducing. He was asked about his industrial experience earlier in the year.

Richard explained, "There were some similarities with Supermarine, but the emphasis was on the production of new stock for the District Line of London's Underground. The development work had been done; it is now a matter of fulfilling the order so that the trains can be operating sometime next year. There is research and development underway, and as with the Spitfire, much of the focus is on achieving greater speed. From the discussions I was able to sit in on I think the days of steam are numbered. We shall see more use of diesel and electricity. Of course, electricity is the motive power for the underground system and the southern region makes extensive use of electric trains. But I don't think I want to enter the industrial world: I didn't feel the thrill that I felt working on Spitfires."

On the way back to Birmingham, Richard found himself thinking about what Stephen had said and wondered how Angela felt about their relationship. The more he considered her attitude towards him, the more he began to think that Stephen could be right and he had not perceived things he should have noticed.

When he returned to his rooms on Sunday evening, he found a letter waiting for him that must have arrived after he left the previous day. The envelope indicated that it was from Prebendary Peter Adams. He wondered about the title and hoped the letter would not contain bad news. He need not have worried, even if fleetingly. First his stepfather explained the new title went with an additional responsibility of 'Rural Dean'. He then went on to ask if Richard would be able to return early for Christmas as the church would be in some difficulty in providing Christmas music. Apparently, Hubert Simms's eyesight had been deteriorating for a few months and he had been offered an opportunity to have an operation under the new National Health Service introduced in July. This would mean that, if he accepted the date offered, he would not be able to play the organ or prepare the choir during the Christmas period. Would Richard be able to help? Richard's first reaction was to think of an excuse, his second was that he was quite capable of doing it, the third that as term finished on Friday, 10 December, with no lectures planned for the last day, he probably had enough time. Accordingly, he wrote back saying he would be delighted to help, would give some thought to music and would come home on Thursday, 9 December, in time to discuss details with Peter and attend choir practice on Friday evening. He assumed Peter would want a service of nine lessons and carols as used in King's College, Cambridge, but as Christmas Day was a Saturday, he didn't know when the carol service would be held, or how many practices he would have.

Discussions by phone or letter resulted in the carol service being arranged for Thursday, 23 December so that it would not be on the same night as the Christmas Eve midnight communion service. Hubert Simms agreed to start preparing the choir for the choir only items for Richard to take the final rehearsals.

It was not until the Thursday morning after his weekend away and his communications with his stepfather that Richard next saw Julia. He had just sat down at a table in the coffee bar in the Students' Union when Julia arrived. She spotted him as she entered and came over saying as she arrived, "There you are; I've been looking for you. I have something to ask you."

Richard replied, "I have something to tell you as well, but go and get your drink and then come and join me."

She was soon back and as she sat down she enquired, "How was your weekend? Did you have a good time?"

"It was certainly eventful. I had a good chat with my brother, who gave me some matters to think about. I went to Matins with Jean, my sister-in-law, and spent time getting to know my god-daughter, which included her encircling my finger with a small, but firm hand grip."

"Oh, how lovely, I have experienced that with my cousin's baby."

"When I returned to my rooms, I found a letter waiting for me from my stepfather who is now a rural dean. The old organist at my home church, who must be nearly a hundred and has been helping out since the previous organist left over twenty years ago, will be out of action at Christmas as he has been offered an operation to improve his sight. I have been asked to play the organ for the Christmas services and to train the choir. So, I shall be away from Birmingham from 9 December, until the start of the spring term. This morning, I had short letters from my mother and my stepsister both saying they were delighted to know I would be home earlier than previous years. Angela seems to have started planning things for us to do as she has asked me if I will read a story to her class. I'm not sure about that, but as one of the possible options when I have graduated is to go into teaching it could be good experience. Sorry, I have told you my news and you haven't had a chance to tell me what you want to ask me."

Julia sounded rather dispirited when she responded, "I think you have already answered my question. I was going to ask you if you would like to sing at the School of Music carol concert again this year and if you had agreed, I was going to invite you to come to Bromsgrove and share Christmas with the family. But it sounds as though you will be more needed in Devon. It would have been nice to spend time together out of term time."

"Yes, I'm sorry about that. I think that is one of the problems with Christmas, especially with carol singing. You can be asked to be in several places at the same time, while there are some people who find themselves alone during the celebrations."

When Julia heard of Richard's Christmas plans, the conversation provided her with three revelations. They were-firstly, that he would not be around to join in any of the concerts and services to which she was committed and secondly, that he was a much more competent musician than she realised if he played the organ and could train choirs. The third revelation, when she thought about it and after a hopeful hint on her part, was that he hadn't invited her to join him for Christmas. As she thought more, she wondered if his thinking had been affected by his visit to his brother. And had he previously referred to Angela as his stepsister rather than his sister? It also sounded as though he was looking forward to spending time with her.

Chapter 12

December 1948

Amongst the ten boys in the church choir, there were six who knew the carols they would sing at Christmas fairly well and they provided a competent top line. However, Richard could not detect among them a soloist who could sing the first verse of 'Once in Royal David's city'. He was generally happy with the progress made at the first practice. His mother had welcomed him warmly when he arrived at lunchtime and he soon discovered that she had several jobs lined up for him. She wanted to know how his studies had been progressing and he assured her that he understood that he was expected to achieve a good degree. She also commented that it was good to have him home well before Christmas and wondered if he had received any invitations to sing in Birmingham before the festive season. He admitted that his friend Julia had been hoping he would stay in Birmingham for Christmas, but he shared his plans with her before she could offer an invitation. His mother told him that Angela would be pleased to see him, although she had not been without male company. In response to his question, she informed him that Hugh Latimer had visited the area a couple of times and spent some time with Angela at the weekends.

The rectory had been promised a Christmas tree by one of the local farmers, who grew them as a cash crop, and Grace wanted some new decorations for it. She suggested that Richard could go into Exeter on the bus with Angela to buy decorations for the tree and then perhaps later he would help Angela decorate it. During the journey Richard asked Angela what her teacher training course had comprised. She explained that in addition to the obvious element of teaching experience, she had studied courses on history of education, curriculum and lesson planning, philosophy and psychology.

"Psychology?" Richard asked. "What did that entail?"

"That course was really interesting and we had a very knowledgeable teacher, even if she did wear some strange clothes. She explained that by observing the behaviour of a child in the classroom, we could identify if there was something worrying or upsetting them. It may be something at home, perhaps the arrival of a new baby, the death of a pet or the child might be enduring some unpleasant bullying or abuse. If the child became withdrawn and didn't want to join in as previously, he could be suffering from some trauma. The trauma could be the result of something he felt he could not tell anybody and no one had realised he had been affected."

She realised that Richard did not say anything so she stole a glance at him and noticed that he was staring into the distance. *Oh dear*, thought Angela, *don't take it any further today, see if he brings it up himself.*

The bus pulled up at a stop and many new passengers got on. Quiet conversation was now no longer possible. When they reached their destination, they explored several shops in Exeter and felt pleased with their purchases: they had time for a coffee before catching the bus home. Richard asked how preparations were going for the school's Nativity Play and as the conversation had turned back to school matters, Angela repeated her invitation to visit the school one afternoon and read a story to her class. He replied that he had never done anything like that, but he'd give it a try if she would help him. They agreed that the following Tuesday afternoon would be a good time and Angela would check with her headteacher that the arrangement was acceptable.

Angela asked, "Have you any plans how you are going to spend your time while you are here?"

"I had thought that with more days than I usually have when home I ought to explore the countryside, but I could do with a guide and you will not be available during the day. I have also planned to do some reading ready for next term."

"Why don't you read during the week when I am at school and then we can spend time together exploring at the weekend? I should love to show you some of the walks I have discovered. I found some new ones when Hugh visited."

"Oh yes," replied Richard. "Mum said he had been down here a couple of times. Is he keen on you?"

"I don't know. He is pleasant company and very handsome, but I am not sure why he came. He said business brought him this way, but I could not find out what the business was that required his presence in Devon."

"It sounds as though the business was an excuse to see you. Do you like him?"

"Yes, but I haven't reached the stage of hoping he will come again soon. What about the girl who hoped you would stay in Birmingham for Christmas?"

"Is it sufficient to say that I am glad your dad signed me up before she had issued her invitation?"

"Would you have accepted the invitation if she had got in first?"

"I might have stayed to sing in the concert, but I felt that I might have found myself under subtle pressure to accelerate the relationship before I was ready to, so I am glad I was able to put the brake on in good time. I think it sounds that neither of us is prepared to commit ourselves yet."

"Agreed, that is one reason I would like to spend time with you. I feel that our meetings have been so short and infrequent that I don't really know you."

"Perhaps our paths have been running along parallel lines and it is time for us to help them to converge."

"Very well put, Richard. I agree entirely."

That Saturday evening, Peter asked Richard to accompany him to his study to check the order of service for the 'nine lessons and carols' as he wanted to take it to the printers on Monday. He asked if Richard had been able to identify a soloist for the first verse of the first carol. No one boy had the voice and ability he was looking for, so he was toying with the idea of having two sing together or else all the trebles. Peter asked if they had to have a boy sing the solo. Richard said it would be strange to have a man sing it, but then Peter asked him if he had heard Angela sing. Richard admitted that he didn't think any occasion had arisen for him to consider Angela as a solo singer and the concept of a female soloist at the carol service was new to him, but he couldn't see why not. He also admitted that he had begun to see Angela in a different light and enjoyed her company. He was searching for words to express the question that had arisen when he had talked with Stephen.

Peter perceived his difficulty and said, "Let me help you. I had a chat with Stephen after you visited him and I think I know what you are concerned about. Let me put it this way. In the table of affinities in the back of the *Book of Common Prayer*, it says that a man may not marry his sister, but there is no prohibition about a man marrying his stepsister. Thus, there would be no harm to anyone if you and Angela were to let your relationship deepen. Does that answer your question?"

"Thank you for putting it so clearly and sympathetically. There are other matters I must also consider, such as what career I should embark on and how to overcome the demons that disturb my sleep."

Peter replied, "I think Angela might have some knowledge and skill that might help you with your demons if you are prepared to talk to her about your experiences. She is very perceptive and understanding and values your health highly. As for future career, what are your options? Did the industrial experience help your decision making?"

"Yes, I think it did. I don't think it is the way I want to go. I am left with three options, as I see it. They are the church, teaching and research, possibly in the very new field of nuclear physics. As the first and third involve more study and more years before I have a secure regular salary, I am beginning to lean more and more towards teaching, which, if I could find a post, I could start in September."

"I know very little about nuclear physics," mused Peter, "but I do know about the church and that would involve more training, although you could seek ordination later in life and in the meantime pursue qualification as a lay reader. Such people are a great assistance to parish priests working in a parish on their own. Obviously, Angela can tell you more about teaching, although her knowledge is biased towards the younger children."

Richard sat nodding his head thoughtfully and then said, "Thank you for your helpful words. I think this could take me forward. I am very grateful."

"Good," said Peter, "I think we have covered all that we came here to do and rather more. Perhaps we had better re-join the ladies. I think I can hear the piano being played."

They could indeed hear the piano and Richard was surprised to hear a beautiful rendition of Schumann's 'Träumerie' and discovered yet another talent of the beautiful Angela of which he was ignorant. When she had finished and the men had applauded, she invited Richard to play. He started to play the carol 'Angels from the realms of glory' and then gradually changed to the carol 'Once in Royal David's city'. He began to sing, turned to Angela and invited her to join in and then allowed her to continue alone. At the end, he turned to Peter and said, "You were quite right. If this lovely clear voice could be loaned to us, I think we have found our soloist."

And then to Angela, he said, "Thank you, that was a heavenly sound, would you sing that first verse at the carol service?"

She replied, "I'd love to sing it, but haven't you got a boy to sing it?"

"No, I haven't found anyone and certainly the sound you produce is purer than even most boys can achieve."

On Tuesday, Richard went to the village school and met Angela's class. They had agreed that he would tell them the story of Androcles and the Lion. He varied his voice to show Androcles' moods and the class loved it when he made the lion growl or roar. Then they were sorry to learn that the lion had a thorn in his foot. He then had the class jeer and hiss when the Christian Androcles was sent out to meet a fierce and hungry lion. They were so pleased when the lion turned out to be the one Androcles had helped, especially when the lion showed Androcles his paw that had healed and they clapped in delight when Androcles and the lion embraced each other. Richard then asked them questions about the story and helped them to realise that sometimes you have to be brave to help someone in a difficult situation and pointed out that you never knew when a good turn offered without any expectation of reward might yield unexpected results. Miss Adams asked the class if they would like her to invite Mr Bailey to come again and tell them another story. The highly positive response was all the answer they needed.

Later, Grace wanted to know how the session had gone.

Angela replied, "Richard was brilliant, sometimes serious, sometimes funny and always keeping the attention of all of them."

Richard then said as he smiled at Angela, "The funniest part was the conversations at the school gate as I was leaving at afternoon playtime." They both began to laugh as they remembered.

"Well, come on, tell us," cried both Grace and Peter.

Angela started, "Two of the girls came up to me and said, 'We loved that story, is he your boyfriend?' so I said, 'Yes, he is one of my boyfriends,' then they replied, 'That's good, because if he is your boyfriend, he will have to come again if you tell him to.'"

Richard, grinning, took up the tale. "Meanwhile, another of the girls, hearing the word boyfriend, said, 'My mum says she is surprised Miss isn't already married,' then another girl offered, 'My mum says perhaps she hasn't found Mr Right yet.' At that point, one of the boys joined in with, 'Why, has she lost him?' to which another responded, 'Mr Wright lives near Perkins farm and he must be a hundred.' Not to be outdone another piped up, 'My dad says Miss is a Real Beaut.' After that I made my escape."

While they all had a good laugh at the things children of that age will say and repeat, Richard thought, *That lad's dad has just about got it right.*

When Friday came, Angela joined Richard and Peter in the church for choir practice. They practised the choir procession from the back of the church during the second and later verses of the first carol after Angela had sung the first verse unaccompanied and then the choir worked on improving the carols they would sing without the congregation. Angela stayed until the end and walked back with her two men. They both told her that there had been many complimentary comments from the choirmen about her solo.

The next day, with the help of Richard, Angela decorated the Christmas tree that had been delivered very early that morning. At one point, they had to revise the location of some of the decorations when they remembered that Stephen and Jean would be with them and Rachel was becoming increasingly mobile. While they worked Angela commented, "Dad tells me that you are thinking you might go in for teaching. I think you would be a good teacher."

"I'm not sure whether I am suited to it, but I think it is becoming my strongest option. Just because I had one successful story telling session, doesn't make me a natural."

"Maybe not, but I wasn't thinking of that. I watched the way you took choir practice last night. Not only did all the choir listen to your instructions, they put them into practice. When you were rehearsing the Coventry Carol and you told them to put themselves in Herod's position and thought everything you held most dear was threatened by a force you weren't sure how to deal with, the difference to the way they sang that verse was remarkable. There was fear and menace in the words that almost made me feel Herod was with us in the church."

"Thank you for that feedback. I shall need to ask you more about what you learned on your course and during your first year's teaching, but I also need to be sure that I have the stamina to be able to deal with the rigours of the classroom."

Angela thought, *Is this the time when I can persuade him to open up?* so she said in as casual a manner as she could while she fixed a bauble to the tree, "Are you still having trouble sleeping?"

Richard thought, *Perhaps I should take this opportunity to tell her a little, but how do I get started?* After a pause he said, "Tell me more about the things your psychology teacher said about people suffering from traumas."

"She told us about some research that had been started sometime after the end of the First World War and how the researchers looked for therapies that might help soldiers who suffered so badly from shellshock. She said it took a long time for people to recognise the symptoms of shellshock and even longer to find ways to help the sufferers. Then she went on to say that she thought the

Second World War had brought another mental illness and there needed to be research to consider what treatment might help the new sufferers. She talked about the terrible sights witnessed by military men and women and the impact those sights had upon them. She also said that the trauma might go on for years. She said that some of the sights and experiences were so horrific that the only way to cope was to try to shut them out of the mind, refuse to talk about them and try to live a normal life. But the memories would lie dormant during the day only to awake with force during the night."

She stopped for a moment, thinking how to proceed, then said, "I don't know if I'm explaining that very well."

They were silent for a few minutes while both sat down, the decorating temporarily abandoned. Then Richard said, "Go on, did she suggest an action or therapy that would help?"

"She wasn't sure how effective it would be, but she felt that trying to shut the memory down wouldn't work, so the sufferer should be helped to talk about the horrible scenes he had seen. She felt that a possible way to exorcise the memory was for the sufferer to describe, even almost to relive, incidents and thus bring them out into the open. She thought it would be a difficult task for the therapist as the scenes described might be so horrendous that they would find themselves greatly distressed. She also said that people would love to hear about successes and daring feats, but tended to shy away from the nasty side of war."

"I don't know whether talking would help, but it might be worth a try if I could bring myself to describe what I saw and still see. And who would be brave enough to subject themselves to the telling?"

"Dear Richard, now is not the right moment, but I would be willing to try to help you whenever you feel you want to talk. I don't think this is something you can arrange by appointment, but we may have opportunities when we are both around. If you feel the moment is right, don't hesitate to tell me and we'll find somewhere quiet together."

"Dear girl, when I feel I can pluck up the courage, I will let you know. Thank you so much."

Again, there was silence. Then they looked at each other, and as with one mind, continued to decorate the tree.

Chapter 13

Christmas Day 1948

The services had all gone well and the congregation loved Angela's solo. They would surely want to hear her sing again. Stephen, Jean and Rachel arrived the day before Christmas Eve and they all sat down to Christmas dinner on a cold but dry day. At the end of the meal and with still an hour and a half of daylight left, Richard turned to his mother and said, "That was a lovely meal. I think it was the best I have eaten since about 1937. Thank you. Now, after we've cleared away and washed up, I need to go for a walk." Then looking at Angela he said, "Do you feel like joining me?" Angela said that she would be delighted to accompany him.

His mother, sensing the walk might be important and before anyone else offered to join them, said, "You two go now. I have other helpers here that will be very happy to help, won't you?" as she looked at the rest of the family.

They walked for a while along well used roads, until they came to a track. Richard asked where it went and Angela replied that it was a footpath that eventually made its way to the next village. From a gateway, you could see the River Otter below.

"Now that is one of the strange things about Malta—a lack of rivers," said Richard.

"So, what was the landscape like?"

"Well, I didn't see it all, even though it's a small island—it would fit several times into Devon. When I was there, it was very hot, no excessively hot, and although the predominant colour seemed to be white or grey of the limestone and not the green we have in our countryside, it was not unpleasant. The people were very friendly and welcoming to the Brits. They are quite family orientated, although the hostilities meant they couldn't often take walks as a family in the evenings. There were bomb craters all over the place."

They walked until they came to the gateway set back a little from the main path.

Angela asked if he had slept well after they returned from midnight communion.

"No, I don't know if I was overtired, but I had some horrible memories. I hope I didn't shout out and wake anyone."

Angela thought this might be the time when he would speak, so she said gently, "Would you like to tell me about it?"

"Yes, I think I need to try, but I'm not sure how to begin."

"Perhaps I can help you. There are three things I have heard you say. If I tell you what I heard, maybe you can say what they were about. The first was, 'Oh no, not the bus, they're all islanders.'"

"Yes, I know what that was about and I see it so often. The bus passed the airfield on its journey from Valletta to Rabat. I watched two mechanics get off and as it continued its journey away from the airfield, I saw a German bomber dive down and fire on the bus. It burst into flames immediately and although I and the mechanics ran towards it there was nothing we could do to save any of the passengers. It was such a worthless loss of life and such a callous action. Why he went for the bus and not the airfield I don't know."

Richard's voice was shaking as he finished and Angela said, "How horrible and unnecessary. No wonder it affected you." She paused a few seconds and then continued, "Another of your memories must have been about fire, because your voice expressed urgency as you called, 'Get the pilot out, there's fire.'"

"Oh yes," said Richard, "that was ghastly. A young pilot, only eighteen, had somehow managed to get his Spitfire back on the ground after being hit by gunfire several times. As he came to a stop, I could tell he was injured and then I saw that the plane already had flames in several places. We had to get him out as soon as possible. All we had were buckets of water and we had to form a chain to get the water to the fire. We managed to open the cockpit and drag him out and as we did so the flames got to the fuel tank creating a fireball. The boy was more dead than alive, not so much from the burns as the injuries he sustained. Amazingly, he survived and none of our burns was too severe."

"You were burned?" gasped Angela.

"My hands were sore for a few days, but I was still able to work with bandages on and I limped a bit for a week or so until the burns on my foot healed."

"You must have been very brave to go to his rescue."

"It's odd, you don't think whether you are brave or frightened, you just act as quickly as you can."

Angela thought for a moment and then said, "Now I can understand what you were shouting about and why the urgency in your voice. But what did you mean when you called out on another occasion, 'How can I tell his family that he was blown to pieces?'"

Richard looked at her then and there was such distress on his face. "That was the worst of all. Two of us were putting a plane in a pen for protection when a German fighter-bomber flew over without warning. I shouted, 'Get down!' I was six paces ahead of him as we dived for cover. The shell must have landed on him and he was blown to pieces." He shuddered and just managed to continue with his voice breaking. "It was a terrible mess and I had to write to his parents and wife to tell them he had been killed."

Richard was nearly in tears as he turned away leaning over the gate with his head in his hands and shaking. Angela was nearly in tears herself. She didn't say anything. She just stood still beside him feeling she needed to put her arm round him. And then she thought, *Why shouldn't I?* So she did. He didn't pull away, but stood as he was for what seemed a very long time, but it may not have been much more than ten minutes.

Somebody walked by on the path, but didn't appear to see them and the spell remained unbroken. It ended when Richard let out an enormous sigh like a great release of pent-up energy, and said in a steady normal voice, "You must be cold. Thank you for listening to me, Anji. I think it's getting late and will be dark soon." He then turned to face her and said with a faint smile, "The family will think I've kidnapped you."

She looked him full in the face and with a twinkle in her eye responded, "Oh, what a delicious thought."

And with that he took her hand and said, "We need to get warm. Can you run?"

In the rectory, Grace noticed that it was beginning to get dark and realised that Richard and Angela had been gone quite a long time. She asked Peter if he would draw the curtains. He got up to do so and then turned. "Come and look at this, everyone." They were just in time to see Richard and Angela arrive at the gate hand in hand and looking flushed and happy.

Next morning, Angela woke after a somewhat fitful night's sleep still tired, but also still excited. She came down to breakfast to find Richard ahead of her in the kitchen making porridge. He came to meet her, took both hands in his and kissed her on the forehead and said, "How did my special lady sleep?"

"Quite well," she lied. "And how about you?"

"Very well, a really good sound sleep like I've not enjoyed for years. It must have been that run or some magic administered by a very beautiful lady who rescued me from a deep pit." He opened his arms wide and she rushed into them.

The embrace might have lasted much longer had not a voice said, "Do you two like burned porridge?" It was Jean.

"I'm sorry to interrupt, but I need to get some breakfast for Rachel before she tells the whole neighbourhood that she is hungry."

The next few days passed very swiftly. Richard and Angela went for long walks, on the bus to Exeter and to Honiton where they visited the pottery and the lace makers, made music together and talked a great deal. On New Year's Day, Richard teased Angela with a question.

"I received a letter from you when I was in Burma with an incomplete sentence in it. Can you tell me now what the missing words were?"

She pretended not to remember, so Richard quoted, "That's one brother hooked, but there's still one left," and she added very quietly, "For me."

"I think," said Richard, "that hook was dangling for a long time before I saw the bait and then I couldn't resist." He also said to her while holding her left hand, "Do you think you could keep this fourth finger free of ornamentation until Easter, because I would like to have something made to put on it?"

"Rich," she replied, "I shall endeavour to make sure no one steals me, because I am still waiting to be kidnapped by you, remember?"

Richard took Angela into his arms and said, "I am so pleased you are willing to put your life into my care because I love you so much."

"I don't know anyone else with whom I would want to share the rest of my life. I think I have loved you since the day your mother took me into your family."

"I am so grateful that you have said 'yes', because I don't think anyone else would be able make me so happy after the black days I have lived through. But, before I go back to Birmingham I need to know the ring size that will fit your finger and then I can make a trip to the Birmingham Jewellery Quarter where there are some very skilful artisans."

Although he didn't tell her then, Richard intended to have the gemstones he had purchased before he left Burma set in the gold ring he would give her on their official engagement.

Later that day, Richard sought an interview with Peter. "You may have noticed that the relationship between Angela and myself has deepened as I think you guessed it might. With your permission and your blessing, we would like to get engaged on Easter Sunday, Angela's 21st birthday and a wonderful time for new ventures."

Peter replied, "I and your mother are delighted and not surprised. We hope you will be very happy and if you pursue a teaching career and find a post not too far away we may be asking you to fill the vacancy for an organist and choirmaster that I think will arise fairly soon."

The next day, Richard shared an idea with Angela, "Before the new term starts, I wondered if we might take a trip to Southampton to visit our parents' graves, as it were to ask their blessing. I am not sure if we could manage it as a day trip. Do you know anyone who might be able to give us accommodation for a night?"

"What a lovely thought. I'll phone Golda Wronska and see if she has any suggestions. In any case, she will be delighted to hear our news, even if it is a little premature. I'll swear her to secrecy until Easter. She will expect an invitation to a wedding in due course."

Angela went off to phone Golda and returned twenty minutes later. "All arranged," she said, "we can go on Wednesday and the church will be open and Dad's successor will meet us and give us a blessing."

So many memories came into their minds when they visited the village in which they had grown up. Much was still the same, but there had also been changes. They were surprised how many people they remembered just happened to be passing the church while they were there meeting the new, to them, vicar. They met the vicar in the churchyard by their parents' graves and then he invited them into the church. As they entered, they heard the organ being played and were overjoyed to discover that it was Dr Helen James who was playing it.

Chapter 14

2 March 1949

With the Adams family in church for an Ash Wednesday service in the evening of 2 March, a visitor slipped into a pew at the back of the church a few minutes after the service started. It was not until the service finished and most of the congregation had filed out to make their way to their own homes that the identity of the visitor became apparent. Well wrapped up against the cold, he asked the rector's wife if he might beg a bed for the night. It was several seconds before she realised that it was her own son. Her exclamation of joy attracted the other two family members and, of course, they wanted to know why he was there. He said he would tell them all when they returned to the rectory.

As soon as they were back indoors, Richard said, "I am here, because it's rather late to return to Birmingham tonight. I've been in Exeter all day at a boys' grammar school and…" He paused and looked at the expectant faces of each of them in turn before continuing, "I have been offered the post of assistant physics teacher to start in September. I think I might accept it. What do you think?"

Angela rushed to him, threw her arms round him and said she couldn't be happier. She stopped and thought, *There is one thing that could make me even happier, but how can I ask him now?*

Richard perceived that there was a question in the air so added, "If you want a silver lining, it is that I haven't suffered a single nightmare in 1949. I think this is going to be our year."

****

Dear Reader

I hope you have enjoyed reading my story. If you wish to amuse yourself further, you might like to complete the local newspaper report below to your satisfaction.

The wedding took place at St Lawrence's Church on Saturday, 24 December 1949 (Christmas Eve) of Mr Richard George Bailey and Miss Angela Mary Adams. The best man was… and the bridesmaid(s) were… The bride was given away by… and the service was conducted by… The organist was…

The author's suggestion for the newspaper notice is below.

The wedding took place at St Lawrence's Church on Saturday, 24 December 1949, (Christmas Eve) of Mr Richard George Bailey and Miss Angela Mary Adams. The best man was Mr Stephen Bailey and the bridesmaids were Mrs Jean Bailey and Miss Rachel Bailey. The bride was given away by Prebendary Peter Adams and the service was conducted by Canon Simon Lane. The organist was Dr Helen James.

Additional information:

The couple left two days after Christmas for a week's honeymoon in Malta, where Mr Bailey served for a few months in 1942.

****

A Battle of Wills

"How much longer, do you think, Owen?"

"Not much more than twenty minutes, dear. We'll put the kettle on as soon as we arrive home."

"Good, I could do with a cuppa. What's that lorry doing? He hasn't seen u!"

While she was screaming her last utterance, her husband was yelling, "I can't avoid him. We're going to cr…!"

The Vauxhall Corsa with four on board smashed into the side of the scrap metal lorry that had pulled out from a side road into their path. The squeal of brakes, the bang of the impact and the noise of metal tearing with metal plates and iron bars falling was followed by a second or two of silence as all other traffic came to a standstill. A voice from the back of the car murmured, "Mum" and then "Dad." He thought he received a groan from his mother and nothing from his father.

Then a female voice from the back asked, "Glyn, are you hurt? My door has been blown open, but I don't know if I can free my legs to get out."

"I don't think I can move, Bridget. I can't feel my legs and there is something wedging my head against the roof."

The sound of footsteps coming from several directions, prompted Bridget to instruct Glyn not to try to move as help was coming.

*

Owen Jones was born and grew up in a small village in Snowdonia. His father was a hill farmer with a flock of hardy Welsh sheep. As they grew up, Owen and his older brother Gareth helped their father with the sheep, particularly at lambing time. It was expected that Gareth would inherit the farm from his dad when the older man retired. It didn't work out as planned as their father died before reaching retirement age and although Gareth did run the farm for a few years he accepted the offer made him by a neighbour who wished to expand his holding. Gareth then emigrated from Wales to Canada where he met and married a Canadian girl and began sheep farming in his new country. Meanwhile, Owen had married Cerys, his sweetheart from school days and moved to a nearby village where he became the local school-teacher in a primary school with just 60 pupils.

A double tragedy in Owen's life occurred when Cerys succumbed to a virulent form of influenza and died in February 1995, when she was four months pregnant. The next two years were dark days in Owen's life until they were brightened when, on an excursion in May 1997, to Aberystwyth, he met Bronwen, from Llangollen, who was staying in the town on holiday with her parents. Although he had enjoyed some female companionship with Gwladys Jones, his part-time school secretary who had comforted him when he was most depressed, it was with Bronwen that he began to live again. Friendship developed into a relationship and within a year they were married in July 1998. Within another year, their son Thomas was born early in July 1999. The birth was not easy and Bronwen was advised that she would not be able to have any more children.

Now that they had a son, they decided that they should make their wills. With the help of a friend, they drew up simple and almost identical wills. They both wished to leave everything to the other and if their spouse had pre-deceased them, to their son. They also included a clause that in the event that both spouse and son had already died, their estate would be passed in the case of Owen to his brother Gareth and of Bronwen to her sister Gwyneth. They signed the wills, had them witnessed, put them in a drawer and forgot about them.

When Bronwen had recovered from giving birth and had established a routine with caring for her son, she found that she could combine the role of mother with that of part-time school secretary in support of her husband. The vacancy for a secretary had occurred when Gwladys left in September 1997. She originally asked for leave of absence to look after her sick grandmother who lived in Pembrokeshire. When she returned in late 1998 with a son Glyn, it was not long before various rumours circulated about the boy's father. Some of these were built on speculation and arithmetic. Others, perhaps stimulated by comments made by Gwladys, suggested that she had married a seaman while he was on shore leave at Pembroke Dock. However, when it became known that Glyn had been born in January 1998, calendars were again produced and memories were racked as to whether Gwladys had been absent from the village nine months previously.

As months became years and as both Glyn and Thomas grew up, questions about the paternity of the former were forgotten. The boys became good friends and had many interests in common, especially sporting. Time spent together was partly because they enjoyed each other's company, but also because Glyn's mother's health was not good and she needed regular hospital visits. Owen and Bronwen were happy to care for Glyn on these occasions. Eventually, Gwladys received a diagnosis of stomach cancer and she passed away in 2012. Owen and Bronwen had no hesitation in offering a home to Glyn as both his grandparents were deceased. It was when they considered a formal adoption that they discovered that there was no father named on Glyn's birth certificate. He had been given his mother's surname of Jones, one of the commonest surnames in Wales and the same as his adoptive parents. The boys were very happy with the adoption arrangement as their relationship was such that they behaved as brothers. When Gwyneth, Bronwen's older and unmarried sister, visited the family at Christmas, she thought they looked so alike that anyone meeting them for the first time would assume they were brothers.

The next two years were happy ones for the extended family and they enjoyed many joint projects, including hill climbing and, for the boys, playing rugby and, in the summer, tennis. Thomas became a very skilful hooker and was selected for the County Youth Rugby Team. In March 2015, playing in an inter-county match watched by national selectors, Thomas sustained a serious injury. He was taken by ambulance to hospital in Bangor where he was treated for his injuries, including a nasty fracture of his right leg.

After three weeks in hospital, he was allowed home, but needed regular physiotherapy sessions. To start with, he made good progress, but then his general health began to deteriorate. Initially, his parents thought he must be suffering from delayed reaction to the accident possibly combined with frustration at being laid up. However, when his decline continued and he exhibited symptoms that gave them considerable concern, their doctor determined to take a blood sample that was sent away for analysis. In the two days while they waited for the results, Thomas's condition worsened. He had difficulty breathing, was running a high temperature, and was confused and incoherent. When the doctor called again, he immediately sent for an ambulance without waiting for the blood test results. Within minutes of arriving in the hospital, the results were available and sepsis was diagnosed. He was consigned to intensive care, but his body failed to respond to the treatment he was given and he died on his sixteenth birthday.

Reflecting on his own losses of both his mother and now his best friend and stepbrother, Glyn realised how devastating the grief must be for his adopted parents. He went out of his way to support and care for them, doing all he could to make their lives bearable. Owen and Bronwen were grateful for the love and attention given to them by the boy they had brought into their care just three short years earlier, but they felt that he should be encouraged to try to take up some of the activities he had enjoyed previously. They persuaded him to start playing tennis again before the season came to an end.

Glyn was not sure how he would feel about attending the tennis club on his own, but he was welcomed warmly and before long he did begin to enjoy both the exercise and the social contact. Owen and Bronwen were pleased to respond positively when towards the end of September, Glyn asked if he could invite a friend from the club to come to the house. Bronwen was delighted to discover that the friend was female, particularly when she discovered that Bridget shared her enthusiasm for horticulture. Bridget's mother ran a small market garden and she was supported by her husband when he could spare time from his practice as a solicitor. As well as producing fruit and vegetables, Bridget and her mother grew flowers for cutting and, although still sixteen and at school Bridget had started designing and constructing wedding bouquets.

At one time, Glyn had toyed with the idea of trying to pursue a career in playing tennis. His coach considered he displayed the necessary skills and qualities to be able to make his way as a professional. When he thought about the amount of time he would need to dedicate to practice and that he would need to be away from home for substantial periods of the year, he abandoned the idea. Instead, after discussion with Owen, he decided to leave school and develop the skills he had already acquired in carpentry to make bespoke furniture and other wooden artefacts. After trying his hand at wood turning and making fruit bowls, superior plant tubs and other small wooden items, he discovered that there was a market for them. When placed on the stall Bridget and her mother had each week in the neighbouring town, not only did they sell well, but he received repeat orders.

One day in August 2017, after Bridget had completed her A levels and left school, Owen and Bronwen took Glyn and Bridget out for the day to a stately home that boasted a nationally renowned garden. The young people came away with many new ideas for designs of garden furniture, indoor wooden items and flower arrangements, particularly using some of the more exotic flowers for which the garden was famous. On the way home, they had been talking excitedly about what they had seen, when Bridget commented that the long wall on their left might contain an estate with unusual plants. On the other side were some rocky outcrops of a hill through which the road had been cut. As the wall on the left came to an end there was a side road out of which a lorry emerged without stopping. Travelling at nearly 60 miles per hour, Owen had no chance of avoiding it.

*

The emergency services were soon on the scene of the crash, summoned by the passenger in the following car. The driver of a removal van which was approaching the junction from the opposite direction pulled up as quickly as he could. The driver of the car behind him was the first on the scene, soon accompanied by other drivers and their passengers. The scene that met the first to arrive was described by them most often as 'carnage'. Much of the car was covered in part of the load of scrap metal. When the fire and rescue service arrived, they found metal sheets, iron rods and other items being removed by people with their bare hands. Metal cutters had to be used to remove parts of the car to reach the occupants.

One rear seat passenger, a girl, was released quite quickly. She was alive and conscious but was thought to have at least one broken leg and possibly other injuries. She was placed on a stretcher and immediately taken to hospital by one of the ambulances. Of the other occupants, the two in the front had died almost instantly. The other back seat passenger was trapped and alive, but slipping in and out of consciousness. Eventually, he was freed and flown to hospital by air ambulance for his injuries to be assessed.

It was several minutes before anyone thought to check on the driver of the scrap metal lorry. He was found still in his cab, apparently uninjured but unconscious. He had a very low pulse and was in a state of collapse, so was also taken to hospital. There was immediate speculation that he may have been unconscious before the collision.

The police were busy taking statements from everyone who had seen the crash. They were pleased to discover that the car following the crashed vehicle and the removal van had clear dashcam footages. From the resting place of the Corsa, tyre marks on the road and the dashcam pictures from the following car, the police were able to judge that the driver had tried to protect his passengers by steering to the left so taking the worst of the impact on his side.

The medical assessments of the five involved in the crash were pretty grisly reading. Owen Jones almost certainly died instantly from multiple injuries including a massive blow to his head. Bronwen Jones died within seconds of the collision with severe injuries to her legs and chest where a metal rod had pierced her heart. Glyn Jones had both legs broken, five cracked ribs, severe bruising and cuts to his face and head. Bridget Llewellyn had a broken leg, two cracked ribs and extensive bruising. Derek Martin, the 60-year-old driver of the lorry, had suffered a stroke minutes before the crash and was probably unconscious by the time of the impact; he was otherwise uninjured, but had suffered paralysis to the right side of his body.

The police had the difficult task of notifying relatives. Bridget was well enough to give details of her parents, who were soon at her bedside in hospital. She was also able to tell them that Bronwen's parents, in their seventies and in failing health, lived in Llangollen and that she had an older sister Gwyneth. From Gwyneth, they learned that Owen's only relative was his brother Gareth in Canada.

When Gwyneth visited Glyn in hospital, she discovered that although seriously ill, his condition was stable and he was expected to recover, although he may not be able to leave hospital for six weeks or longer. He asked her about Bridget's condition, so she went away to find out. As an investigative journalist for a national newspaper, she was adept at obtaining the information she wanted and before long she was at Bridget's bedside and talking with her parents. It did not take many minutes before Geraint Llewellyn, Bridget's father and Gwyneth decided that they were the most appropriate people to deal with funeral arrangements and legal matters. Geraint agreed to ask one of his colleagues to deal with wills and financial costs and payments. Gwyneth said she would make the arrangements for the funerals with a funeral director and the local Methodist minister and then inform Gareth.

The next time Geraint and Gwyneth spoke, there were still two questions to resolve. They did not know if Gareth would wish to come to the funerals and whether Glyn would be well enough to attend. It was decided that there would be a joint funeral and burial followed by a wake in the hall next to the chapel and then the family would return to the Jones's house for a formal reading of the wills.

By delaying the funerals for three weeks, there was enough time for Gareth and his wife to book flights to join them. It was his first visit to Wales and the place of his birth since he had emigrated more than twenty years before. The delay also gave Glyn just enough time to reach a stage in his recovery to be able to attend in a wheelchair with his right leg in traction and a nurse in attendance.

The chapel was packed for the service and although there were few relatives a large proportion of the village population was present to honour the village schoolteacher and the school secretary. Many former pupils also attended showing how much the couple had been respected in the community. When she saw how many stayed for the wake, Gwyneth was pleased that she had ordered refreshments on the side of generosity.

Present for the reading of the wills were Geraint Llewellyn and his solicitor colleague, Glyn with a nurse in attendance, Gareth and his wife, Bronwen's parents and Gwyneth. Geraint's colleague explained that the wills were simple and very similar. He read each of them and checked that there was nothing that needed explanation in the wording. He then pointed out, "It had been anticipated that one will would have been read when one death had occurred. Although taken together, the wills allow for the situation when both Owen and Bronwen had passed away, it had been assumed that the deaths would not occur simultaneously. Nevertheless, both wills make provision for the inheritance to be passed to a surviving son, but the son Thomas has pre-deceased them. Now, we have to consider whether there is another son, namely Glyn. Does he have a claim as an adopted son, rather than a natural one? I will pause there for you to consider and to ask any questions."

Gareth was first to speak, "This is how I see it. We may have to leave Glyn out of the reckoning, although we may wish to make some provision for him. If we assume that Owen and Bronwen died at the same time, Gwyneth and I share the inheritance. If it can be proved that Bronwen died first, it is mine to claim. If Owen was the first to die, then it goes to Gwyneth."

Then Gwyneth spoke, "I would be very happy to see the inheritance go to Glyn, particularly after what he has suffered and in recognition of the way he cared for Owen and Bronwen after Thomas died. However, that may not be legally possible, especially if he is not the natural son of Owen or Bronwen. I think there are two issues that need to be resolved and it may need to be a court decision—I don't know, I am not a lawyer. The first is whether Glyn has a justifiable claim, either by adoption or even by parentage—it is not known who his father is or was. Could Owen have fathered him? A DNA test might tell us or are we too late having buried Owen? The second issue relates to the fact that the son mentioned in the wills is not named, but if Glyn does have an admissible claim we have to recognise that Glyn was born before Thomas although both were born before the wills were drawn up."

The solicitor then turned to Glyn, "Have you any comments?"

Glyn thought for a moment or two and then replied, "It is obviously not clear at this stage whether any money will come to me, but whether there is or not, partly to acknowledge the respect in which they were both held as evidenced this afternoon, I would like there to be some memorial in the village or the chapel or possibly a garden or quiet space." He continued, "I have no idea whether Owen was my natural father and I am surprised by the suggestion."

"Sorry to mention that possibility, Glyn," interposed Gwyneth, "but I have always been struck by the similarity between you and Thomas whenever I saw the two of you together."

The solicitor summarised very briefly, "We have seen there are some issues to resolve before we can say definitely who should be the beneficiaries and we may need expert guidance. I am willing to seek that guidance if you wish me to, both in respect of interpretation and in answer to questions we have raised. Glyn, if it is possible to check DNA, would you be prepared to provide a sample. Also, Gareth, as Owen's brother, would you be prepared to have a sample taken before you return to Canada?"

All agreed to further investigation and both Glyn and Gareth agreed to provide samples.

While the proceedings had been in progress, Glyn's nurse had been busy sending a text on her mobile phone. As the meeting was about to be concluded, the nurse's phone rang. She held up her hand while she listened as if to signal that this was a call with some relevance to the debate. At the end, she looked to the solicitor and said, "I sent a text to the hospital to ask if they had collected any DNA. Apparently, they do as a routine for identity purposes. There is a definite match between Glyn and Owen, suggesting that Owen was Glyn's birth father."

The solicitor responded, "Thank you for that information, but I am not sure that it clarifies the inheritance situation. In fact, it may muddy the waters rather. I think this points to the need for a court judgement and the wisdom of Solomon."

Gareth asked, "May I make a suggestion; that you offer the court a solution that the inheritance be split three ways, being Glyn, Gwyneth and myself."

Gwyneth responded, "I don't agree. I think it should all go to Glyn, because I am sure that is what Owen and Bronwen would have wanted, especially if they had known that Glyn was their son which was how they had considered him."

The solicitor looked to Glyn who stated, "Leave it to the courts and stop squabbling about it. I am getting tired and I need to rest."

Bridget and Glyn continued to make good recoveries. After she had been discharged, Bridget and one of her parents made regular visits to see Glyn and learned how to assist him with his physiotherapy. Their relationship flourished as they began to make plans for the future. In particular, they were encouraged to learn that the idea of a memorial garden had already attracted many generous contributions, including an offer of a suitable plot of land in the village.

They were both able to attend the inquest into the crash. The police presented a technical report in which they stated that Owen had no chance of avoiding the lorry, but had tried to protect his passengers by steering to the left. The state of health of the lorry driver had been examined. There was nothing in his medical history to indicate a susceptibility to strokes and he had had a full check-up sixth months earlier. Both vehicles had been thoroughly examined and, although they would not have contributed to the crash, some deficiencies were found in the lorry's braking system and the state of its maintenance was inadequate. A separate investigation would lead to a prosecution of the firm owning the vehicle.

Three months after the accident, the court made a ruling in favour of Glyn. In the report of the court's deliberations, it was stated that if Glyn's claim had not been upheld, the beneficiary would have been Gwyneth as it appeared that Bronwen had survived her husband by a few seconds.

Glyn accepted the verdict, but stated that although he was grateful to receive the legacy, he found it poor compensation for the loss of two lovely parents. Gwyneth was delighted by the ruling. There was no reaction from Gareth in Canada as his hopes for a pay-out had not materialised.

Behind Closed Doors

1

"They're here, Mike," shouted Lucy to her husband from the kitchen where she could see the road outside.

"What's that, dear?" Mike called, as he was standing somewhat precariously on a chair changing a bulb in the ceiling light above the dining room table.

"It's Eric and Pat; they are just pulling on to the drive."

"Go out and greet them, Lucy, while I put these tools away. I have just finished the last job, so they have timed it perfectly."

While Lucy went to the door that was in the centre of the front of their detached house, Mike came out of the dining room that was behind the kitchen and out to the garage to replace the tools he had been using. When he returned, Lucy was showing their guests through to the sitting room on the other side of the house behind the study that looked out onto the road.

Eric turned to greet Mike and after responding to Mike's query about their journey asked, "Would it be possible to put my car on charge?"

"Certainly," responded Mike, "so you have gone electric since we last saw you; let's do it now."

It was some minutes before they returned to the ladies who were chatting with mugs of coffee in their hands. Pat was saying, "I expect Eric has been showing his new car to Mike."

"Exactly, Pat," remarked Mike, "it's a beauty, but not as beautiful as you," as he went to her and kissed her. "It really is good to welcome one of my favourite girlfriends back to our house."

Pat, sharing a grin with Lucy responded, "It's good to be back in the village, Mike, but I perceive that you are still the village charmer, especially where the ladies are concerned."

Lucy joined in the teasing, "Oh, he hasn't changed. I don't think I would want him to, except when I ask him to fetch something from the village shop and he has so many conversations on the way that I never know how long it will be before he returns.”

“That’s something that I remember about the village when we lived here: everyone is so friendly and there is such a good sense of community,” commented Eric.

“That’s true,” replied Lucy, “but not even Mike has been able to get more than a reluctant ‘good morning’ from the new people over the road.”

“I noticed the change to the property opposite you as we arrived. High fences and formidable eight-foot double gates! It looks as though they have barricaded themselves in as though preparing for a siege. I wonder why?” A pensive frown on Eric’s face accompanied his last three words, spoken slowly.

Lucy was quick to say, “Now, Eric, you have come for a holiday; you can give your suspicious police mind a rest for a few days. I don’t think you’ll notice many changes since you moved away three years ago. Are you still pleased with your Thames Ditton house and being so close to the Met’s police horse training centre?”

Before Eric could reply, his wife interrupted, “We are pleased with the house and we have very friendly neighbours for which I am grateful, but we don’t feel the sense of community in suburbia that exists here. I miss the country walks with the peace and quiet, although a walk along the Thames towpath is enjoyable. The path is quite well populated but very few speak or even smile.”

Eric added, “The location is very convenient for the work I have to do in my current role, although I am not allowed to say much about that. It is not a bad run to Guildford if I need to liaise with the Surrey police and London by train is easy enough if I need to visit New Scotland Yard or anywhere else in the city. Now, other than your neighbours at ‘Fort Knox’ over the road, are there any other new people in the village?”

Conversations between the four friends continued as they caught up with news of the family members of each pair. They also made plans for how they would use the week they had together. Other than a few days when Mike and Lucy had visited the Thames Ditton house, this week was to be the first opportunity they would have to continue the exploring they had been accustomed to for the several years when they were near neighbours.

After lunch, Eric and Pat brought their luggage in from the car and put it in the front bedroom Lucy had prepared for them. Then they began the walk around and beyond the village. Lucy was intrigued to notice that Eric seemed to be taking an interest in the back of the fortification he had nicknamed 'Fort Knox'. She wondered what was going through his mind, but then other matters took his attention. She also noticed how Mike expertly manoeuvred the disposition of the party so that he accompanied Pat. However, she found Eric entertaining and realised that his observational skills were highly developed as he pointed out things she would have not given a second glance.

After three days with fine June weather when they visited both familiar and unfamiliar places in the county, they decided to have a morning shopping. Lucy and Mike were downstairs first and while Mike fed the birds, Lucy began getting breakfast ready. She had nearly finished before Pat and Eric appeared together.

Pat apologised for being later than she had intended and so had not helped Lucy with the breakfast. She explained, "I slept late, and Eric didn't wake me as he was reading. I woke during the night and after visiting the bathroom I looked out of the window where I saw some activity over the road."

Eric was suddenly alert. "What did you see, Pat?" He clearly wanted to know about the house.

"It was just after 2.30 a.m. and very dark, but the road was suddenly lit up by a vehicle. As it approached, it switched off its headlights and then I saw torches and the big gates of the house opposite being opened. The van, one of those long transit types, reversed through the gates, being directed by the torches. The gates were quickly shut but not before the light from one of the torches shone on a shed or outhouse in which a light was also shining. Then everything went quiet, so I returned to bed, but it was a long time before I went to sleep again."

"How curious," pondered Eric. "I can understand the headlights being switched off to avoid disturbing the neighbours at that time of night. But who would be working then? Did you see anything else?"

"Oh yes; by replaying the scene in my mind, I can remember something else. I caught sight of some lettering on the side of the van. All I could read was MFORT and then a gap and B, but I don't know what the rest was. I don't think we can find out, because just as I was drifting off to sleep I heard something, so I looked out of the window again and I saw some tail lights of a vehicle larger than a car disappearing down the road. I looked towards the gates, and they were just closing, so I assume the van had just left. That got me puzzling again so I lay awake for several more minutes."

Eric turned to Lucy and asked, "Have you ever seen any nocturnal activity over the road?"

"No, as our bedroom is at the back of the house, we don't have occasion to look out the front during the night. I can remember looking out at the fireworks on bonfire night, but that was earlier in the evening; it must have been about two weeks after the people moved in and before they started their alterations."

"I wonder if last night was a one-off or a regular occurrence," mused Eric. "If you hear anything again, Pat, please wake me up. I am curious and should like to know what is going on and what the other letters are on the van. MFORT B—Anyone any thoughts?"

"Any thoughts about what?" Mike inquired as he entered the room.

Lucy explained for her husband, who had not been in the room when Pat shared her news. Eric repeated the letters, then both he and Lucy spoke at the same time "Comfort?"

"Comfort Beds," exclaimed Pat. "That's where I should have been when the van arrived."

"And maybe that is where they hoped all the residents of the village would be at that time," commented Eric. "If you will just excuse me for a few minutes, I think I'll phone my office and ask them to find out if there is a company called 'Comfort Beds' anywhere around here."

When he returned from making his call, having found a location where he obtained a good signal for his mobile, he asked the others if they would like him to drive and if they had a specific destination for their shopping trip in mind, such as Poole or Salisbury. They chose Salisbury, as Lucy had heard of a good place to eat, and they could also include a visit to the cathedral.

2

As they left the cathedral in the afternoon and began to wander around the Cathedral Close, Eric's phone rang. He spotted a convenient seat and sat down while the others continued to admire the exterior of the ancient building. His phone call finished, Eric re-joined his group and reported, "We were nearly right: Comfort Bedding, such things as mattresses, pillows, sheets, duvets and blankets. Their main premises are on the eastern side of Bristol, and they have a successful export trade to the continent by ferry from Poole or Portsmouth. And, your new neighbours recently relocated from Bristol. They are a couple with two sons in their early twenties."

Mike thought about the information for a moment and then commented, "You have been busy investigating. Are you happy now, because it all sounds legitimate?"

"Do you think so?" Eric responded somewhat dubiously.

"Well, try this. Our neighbours decided they needed new mattresses and ordered them from a firm with whom they had had previous dealings when they lived in Bristol. The firm said they could delete carriage costs if they could drop off the goods on the way to the early morning ferry, provided they would accept a night-time delivery."

"It seems plausible, but I still don't understand the need for such high gates."

On the way home, the phone in Eric's car became active, indicating an incoming call. Eric pressed the appropriate button and, while he still had both hands on the steering wheel, said, "I'd better answer this, but I may need to pull over."

Seeing a suitable place to stop, he drove towards it at the same time beginning his conversation. "Hello, Colin, is there something important? I'm in the car with passengers."

A voice at the other end replied, "I understand, Chief, but I think you should know that Herr Bruck from Frankfurt would like to speak to you."

"Thank you, Colin. I have his number and I'll phone him as soon as I can."

"I'm sorry to have to call you while you are on holiday. I hope you had a good day in Salisbury, and you haven't cricked your neck looking at the top of the 404-foot cathedral spire."

"I'm quite fit, thank you, lad. You needn't spend your time star gazing while I am away; just keep your nose to the grindstone!"

"Yes, sir, goodbye, sir."

Having completed their return journey, while Lucy and Pat prepared a snack and Mike watered the garden, Eric went for a walk. He found a suitably private place from which he phoned his contact in Germany. After initial pleasantries, they agreed to converse in English as Herr Bruck was not certain that he could not be overheard. Eric began, "You have some news for me, Kurt?"

"Yes, indeed. We think we may have a lead on those forged Euro notes that keep appearing. The forgery is so good that very few people can spot them. Today, a bank clerk had three of the forged twenty Euro notes handed in by a lady when she was banking her—how do you say it?—guest house or B&B takings. Fortunately, the bank clerk remained calm and thought quickly. She casually remarked to the lady that she hadn't seen such clean notes for some time. The customer seemed happy to enter into conversation and volunteered information that she had received them in change when she paid two 100 Euro notes for four pillows costing 35 euros each. The bank clerk asked if they were good quality pillows to which the lady replied that they had come highly recommended from a firm in England."

"Do you know the name of the firm, Kurt?"

"Yes I do, thanks to the young assistant in the bank. She expressed interest in possibly buying some pillows for her parents and the lady took a receipt from her handbag. The firm is based in Bristol and is called Comfort Bedding—have you heard of it, Eric?"

"I heard of it today when I asked my team to check on a vehicle that attracted my attention. The information they passed to me did not arouse my suspicions particularly, but now, on the basis of your intelligence, I think I shall investigate further. They export their products to the continent by van, crossing the English Channel by ferry into France. I wonder how often they cross and where they go to once they reach the French ports. We may need to involve our French colleagues. Kurt, I will make enquiries here and keep you posted. Many thanks and I think your alert bank clerk might be in for a reward."

Eric had much to think about as he walked back to join the others. He was part of a small team that investigated and monitored national and international currency violations, including money laundering, forgery and abuse of crypto currency and bitcoins. Were these forged Euro notes being printed in this country? Was Comfort Bedding in any way involved? Was the 'Fort Knox' house in the village part of a fraudulent exercise? He decided that he would ask for more detailed information about Comfort Bedding, which must be done without arousing concern.

While he had been walking and thinking, Eric had taken a detour which required him to pass the village pub. He hadn't asked his hosts how the pub was doing. On arriving at his hosts' house, he inquired about the pub and was told that it was thriving under new management and had become very popular. He suggested that he and Pat should treat Lucy and Mike to a meal there on the next evening. Everyone being agreeable, he booked a table for four.

When they arrived at 'The Six Bells' the following evening, they were shown to their table, ordered drinks and then perused the menu. Having made his choice quickly and while the others were trying to make up their minds, Eric looked around the room and noticed a few changes that had been made in the three years since he was last there. He also noticed two young men at a nearby table in quite animated conversation. They were both wearing shirts in the colours of rugby teams that he recognised. Asking Pat if she would order his choice if he wasn't back in time he excused himself from his table and went to talk to the two young men. "Good evening," he began, "excuse me for butting in, but I noticed you are both wearing the colours of rugby teams. Does that mean you are both fans, but not of the same club?"

The lads both looked up and initially did not look too pleased to be addressed by a stranger, but the chance to talk about rugby brought about a change of countenance. "That's right," said the one Eric assumed to be the elder, although the striking similarity in their appearances suggested to him that they were brothers. "We were arguing or debating the merits of each team with a needle match coming up on Sunday."

"So, who supports Bristol and I assume the other roots for Bath?"

The same brother continued as spokesman, "I am the Bristol man because we used to live fairly close to their ground, but since we moved house, my brother decided to follow Bath as it is closer to here. Are you also a rugby fan and which is your team?"

"In my youth, many years ago, I played a few games for Exeter Chiefs' second team and played against both of your clubs. But I am only a visitor in this part of the country, although I do sometimes get to see international matches and some of the six nations matches as I now live about five miles from Twickenham. So, will you both be going to Bristol on Sunday?"

"He is," said the younger brother, "as he has helped with the design and printing of the match programme." Disregarding a restraining hand on his arm and seeming to desire to make a contribution to the conversation, he continued, "I cannot go as I have been asked to help a friend who has a job to do in France."

At that moment, the boys' meals were brought to them.

Eric bade them goodbye and hoped they both enjoyed their weekends. As he sat down, he wondered if the two lads he had spoken to were the sons of the couple at 'Fort Knox'. The conversation at his table was now in full swing about whether a buyer would come forward for the village shop and post office. Their meals, when they were served, were very good. Eric noticed that the two rugby brothers left as soon as they had eaten their meals and didn't speak to anyone else.

When the landlord stopped at their table to ask if everything was to their satisfaction, Eric took the opportunity to ask a question. "The young men in rugby shirts, are they regulars and village lads?"

The landlord replied, "I know most of the regulars quite well, but not that pair. They come in about once a month and I think, although I don't know, that they may have to fend for themselves on those evenings. Perhaps their parents go out and do not cook on those days, but they keep themselves very much to themselves. I was really surprised they talked to you—our waitress attracted my attention as it was such an unusual occurrence."

"Maybe they are 'townies' and not accustomed to the caring gossips you find in village communities. Perhaps they are still getting acclimatised, although the village pub is one of the best ways to get to know people and to get known, unless they do not want that sort of familiarity," commented Eric.

The two couples left the pub to walk home just before 8.30 p.m. when it was still light, being midway through June. They had completed about half their journey when a small helicopter came from behind them flying quite low. They watched as the chopper spent a few minutes going forwards and backwards over a nearby field, before slowly making its departure over Lucy and Mike's house before passing over 'Fort Knox'.

"What do you think that was about?" Mike asked. "Do you think they were taking pictures, perhaps for an archaeology survey?"

It was Pat who responded, "If it was for archaeology, it was a sensible time to take photos because the sun is low and bumps and undulations could show up more clearly on the film."

Eric commented, "I wonder if they had the cameras still running when they passed over 'Fort Knox'. I'd like to have a peek at the footage if they have any. I wonder where they came from."

"You really have got a thing about that house, haven't you, Eric?" Lucy said. "I think I know whose field they hovered over. I'll see if I can find out, if you wish."

"I should be grateful for that information. I'll tell you why when we are indoors."

When they reached home and were drinking coffee, Lucy turned to Eric, "Now, why are you so interested in our neighbours? Spill the beans!"

"What I am going to tell you is in strictest confidence, you understand. Not a word to anyone. We have been getting reports from different parts of Europe of forged Euro bank notes being circulated. The financial institutions in Frankfurt are getting very twitchy about the situation as the notes are excellent forgeries and difficult to detect. The amount of illegal cash floating about is reaching significant proportions. That call I had this afternoon alerted me to a possible area of investigation. My contact informed me that some of the notes may have come from somewhere in this country as they were able to link them to a purchase of pillows supplied by Comfort Bedding of Bristol."

"Wow, that's extraordinary," cried Pat. "If I hadn't visited the bathroom in the middle of the night, we wouldn't have known anything about Comfort Bedding."

"So, do you think there is some criminal activity going on over the road?" Mike inquired.

"I didn't say that," responded Eric. "Even if the firm is involved, and that is far from certain, your neighbours may have nothing to do with it. Nevertheless, I intend to make some enquiries, especially after my conversation with those two lads this evening. One has some knowledge of printing, and the other is going to France this weekend to help a friend. Again, I ask you, Lucy and Mike, not to say anything to anyone, even if you hear other tongues wagging. But if you hear or see anything you think may be relevant, let me know."

Lucy took the coffee mugs into the kitchen to wash them up and while she was there, she phoned the farmer over whose field the helicopter had been hovering. When she returned, she reported to Eric that the farmer didn't know who owned the aircraft, but he had given her the name and telephone number of the archaeologist who was interested in examining the contours in case there may be something that suggested an exploratory dig might be worth considering. Eric thanked Lucy, made a note of the details and said he would make contact the following morning.

The next day, Friday, and Pat and Eric's last day, Eric made two telephone calls, and as a result, invited the other three to join him in a little excursion to visit a Dr Mortimer to look at the photos from the aerial recognisance. The expert explained how the markings suggested there could be the remains of a structure of some sort, possibly a village and maybe a manor house or even some form of religious building. He then showed them some discolouration in the lawn in Mike and Lucy's back garden. He told them they would not be able to see the line with a different colour with the naked eye at ground level, but it appeared that there could be an old path or roadway in their garden that continued past their house and across the road to the house opposite. Lucy noticed that Eric studied the film of the house and grounds of their neighbours most assiduously.

On their return, it was obvious that Mike and Lucy were most excited about the prospect of an old roadway in their garden and wondered if there could be buried treasure in the garden. Eric pronounced himself very interested in what he had seen but did not divulge what had attracted his attention. He also did not tell them that in his second phone call he had asked for observers at the channel ferry ports to watch for a Comfort Bedding van and, if one made the crossing, to alert French police to monitor its progress on the continent.

In their last afternoon together, they sat in the back garden having a cup of tea and pondering where the track of the roadway might be. They gradually became aware of an increase in bird activity, with rooks and jackdaws and even sea birds creating a clamour as they wheeled about in the sky above them. The air became close and humid as though a storm was brewing. It began to rain before they went to bed, but it was when they retired that the storm really broke with lightning and thunder and a torrential downpour.

The continuing heat made it difficult to sleep and they were pleased to open windows as the storm moved away. Eventually, Eric and Pat did sleep, but it seemed only a few minutes to Pat before she heard something and was suddenly wide awake. Eric was not very pleased to be woken, but when he realised that something was happening over the road, he was immediately very wide awake. The Comfort Bedding van was in the road waiting. A late flash of lightening lit up the scene as the younger of the rugby fans emerged from the gates opposite and got into the van, upon which it drove away. Eric checked his watch and found the time to be a little after four in the morning. It was just getting light. Probably going to Portsmouth for the 8.00 a.m. sailing, thought Eric, which would suggest they are bound for Caen. He hoped the observers were ready.

Just under four weeks later, on a Thursday evening, Eric and his sergeant, Colin, were sitting at a secluded table in the Six Bells Pub. "Do you think they will show up?" Colin asked.

"I don't know, Colin; I'm playing a hunch. If it is their usual evening and they appear, I think we can rule out them knowing or having involvement in the crime we are investigating, but they may have seen something relevant. Ah, here they come. You stay here. I'll see if I can invite them to join us."

As the brothers approached the bar, Eric arrived at the same time. Eric caught the eye of the elder boy and said casually. "Oh, hello, my rugby mates, how are you? Do you remember me? I hoped I might see you as I have something that I think might interest you."

"I remember, it was the last time we were here, just before the derby match."

"That's right. It turned out to be a close contest—just one score in it if I remember correctly. What are you two having to drink? Then come and meet my friend who needs a little educating on rugby."

"That's very kind of you. We would both like a lager."

The barmaid checked the table number and said she would bring the drinks over together with some menus.

Introductions completed Eric asked, "Do you two ever have a chance to watch rugby at Twickenham?"

"No," replied the younger. "We've never been."

Eric produced two tickets for the first Six Nations fixture later in the year, England versus Wales, and said, "Do you think you could use these?"

Eyes nearly popping out of their heads the elder replied, "We certainly could, but why us—are they genuine?"

"Oh yes, they are kosher alright, but let's choose our meals and then I'll tell you why I am offering them to you."

After they had chosen their meals, Eric looked carefully at the two lads to make sure he had their full attention. "Now, I already know that one of you supports Bristol and the other Bath. I have already told you that I had some experience with Exeter, but you don't know that Colin was with Leicester Tigers for a couple of years while they were the team everyone wanted to beat. Colin and I may not be able to use these tickets, which we have been able to obtain before general release, but I want to see them used by true rugby fans, not those who go to matches to cause trouble. Occasionally, you see shots on TV of police horses having to be deployed to control crowds. What you don't see is the horse boxes outside the ground with the horses kept inside in case they are needed. For a time, I was involved in the management and care of those horses, although I have a different job now."

"Does that mean you are policemen?" The younger brother asked.

"Yes, although our role is not the usual one you would normally associate with the police, which brings me on to the second thing I want to talk about. Much of our time is spent on what you would probably call under-cover investigations. I said I hoped I would see you today." While he had been speaking, Mike and Colin had shown the lads their Police ID. "The fact that we are chatting with you today does not mean that you are in any trouble. If you were, we would not be chatting in a pub, so don't look so worried. I want you to stay out of trouble, but I believe you are both in danger of being sucked into a major criminal activity, of which you probably know nothing. However, you may have information that you can help us with."

"This has come as a shock," said the older sibling. Then with a warning look at his brother which suggested, "Don't say anything and leave this to me," and looking at Eric continued by asking, "What has it to do with us? Can you tell us what it is all about?"

"I can and I will, but before I share some sensitive information with you, I want your assurances that you will keep this to yourselves. Ok?"

"Yes, but can we tell our parents?"

"I must ask you to wait until I have told you more before I answer that question. But here come our meals. Relax and enjoy them and let us talk about the Bristol/Bath match you saw, Philip. Yes, I know your names; I wouldn't be much of a policeman if I hadn't found that out, would I?" Eric was smiling as he made the last remark, which caused the other three to smile and the boys to relax, especially as Colin asked Philip to tell him how the match progressed and the nature of the scoring. The younger, Trevor, who had not been at the game, had obviously made himself aware of most of the major action, and joined in the description.

When they had eaten and while they waited for another round of drinks, Eric turned to Philip and said, "Tell me about the printing you do, Philip."

"It's not very much yet. I work in a small printing firm and they do posters, notices, business cards and anything anyone asks for. But I met a guy in Bristol who uses printing as an art form. He has produced some really fine and intricate patterns and does some very clever stuff with colours. I think he has experimented with holograms and other unusual techniques. He is a real master craftsman and he has given me a few tips and promised to teach me more, but that means visiting Bristol which I can't do very often. Dad has bought me a small printing press which I have in a shed at home."

"It sounds as though you find printing exciting. What about photography?" Colin asked.

"Oh yes, I've done some work with combining my photos with articles I have written. I can also enlarge or reduce or superimpose, but there is so much I don't know yet, but I want to learn."

"How did you meet this expert?" Colin continued.

"It was when I went to a factory with my dad. The firm was keen that my dad would work with them."

Eric then turned to Trevor, "Tell me about your trip to France when you left in the middle of the night following a thunderstorm. I think you went in a van belonging to Comfort Bedding. How was the crossing after the storm?"

"It was rough and I think we took longer than usual. We had to make up time when we landed, but fortunately, the French rushed us through passport control. We had to deliver most of our load to a warehouse just outside Paris. I don't know the district, but it wasn't a smart place like the pictures you see of places like Amazon or IKEA. My friend, the driver, asked me to help him off load the mattresses so that they could be checked and additional labels added. We then had to load another batch that he had brought on his previous trip. After that, we had three addresses to go to with bedclothes, including the pillows that our parents make. Finally, we visited another warehouse, somewhere near Nantes, a much classier place, where we left the reloaded mattresses. The driver said that the next time he visits, he will have to take his load with new labels to somewhere near the German border, but he will have his usual mate with him then. I don't think I would want that job regularly, but he said he was well paid."

"Your parents make the pillows? Are they special or high quality and square rather than rectangles we use in this country?"

"That's right," replied Philip. "Dad has developed a filling as soft as duck down but made of processed vegetable material. The pillows also have an internal webbing that enables them to keep their shape. Comfort Bedding supply the cotton and other materials and Mum and Dad put it all together with the machinery they have in the outhouse." Philip stopped talking and looking worried asked, "Is that what this is all about? Will they be prosecuted for having a business in unlicensed premises and not paying taxes, or something like that?"

"So, your parents make all the pillows on your own premises?" Colin responded. "Do you know where the mattresses are constructed?"

Philip replied, "They make those in the factory near Bristol. When I went there with Dad, we saw them being made. The man who showed us around was very proud of what he called the ventilation holes that stop people sweating."

"And does the Comfort Bedding van call for your dad's pillows every week?"

"One van calls here, usually early on a Wednesday, but another trip is made at the end of the week."

Eric smiled as he said, "Thank you, Philip. Just answer one more question. Where are your parents tonight?"

"Oh, that's easy: they love old films, you know, some of the black and white ones. They belong to a club that meets once a month in the house of one of their friends who has a cinema room with screen and projector. They meet every third Thursday of the month, which is when we come here to eat. Do you want the address and telephone number?"

"If you know it, yes please, I would like Colin to check that they are there, and Colin, you can say that Philip and Trevor may be late home as they have met some friends."

Eric continued, "Now, lads, let me put you minds at rest. It may be that your parents are operating outside the strict letter of the law, but I am pursuing something much more serious. Customs and Excise might be interested in what your parents do, but only if they find out. My investigation is of a different nature. You might be advised to suggest to your parents that they operate within the law and if your dad's pillow filling is as good and revolutionary as it appears ask him if has taken out a patent on it."

"Thank you," said both boys. Trevor continued, "Does it mean that if Dad has a patent, then he would have the credit for his invention and Comfort Bedding couldn't steal it from him?"

"Absolutely, now let's move on. You have helped a great deal tonight. Have you heard of money laundering, and have you also heard of counterfeit money?"

Both boys nodded. Eric continued, "My investigation is related to serious financial irregularities, not on whether individuals like your dad are paying their taxes. I am advising you to keep clear of trips to France, Trevor and Philip, I suggest you do not have any further contact for the time being with your printer friend in Bristol."

"Yes, sir, I think we understand and thank you for your guidance."

"Now, if you're ready, I think we should walk home with you and meet your parents. Colin has just told me in the note he passed to me that they have just left their meeting."

Gordon and Bridget Collins, the lads' parents, had just driven in through the big gates, when Eric, Colin, Philip and Trevor arrived. The boys made the introductions and when Gordon heard the visitors were policemen, he looked very apprehensive and nervous, but then he saw his sons smiling and his expression changed to puzzlement. He invited them to join him in the house, but Philip intervened and suggested they gather in the outhouse. Gordon's puzzlement turned to worry, but Philip assured his dad that he knew what he was doing. When inside, Eric explained the situation and said how helpful the information was that the brothers had provided. Then Philip showed Eric and Colin his printing press and his parents' pillow making operation.

Gordon, seeming to understand, was still worried and asked, "Are you going to arrest me for having a business in my backyard and for not declaring it?"

Eric replied, "No, that's not my concern at the moment, but I would advise you to put the record straight with the authorities and pay your taxes. But, more importantly, get your invention patented and seek to sever your connection with Comfort Bedding. It seems they have been using you and your product to give their activities a veneer of legitimacy. By now, your pillows should be getting known on the continent, so seek reputable merchants to handle your trade."

Gordon and Bridget began to look happier, while still expressing shock at the way they were being used by a business they thought was doing them a favour. Bridget asked, "Is there anything else we should do?"

"I'll mention three things: Consult someone who can give you good sound business advice on trade with the continent, get in touch with the patents office, and integrate yourselves with the community in this village. You will find there are some really friendly, helpful and caring people among your neighbours: hiding behind screens invites people to invent rumours of criminal activity that could do you no good. Join your sons when they go to the pub, greet people in the street and get yourselves known."

Eric spoke quietly to Colin, "I think you can fire the gun and start plan A."

As he left the room, with his phone in his hand, Colin briefly responded, "Ok, Chief and I'll advise the French. Do you want me to contact Kurt?"

"Yes please, Colin." Turning to the family, he spoke to them again, but this time they were in no doubt that he was talking with his police hat on. "Thank you for your co-operation. I trust that you have told me the truth and have not concealed anything. I now command you not to breathe a word about what you have learned this evening—you may even wish to leave your phone off the hook. You have been very close to being drawn into a criminal activity, much more serious than running a business in your backyard. There are likely to be some arrests this evening, an experience you will escape. If any further information comes your way or you remember anything you should have told me, call me on this number. Now, we shall leave you, but do not be surprised if you hear from me again." Handing a card to Gordon, he left as Colin returned. The last the family heard was Eric saying to Colin, "Now to our car and head for Bristol."

5

Three weeks later, Bridget Collins joined her husband in his workshop holding a sheet of paper in her hand. "Look at this, Gordon: we have an invitation to a buffet supper next Saturday from Lucy and Mike of the house opposite. They say that it is to meet a Dr Mortimer, an archaeologist who can tell us about some aerial research that was conducted a couple of months ago. I seem to remember the boys talked about a helicopter hovering in this area at that time. Do you think we should go—we are all invited?"

"I don't know: perhaps we should. That police chappie suggested we should get to know our neighbours better and it might be interesting if there is some archaeology around here."

When the Collins family arrived at the house across the road, they were greeted by Lucy who introduced them to her friend Pat. "Our husbands have just gone for a walk with Dr Mortimer who wanted to show them something and to take some photographs. I don't think they will be many minutes."

Less than five minutes later Mike and Dr Mortimer joined the party in the living room and further introductions were made. Mike explained that the last member of the party would join them as soon as he could, but he had just received a phone call, which he said he needed to answer. Mike also suggested that Dr Mortimer should start his talk as everyone else was present.

Dr Mortimer proved himself to be a very good speaker and had his audience listening to every word, so that they were transported to a time when the landscape around them would have looked very different. He explained that he hoped soon to have permission to begin some exploratory excavations in the nearby field. He also informed them that he may wish to ask them to allow some digging in their gardens. So engrossed was everyone in the charismatic talk that no one noticed when Eric slipped quietly into the room.

The talk was followed by general debate and questioning, during which Lucy called across the room, "Eric, will you help me take the supper dishes into the dining room and then our guests can help themselves when they are ready."

Philip looked up to see Lucy and Eric leaving the room. He dug his brother in the ribs and whispered, "Did you see who that was?"

"No, who?"

"The policeman who gave us the rugby tickets." Further whispering shared the news with the other members of the Collins family. Shortly after, Lucy reappeared and invited the company to adjourn for supper. As Bridget Collins led her family into the dining room she was greeted by a smiling Eric, as were the rest of the family and he just said, "I have some news for you, which I'll give you when we have the right opportunity."

After supper, during which period Eric talked rugby to Philip and Trevor, Dr Mortimer bade them all farewell and expressed hope of seeing them all again in the not-too-distant future. Conversation continued as Bridget and Lucy became better acquainted, Pat chatted to Philip and Trevor and Mike discussed the implications of the archaeology exploration with Gordon.

Eric then asked their hosts if he could make a statement. "Lucy and Mike, you know that when Pat and I spent a most enjoyable holiday with you a few weeks ago, I was in the middle of an investigation, of which I told you a little. Since then, I have spoken to all four members of the Collins family, and they have been able to provide me with information that has been valuable in helping to bring the matter to a conclusion. I am not able to go into detail, but I can tell you that a criminal activity that could have had massive political and financial repercussions has been uncovered and stopped. As a result, several developments have occurred. The firm Comfort Bedding will not be trading again. A very talented printer and forger, Philip, will be sewing mailbags or undertaking some other activity as will several others. A scruffy warehouse in France, Trevor, will be emptied and probably demolished. How were they all involved? The mattresses designed and constructed by Comfort Bedding had false compartments that could hold a significant quantity of forged Euro bank notes. In the French warehouse, the notes were removed and began circulating through a network of couriers throughout the continent. The mattresses were then re-built and delivered to sales outlets throughout France and Germany, along with other bedding items including a very good quality pillow. You, members of the Collins family, were all caught up on the periphery of this crime, but all were wise to tell me what you knew. How did I know to question you? What made me suspicious? A fortress residence in a village, a delivery van calling in the middle of the night, a family that seemed to shun the village community in which they were living, a remarkably good image of machinery in an outhouse that was on the film taken with low sunlight from the helicopter when it banked round to leave the scene and finally some smart observation and subtle questioning by an alert bank clerk in Germany."

"I don't understand the last bit about the bank clerk," commented Gordon.

"She discovered that some forged notes were being paid in and commented on how clean they were. In conversation, she learned that the lady had received them in change when she bought some pillows supplied by Comfort Bedding from Bristol in England."

"She should get a reward, as should you," commented Gordon. "She for her quick wits and you for not jumping to wrong conclusions and keeping us from being swept up with all the criminals."

"Thank you, Gordon," smiled Eric. "I hope you have taken steps to ensure that another government department doesn't sweep you up if they come asking questions about your backyard factory!"

Is My Twin My Sister?

Anyone glancing in the bay window of the Rose and Crown in Fulton at lunchtime on a particular market day would have seen two blazer-clad gentlemen sitting at a table poring over maps. On the breast pocket of each was a badge that informed that they were representatives of the Western and Eastern Bus Company or WEBCo. The maps they were viewing had been over marked with plans for a new town that was to be built midway between Fulton and the county town eighteen miles to the east of Fulton.

The two gentlemen were Dennis, who lived and was based in Fulton, and Guy who worked in the head office of WEBCo in the county town. Amongst other responsibilities they planned the bus routes and timetables. Much of their conversation was conducted by telephone or email, but on this occasion they felt the need to meet to examine how the bus company could serve the new town.

They had been served with drinks and decided to start their discussion while they waited for their meals to be delivered to their table. From time to time, one or other would look up and glance at other customers or look out of the window. On one such occasion, Dennis raised his head just as a lady passed his table. He recognised her, but she was walking on. He left his seat, saying to his colleague, "Excuse me a minute" and called after the lady, "Good afternoon, Heather. I have it right, haven't I? You are Heather?"

The lady turned and responded warmly, "Well, hello, Dennis. I didn't see you sitting there. Yes, you have my name correct this time; not like the first time we met. But I can't blame you for that; when Hazel visited me last week for the day my brother called unexpectedly after six months in the States and couldn't decide which of us was me."

"Poor fellow, I suppose you hadn't had an opportunity to introduce him to you newly found Sister."

"Well, he knew about her, but hadn't even seen a picture of her. But what are you doing in here at lunchtime?"

"A working lunch with my opposite number from head office. We are considering what changes we shall need to make to bus routes when the new town is built."

"Is that very difficult?"

"There are many things to consider. It's not just the routes, but the frequency of the buses, the timetables, especially if there needs to be connections with other services, and how many buses we shall need for each route. We have to check that we have the manpower, or person power, to deliver the service. There is a lot of economics involved."

"I'd better leave you to it. Have fun! Oh, will you be going to the village fair at Nether Fulton on Saturday; I understand they are planning a special display including a parade of goats in fancy dress?"

"That sounds fun. I hope to see you there. Bye now."

Returning to his table, Dennis apologised for abandoning Guy. His colleague commented, "A very attractive lady; have you known her long?"

"Believe it or not, that is not an easy question to answer. I met her many years ago, but I have only recently found out who she is. To make it more complicated, I found out who she is when she discovered who she is. What do make of that?"

"What did you say? You found out who she is when she discovered who she is? Certainly confusing! It sounds like the programme 'Long lost family'."

"Pretty good, Guy, I had better tell you the story, but it might take some time."

"Ok, you tell me during our meal, which I think is just coming. We'd better move these maps and make space."

"I think we have to go back to a time when I was about nine and living in London suburbia. My mother had a friend living two or three streets from us. This friend had two daughters, twins. During the school holidays, the two mothers planned day trips, sometimes to the country, sometimes to the grounds of a stately home or a large botanic garden. The girls, my brother and I were taken along. The twins were named after trees, Hazel and Holly, but they weren't alike."

"I thought Hazel was really pretty, but Holly was quite plain. Hazel had fair hair and blue eyes, whereas Holly had dark hair and her eyes were a sort of greenish-brown. Hazel was clever and artistic, but Holly was slow and seemed withdrawn. The only time I remember seeing her enthusiastic was when we visited a farm. I don't remember having any contact with the family after we reached secondary school age when I lost touch for many years. I did think I saw Hazel on one occasion soon after I had joined secondary school. For some reason, I was with my aunt, my mother's unmarried sister. I think we visited a nature reserve and met some of my aunt's friends and they had a girl with them who looked just like Hazel. I never discovered her name, and being rather shy with girls, kept out of her way, in spite of my aunt's attempts to bring us together. I think the girl was probably less embarrassed than I. Afterwards I thought about the girl and wondered why she looked so much like Hazel, whereas Holly didn't."

"About three years ago, I was walking past the window of an art gallery in Baybridge when I noticed some striking landscape paintings of local areas. The name of the artist was given as Hazel Willson with two 'ells'. This was the name of the pretty twin and although Wilson is not uncommon, spelt with a double 'ell' it is unusual. I couldn't see the price ticket, so out of curiosity, I went into the shop. The owner was talking to a lady, but he came to me and asked if he could help. I asked about the paintings by Hazel Willson. 'Why don't you ask the lady herself?' was his reply at which point the lady turned to face me, raising her eyebrows and smiling."

"The face was no longer pretty, it was beautiful, the raised eyebrows, the right slightly higher than its companion, left me in no doubt. Without preamble I burst out, 'Hazel, it is many years since I last saw you, but I doubt if you will remember me from your childhood.'"

"She looked at me puzzled then queried, 'Childhood, you said?' So I replied with the name of two of the places we had visited with our mothers. I watched as remembrance gradually dawned on her face, then she exclaimed, 'Dennis! Dennis Edwardson! What are you doing here?'"

"I live and work in Fulton and have done for nearly twenty years."

"Well, that is extraordinary. My husband and I moved to Fulton just over two years ago." Then she turned to the owner of the gallery who was standing listening with his mouth open. "Sam, are you trying to imitate a goat or a donkey? Do you think we could borrow your back room for a chat, my friend and I have more than thirty years to catch up and we need to make a start?"

"We met several times over the next few weeks and we met with our spouses, but only after her husband, Jack Cattaway, had come home from hospital after serious heart surgery. I learned that her twin, Holly, is now living in New

Zealand. Although Hazel has artistic flair, Holly seems to have inherited a creative gene that she uses in rearing rare breeds of sheep and goats with her husband, a true Kiwi ranch farmer."

Guy asked, "The lady you spoke to just now was this Hazel?"

"No. If you think what I have told you so far is extraordinary, what I am about to relate will really take some believing."

Taking a deep breath, Dennis started on the next part of his story. "It must be about nine months ago; I attended a concert in Fulton Town Hall with my wife. Refreshments were offered during the interval and as I thought the programme would appeal to Hazel, I wasn't surprised to see her approaching the refreshment bar with another lady. The ladies were in conversation as they came towards me but I interrupted them by saying, 'Good evening, Hazel, are you enjoying the concert?'"

"She looked at me without recognition and at her companion and then replied, 'I'm sorry, I don't think I know you and neither of us is named Hazel.' I was dumbfounded, confused, but just managed to be sufficiently coherent to offer an apology, saying that I had mistaken her for another lady to whom she bore a striking resemblance. She kindly accepted my apology and added with a smile that she was enjoying the concert greatly. But that smile made the resemblance even stronger."

"My wife and I withdrew, but she said she was as flabbergasted as I was when the lady was not Hazel. I'm sure the second half of the concert was just as good as the earlier part, but my mind was so exercised thinking about the conundrum of the lady who was so like Hazel, but wasn't, that I hardly listened to any of it. She was so like Hazel, whereas Hazel's twin, Holly, hardly resembled her in any way. Could Hazel and the stranger be related? I had heard of a case where babies were accidentally swapped minutes after birth. Could that have happened with Holly and this unknown lady? Was it possible to find out?"

"I could hardly accost the lady who I thought of as Hazel's double unless I had something of importance to say. Then I realised that two weeks earlier, Hazel had celebrated a birthday. I also knew the year of her birth as it was the same as mine. I left my seat immediately as the last note of the concert sounded and made my way to the exit. As the lady and her companion came out of the hall, they saw me and she smiled (oh! that smile; it nearly put me off). Again, I began with an apology, 'I am sorry to waylay you like this, but you look so like my friend I feel you must be related. I know I should not ask this of a strange lady, but the date my friend was born is written on my programme.' She took one look at it and exclaimed, 'That's my birthday too!' Then she turned to her friend saying, 'Do you mind if we investigate this further?'"

"As this place was still open, the four of us came in here. We introduced ourselves and the new lady said her name was Heather. I told them about Hazel and how I had known her as a child, but had only made her acquaintance again after she had moved to this town. Heather said she had spent most of her early and teenage years with her parents and her younger brother on a farm in Berkshire. Her father had inherited the farm soon after she was born. He had always lived and worked on farms, but her mother was a Londoner. I decided to venture a question and asked Heather if perhaps she might have visited a nature reserve with her family when she was about twelve and did they meet a rather shy boy of about the same age with his aunt. She looked at me and said that she did remember the occasion and had felt sorry for the boy who was obviously embarrassed by his aunt's remarks."

"It was at this point that I became convinced that I had met Hazel and Heather separately on two occasions some thirty or more years apart. On each occasion, I felt that they could be related and possibly twin sisters. The next thing was to tell Hazel what I believed I had discovered and to arrange for the two ladies to meet."

"And are they related? Is there more to the story? The chances of them being swapped as babies and then meeting up and you being involved must be millions to one."

"Yes, Guy. At Heather's request, I arranged for her to meet Hazel. But first I related to Hazel what had happened at the concert. My wife and I invited both ladies to our house. Although their hairstyles were slightly different, they really did look identical. They looked at each other and both at the same time exclaimed, 'It's like looking in a mirror.' It was Heather who took the thinking a stage further by suggesting that if there had been a baby swap, then she and Holly must have been exchanged. Again, they spoke as one remarking that they needed to do DNA tests."

"Heather had a question for Hazel. 'Is your, no, our mother still alive and able to tell us about the births?' Hazel's response almost sealed the debate. 'Yes, she is, although she is now in a care home. Although she is physically weak, her mind is still razor sharp. After Dennis had told me about you, I phoned her and asked her if there was ever any doubt about Holly being my sister. She replied that she loved us both but did wonder at times about the differences between us. Then she said that the night of our birth had been particularly hectic with half the maternity staff missing with 'flu' and twice the normal number of mothers in labour. The staff were so frantic trying to be in several places at the same time that it could have been possible that a baby had been given to the wrong mother. If a mistake had been made, she had no way of knowing which her true daughter was and this was before the days of DNA.'"

"So, Dennis, have DNA tests been done and, does Mrs Willson know who her true daughters are?"

"Yes, and yes she does. She has met Heather and the two of them have bonded as though they have known each other for years. Holly knows the situation and Heather's brother Piers, who is biologically Holly's brother, flew out to New Zealand two weeks ago."

"So, end of story and everyone will live happily ever after?"

"Just one afterthought or epilogue, I said that Hazel had always been artistic. In addition to painting, she is a very accomplished pianist. Heather, although not living with a musical family, had displayed a wish to play the piano and her parents had indulged her. At the end of this month, the twins will take to the stage in a concert in Nether Fulton church when the programme will include one or two piano duets performed by the twin sisters."

Life after the Graveyard

On a bright and still but chilly Saturday afternoon in mid-January, Daniel Hammond spent time in the churchyard of All Saints Church in Foxhaven. The purpose of his visit was to scatter the ashes of his wife who had died at the beginning of the previous month. Their marriage had lasted just under two years, during the last six months of which Daniel had watched Amy fight and finally succumb to a virulent form of brain cancer.

Amy's valiant battle reached its conclusion two days after her thirtieth birthday and now two days after reaching the same milestone, Daniel was fulfilling her last wish. In one of her last lucid moments, Amy had asked that her ashes be scattered on her parents' grave. She said that as Danny, as she had always called him, was still young enough to marry again, she did not wish him to be encumbered with maintaining her grave. Before visiting the churchyard, Daniel had interrogated the internet and found prayers which he thought suitable and with which he felt comfortable. He read these aloud and then scattered the ashes. He stood for several minutes in silence reviewing the three years he had known Amy and the activities and experiences they had shared.

He turned and made his way slowly to the church gate in readiness for returning to their, now just his, home in the village of Plover Green some fifteen miles away. Just before he reached the gate, a young lady came through it with arms laden with buckets, tools and plants. He thought she seemed familiar and as she struggled with her burden he felt he must offer help, especially as she dropped a trowel and a small fork and was finding it difficult to retrieve them. As he stood up with the escaped tools in his hand, they looked at each other and both realised they had seen each other before.

Daniel spoke first, "Hello, haven't I seen you before in Plover Green?"

She smiled as she responded, "Yes, and I have seen you there, but what are you doing here? I assumed you lived in Plover Green like me."

"I do, but how odd. We live in the same village, have seen each other about, but have never spoken, and now fifteen miles from home we get into conversation."

They had continued to walk together as she made her way to a point where she was able to unload the items she was carrying. "This is my grandparents' grave and I try to keep an eye on it. I'm afraid I have rather neglected it for the last four or six months. My parents, who live nearly two hundred miles away have told me they are going to visit me at the end of the month and I expect Mum will wish to inspect the grave."

"I too have been visiting a grave. It is the grave of my in-laws but, unlike you, I don't have any responsibility for its maintenance."

As she started to work on the grave in order to tidy it and then set the plants into the soil on it, she continued, "So, if you have not been doing any maintenance, why are you here? Oh, sorry I shouldn't have asked."

"It's alright. I suppose it does seem a little odd. I have just been scattering my wife's ashes on her parents' grave as she wished."

"Oh, I'm so sorry. Now, I come to think of it, I used to see you out together, but you were on you own the last time I saw you. How did she die? Oh, sorry again." And she clapped a muddy hand over her mouth.

"Yes, the last six months have been hard. Amy had a cancer in the brain and although she fought bravely she knew we didn't have long together." While Daniel had been explaining, he had bent down to help with planting and to try to hide his emotion while he talked about Amy.

"I suppose you had to devote all your free time to look after your wife. Will you be able to join in some of the village activities now and meet people?"

"I think I might and perhaps I have started. My name is Daniel Hammond and you are?"

"Susan Reece and I teach in the primary school in Plover Vale. Well, look at that. Just two plants to go in! That was quick work, thanks to your help. My boyfriend wants me to go to see a film this evening—now I shall not have any excuse not to join him."

They began walking back to the car park as Daniel remarked. "You don't sound very enthusiastic."

"Well, I suppose I'm not very keen, but it is a way of spending the evening, although I have plenty of school preparation work to do."

"Perhaps it's my turn to be undiplomatic: is it the film or the boyfriend you don't find inspiring."

"Maybe it's a little of each. I haven't known him long and this evening could be a trial to determine whether I want him to accompany me to the village pantomime."

"Oh, when's that?"

"The second weekend in February in the Village Hall, it's usually very good, performed by the Plover Players. This year's choice is 'Aladdin'. Will you go?"

"I might well put that in the diary. Is it entry by ticket?"

"That's right. Performances are Friday and Saturday evenings and Saturday matinee. All tickets are the same price, and the earliest arrivals choose the best seats. I could get you a ticket if you like and drop it in to you if you give me your address."

"That is very kind—yes, please, as I shall be working away from the village for a week from tomorrow. I live at 14 Lapwing Close."

"Oh, the opposite end of the village to me, that may be why our paths have not crossed very often. I have a flat in Cedar House. Will you be far away and have to stay somewhere overnight?"

"I am an accountant and a friend in the Midlands has asked me to help him sort out the books of a largish construction firm so that he can submit their tax return before the end of the month. According to him, their books, and probably their finances, are in a mess."

They had reached their cars and had continued their conversation while standing beside them. Before they parted Susan asked, "Which performance of the panto do you wish to attend?"

Daniel replied, "I have no preference. I'll leave the choice to you: see how the tickets have been selling."

Driving home, Daniel did a mental check of the items he would need to take with him: laptop, calculator, and notepads, law books, particularly financial and company law, pens, pencils, highlighters, paper clips… His thoughts wandered to considering what sort of preparation Susan had to do. He realised he did not know what age range she taught. Other questions followed. How long had she been teaching? How old was she? She had been so wrapped up against the cold that, other than her height, which he thought might be described as average, he could not really determine her features. He did know that she had a clear pleasant voice and a friendly inquisitive manner. Did she sing or perhaps she was into drama? This pantomime: was she going to watch it, or would she be appearing in it? What had she actually said about it? Well, what did it matter anyway?

He reached home and began making preparations for the next day as he needed to make an early start. He was due to join his friend for lunch in the hotel in which he would be resident. They hoped that a briefing session over a meal would enable them to make a prompt start on Monday. By the time he had checked and double checked that he had everything, there was little time to continue the task that he knew he had to do and over which he kept procrastinating. This was to sort all Amy's clothes and effects. It would have to wait until he returned. That was when he was surprised to find his thoughts returned to Susan: how did she compare in size to Amy and how similar in style would her dress sense be to that of Amy's?

Daniel's work went well and he was able to book out of his hotel a day early, arriving home in the late afternoon of Thursday. He chided himself that he must not let this opportunity of a free day for sorting Amy's clothes be missed, so he made a start by emptying her wardrobe. He had just come downstairs to fetch a black sack when he realised someone was trying to push something through the letter box. He opened the door and found Susan on the other side trying to balance on a pedal cycle while delivering an envelope. After the first shock at being discovered, Susan explained. "This is your ticket for the pantomime; I picked it up last night, but I didn't think you would be back until tomorrow."

Daniel also having recovered from the unexpected meeting replied, "Come in for a moment and I'll get some cash to pay for the ticket. You can put your bike in the porch, it should be quite safe there." When Susan was safely inside, he continued, "Now, how much do I owe you and which performance is the ticket for?"

"It's just £10 and for the Saturday evening. But it doesn't matter now, it looks as though you are busy, I didn't mean to disturb you as I didn't think you would be home before tomorrow."

"You aren't disturbing me, rather you are giving me an excuse to stop doing a job I don't like doing, sorting out Amy's clothes."

"Would you like some help; I have an hour to spare now?"

"That is very kind of you, if you are sure you can spare the time. It really is a task for which I have very little enthusiasm."

The hour passed quickly and much was achieved. When Susan, who became Sue as they worked on the task, had taken off her coat, Dan discovered that the person under that top layer was a very attractive young lady. He found out that she was 27, as yet unmarried, had been teaching at Plover Vale primary school for two and a half years, following two years in another county. She was now teaching year five and was responsible for creative and dramatic arts in the school, although before teacher training, she had spent a year in the finance department of a well-known chain of department stores.

He asked her if she was involved in the panto to which she responded, "Yes, I do have a small part," and then teasing him, continued, "but I'm not going to tell you who I play. You will have to wait until you see the production. You are allowed to speculate, but I shall not give you any clues or tell you if you are right."

"You won't know if I guessed correctly."

"If you accept the invitation I am now giving you to come as my guest to the cast party after the Saturday evening show, you can tell me then. Will you come?"

"Thank you. I will accept, but I don't suppose I will know anyone else there."

"A wonderful opportunity to meet people and after your past few months, I reckon you deserve some relaxation in what I am sure will be a convivial atmosphere."

Dan decided that it was his turn to tease. "Did your choice of the Saturday evening performance have anything to do with this invitation? And what about your boyfriend… won't he be put out if you spend any time with me?"

"David probably won't be at the party, unless someone else invites him. He is not what you might term a regular boyfriend. Actually, he is the deputy head of the school in which I teach and his classroom is next to mine. He has only been in post since September and is a few years older than me. He and his wife have separated and he is living with his widowed mother about eight miles away. His children live with their mother, but they visit him every other weekend. I suppose it's because I feel sorry for him that I keep him company with the odd cinema trip and occasional meal. I think he is gradually getting to know other people outside school."

As they parted after what was, for Daniel, a very productive hour, Sue said, "I'll watch out for you arriving at the panto and note where you sit so that I can fetch you afterwards."

The panto was not the next time they met for when Daniel called at the village shop a week later Sue was just leaving. They had just exchanged greetings when another lady exited the shop. Sue introduced Daniel and Jenny to each other and explained that Jenny also had a part in the production. When Jenny went on her way saying that she had 'a million things to do', Sue breathed a sigh of relief. She explained, "I was afraid she would give the game away and tell you what part I play. Jenny is part of the chorus. This is her first production, and joining in is part of her way of keeping busy as she is finding it hard to come to terms with her husband's death. He was a passenger in a light aircraft that crashed in the sea killing him and the pilot. It was several days before his death was confirmed."

"That's sad," responded Daniel, "I am beginning to wonder if there are any couples in stable married relationships in this village!"

Having been told by Susan that he should get to the Village Hall early, Daniel joined the queue waiting for the doors to open. He did not have to wait long. Susan was just inside the door with her coat over her costume, a scarf over her head and stage makeup applied to her face. As soon as he was through the door, she was beside him offering him a programme for the show and then hustled him through to a seat in the third row.

After looking around and getting a feel for his surroundings, Daniel was pleased to note that there were several families present and a wide age range in the audience. Judging by the noise level, it was clear that this was a time to greet friends. Next, he realised that he hadn't looked at his programme. Now he could find out what part Sue would be playing. It wasn't until after he had read the introductory comments and the blurb about the Plover Players that he noticed that his programme had been 'doctored' as there was no cast list. He tried to look at his neighbour's programme, but although he could see there was a list he was too far away to read it. He was wondering if he could ask to check his neighbour's programme when it was passed down the row to someone else.

It was halfway through the first act and most of the characters he remembered from the story had appeared that he began to wonder if Sue had a part or if she had been so cleverly disguised that he had missed her. Several characters appeared that he did not remember being in the story. It was these characters that caused the greatest laughter as pointed remarks were made about some of the village organisations and people. The vicar, shopkeeper and publican, the Bingo evenings and the WI were all subject of critical 'acclaim'. The story was resumed and mention was made of a search for an old lamp. Daniel was just calling to mind that there might have been a ring as well, when there was a loud bang, the lights went out followed by a flash and there centre stage lit by a spotlight was the genie of the ring. The genie was a scantily clad maiden, who looked about 16 with dark hair in which there were highlights in three different colours. Her appearance was greeted with applause, stamping of feet from one quarter and wolf whistles in which he was tempted to join such was the impact that this delightful creature made upon him. It was only when she spoke in a clear musical voice that filled the hall that he woke up to the fact that Sue was the genie. Well, he hadn't guessed that she would be playing that role or that she would look so gorgeous. He wouldn't be surprised if most of the men in the hall would be half, or more, in love with her.

Daniel thoroughly enjoyed the performance, joined in the applause and the song the audience were invited to sing, laughed at the scripted jokes and the mistakes that were covered up by 'ad libs', and caught one of the sweets that was thrown into the audience. As the audience filed out at the end in good humour, he waited for his genie to appear. When she came for him, her multi-coloured hair was wrapped in the scarf, but she still had her face paint in place. She wore her coat, this time unbuttoned and he could see that she had dispensed with her costume and was dressed normally and discretely.

As she came to him smiling, he congratulated her, and without realising he was doing it, opened his arms to embrace her and was delighted to find her responding. When he told her that he had forgotten that there was genie of the ring as well as one for the lamp and he had been taken by surprise, he said that he would think of her in future as his genie.

"Let's go," she replied with eyes sparkling with pleasure and putting her arm through his. "We have a room set aside for us in the 'Feathers' down the road."

"Do you know who the people were that were stamping their feet when you appeared?"

"I have a feeling it was some of the staff from school, but I shall pretend not to know. Thank goodness it is half-term next week."

"I expect you could do with a rest after these three performances. You might need to lie low, as I'm sure you will have acquired a host of admirers."

Looking up at him as they passed under a streetlight she somewhat coquettishly inquired, "Are you among them?"

He looked at her carefully and seriously, "Is my answer important?"

As they stood still looking at each other she said quietly, "I believe it might be."

Dan replied, "I think I would like to find out and perhaps we can explore the possibility during your half-term break."

When they reached the party, it was already in full swing. As he expected, Sue was immediately welcomed by other cast members. She held onto Dan so that he didn't get lost and introduced him to several people the names of most of whom he immediately forgot, but some he did recognise from seeing them on the stage. One he had met previously, as Sue had introduced him to her outside the shop. She was Jenny whose husband had been killed in the plane crash. She had an older man with her whom she introduced as David. "David teaches in the same school as Susan."

Daniel spoke to the other man, "I think I may have heard of you. Were you in the cast or just a spectator tonight like me?"

"No, on both counts, I went last night and met Jenny as we left at the same time. She invited me to join her tonight as she said Susan already had an escort."

"An escort! Yes, I suppose so, but one unexpectedly chosen by her."

Sue, who had disappeared to the bar, returned with two glasses of wine. Addressing David, she said, somewhat formally, "Good evening, David, I didn't know you were here this weekend. I thought it was your turn to look after your children. But it is good that you can look after Jenny instead." Then turning to Daniel, "Dan, I want to introduce you to our producer—he is quite a livewire in the village and is always planning future productions."

Wondering where this introduction might be leading, he allowed himself to be led away from Jenny and David. As they moved away and through the throng of panto people and guests, Sue muttered, "What's he doing here? I thought I was free of him this weekend."

At the end of the evening as they were about to depart to their own homes in opposite directions, Daniel informed Susan, "I am working at home this week, a fair bit of number crunching to do as well studying a recent court case that may result in some changes to company law. If you have a spare hour, would you like to call in for coffee Monday or Tuesday morning?"

Without hesitation, Sue replied, "Yes please, how would 10.30 on Tuesday suit?"

On Tuesday, they both had information to share. Sue was pleased to report, "I shall have a few days without David as he has his children staying with him. He phoned me yesterday to invite me to join him and his children today on a visit to a wildlife park. I was able to say truthfully that I had another commitment and before he suggested an alternative excursion I told him that for the rest of the week I would be preparing for my parents' visit and entertaining."

"Didn't you wish to meet his children?"

"I certainly don't wish to be put on trial to see if I would suit as a future mother to them."

"Is that because you see enough of children during the week at school?"

"It's not that, but when the time comes for me to be a mother, I want to look after my own kids, not those of someone else with whom I would have to share them. My mother is coming for a couple of days, but it is not her I was thinking of entertaining. I wondered if you and I could go for a meal next Saturday."

"That sounds a great idea. Saturday is fine unless you would prefer the next week."

"No, I have a busy week at school after half term. We have a mature student teacher joining us for six weeks and he is to be attached to my class."

"I hope it's not another 'lame duck' you are rescuing from some trauma."

"What do you mean, 'lame duck?' Are you referring to David? If you must know, Matthew is 26, an ex-Marine and engaged to be married in the summer. Now, what's your news?"

"Not as juicy as yours. I met Jenny in the shop yesterday and as she was going my way to visit someone about joining the WI we walked together. She has clearly been through a bad time, but seems to be prepared to talk about her problems. Did you know she was pregnant and the loss of her husband caused her to miscarry? She seems to have been quite impressed with David and the way he looked after her at the party. We discovered that, in addition to having both recently lost a spouse, we both grew up in the same London borough. We must have gone through secondary education at about the same time, I at the boys' grammar, while she was at the girls' school."

The Saturday meal was a success at an Italian restaurant and the following Friday, they were fortunate to secure two tickets at the local cinema for a live relay of Shakespeare's Hamlet from Stratford. They learned more of each other and their conversations never lagged for lack of something to say. March turned out to be a busy month for both Daniel and Susan. Twice they tried to make arrangements to spend time together and on both occasions, something occurred that led to a postponement. They had to be satisfied with several brief telephone conversations. Sue talked about the support she needed to give Matthew and the teaching strategies she showed him. They worked together on their lesson plans and towards the end of the month they were absorbed in report writing. Dan began to wonder what sort of relationship was being established between them.

From Dan, Sue learned of Jenny's gradual emergence from the shell she had built around herself. In addition to joining the Women's Institute, she had acquired a part-time post as a dentist's receptionist. She had decided to explore the countryside and had joined the village walking group. When she told Dan of this new hobby, he was persuaded to join the group. During these walks, they talked about their teenage years and remembered places, shops and characters they both knew.

As the month neared its end, Daniel was surprised to hear from his accountancy friend with a suggestion that they join two of his friend's acquaintances hill walking in Scotland immediately after Easter. He would be away for ten days during the school holiday. When she heard his news, Sue decided to revise her hopes and plans. With Matthew having completed his teaching experience in the school and gone home to reunite with his fiancée, she had expected to be able to spend some days in Dan's company. Instead, she left the village to spend a few days with her mother as she would be alone while her father was away on a business trip.

As Sue neared her village as she drove home, after spending the few days with her mother, she came to a point where her road was crossed by a footpath. At the side of the road, waiting for an opportunity to cross was a group of walkers. As she was in a line of slow moving traffic Sue looked at the walkers to see if she recognised any of them. What she saw caused a shock to her equanimity, for Jenny was being helped over a stile. David was just behind waiting his turn, but it was Daniel who was assisting Jenny and holding her hand. But Dan was in Scotland, wasn't he?

What Sue didn't know was that the Scottish break had been terminated prematurely. Firstly, the Scottish weather was atrocious with heavy blustery rain and, secondly, one of the walkers slipped and fell hurting his foot, either breaking a bone or bones or suffering a bad sprain. He could not continue.

What Dan did not know was that Sue saw him hand-in-hand with Jenny. She drove back to her empty flat and tried to make sense of what she had just seen. Had Dan ever gone to Scotland? How much time had he been spending with Jenny? Did it mean that her own relationship with Dan was over? She tried to replay the conversation they had shared under the streetlight on the way to the panto party. Had she read too much into what he had said and the times they had spent together? What if Dan and Jenny, both having recently lost their spouses and coming from the same London borough, were to get married, how would she feel? Did she mind? This was a question she realised she could answer. She had had boyfriends before, but nothing serious had come of the times they had spent together—they had shared some good times, but parted amicably. She felt differently about Dan. The more she thought about him the more she realised that she loved him and couldn't bear the thought of seeing him regularly with someone else. She went to bed in tears asking herself what she could or should do.

In the morning, she had no answer. She had had a wretched night and when she looked at herself in the mirror her face reflected her miserable dark hours. Dan was not due back, even if he had already arrived, for three days, two days before the start of the summer term. Would he phone her? If he did what would she say to him—should she wait to see what he said? Should she ask him about his feelings for Jenny? No, she couldn't do that. She was imagining something that did not exist, or did it? What if he didn't phone her, should she phone him? But what if he told her that he and Jenny were seeing each other regularly, what could she do? Go back to school and be pursued by David? No! No, then what? Another term and then another year! Then she remembered that Matthew had been talking about a vacancy in the church school near where he lived, but he wasn't going to apply for it because it was too close to his home. By the end of the summer, she would have completed three years in her present post; she could look for a move to another school. That was it. She would use the next three days looking in the educational press for suitable vacancies for September. Perhaps she could apply for the post of deputy head in a small village school.

On Friday, the day Dan was scheduled to return from Scotland, Sue drove into the nearest town. She bought a copy of the weekly educational paper which might have details of teaching posts that she had not noticed on the internet. She thought she ought to read some of the articles to make sure she was aware of the latest developments in case she was called for interview. Driving back through the village, she saw Jenny and Dan in conversation outside the village shop. It might all be quite innocent and they just happened to meet, but it might confirm her worst fears. He hadn't phoned her, unless there was a message on her answerphone.

As she drove on, continuing to survey the meeting in her rear-view mirror for too long, she only looked ahead just in time to be able to take evasive action and avoid a car coming towards her. Struggling to come to terms with the shock of nearly causing an accident, she suddenly realised that she knew the car with which she almost collided. It belonged to David, but what was he doing in the village when he lived eight miles away?

Susan had been home about twenty minutes when her phone rang. She checked the screen and recognised Dan's number. As she picked it up, she wondered why they had always contacted each other on their landlines when they both had mobiles. She offered a very flat 'Hello' and waited for the caller to speak. Dan's voice sent a tiny tingle down her spine as he said, "Hello, Sue, I hoped you might be in and back from your trip to see your parents. I hope you had a good time and better than my trip."

She couldn't help herself when she heard his last few words and responded, "What was wrong with your trip?"

"Just about everything, foul weather; cold, windy and always raining and then an injury to one of the party, so we abandoned after four days. I have been home four days waiting until you returned, but I had forgotten when you were due home."

"So, what have you been doing with yourself? Finding other company?"

"Finding other company? I joined the walking group on one of their hikes, but otherwise I have been kicking my heals until I could see you."

"You didn't try phoning me in case I was at home, nor did you try contacting me on my mobile. Instead, you went walking with Jenny, holding her hand while she climbed over a stile."

"How did you know about me helping her over the stile?"

"I was just driving back into the village after a 200-mile journey and saw you and then this morning, I saw you chatting with Jenny outside the shop."

"Ok, you saw me helping Jenny. She was the fourth person I helped. I don't suppose you saw me help two other ladies and the oldest man in our group. And this morning I met Jenny outside the shop while she waited for her escort. But where had you been so early this morning? Sorry, I shouldn't be questioning you about your movements, but can I come and see you?"

"Yes, but give me a few minutes. Come about 11.15."

"Thank you, I'll see you then."

Sue washed her face, brushed her hair and applied make-up and lipstick and was ready by 11.00. While she waited, wondering whether Dan's arrival time could give her any indication of how he felt about her, she started looking at the teaching posts in the paper she had bought. She placed a pencil cross against a couple.

At 11.13 (two minutes early!—a good sign?), her doorbell rang. She opened it to a very smart Daniel. He opened his arms to her and as before at the panto, but with rather different motivation, she found herself responding. No words were spoken, neither felt them necessary at that moment, and then Sue asked, "Coffee?" Receiving the prompt answer, "Yes please" she went into her kitchen.

Dan sat down, noticed her newspaper, picked it up and then realised it contained details of vacant teaching posts. What does this mean? Is Sue planning to move somewhere else? If so, why? Do her statements about Jenny have anything to do with it: surely not?

When Sue returned with the coffee, Dan didn't waste any time on pleasantries but held up the paper and asked, "Are you applying for other jobs and do you intend to leave the village?" And then added quietly, "And me?"

Unable to stop herself Sue replied, "Oh, Dan, my mind has been in turmoil since I saw you with Jenny. I thought it would be so understandable if you and Jenny got to know each other as you had both lost your partners. You had told me so much about the conversations you had with her. It's been bearable at school since I got to know you and Matthew provided a buffer between me and David. The thought of David pursuing me this term, made me think of moving elsewhere."

"Sue, my dear, I am sure you are worthy of promotion and also that you would make a very good deputy head, but you should not be seeking another job as a means of escape. Anyway, I don't think you need to worry about David anymore. You saw me with Jenny this morning. I only stopped to pass the time of the day while she was waiting for David to pick her up. They were going to plan a little excursion that they could take David's children on during the weekend."

"Oh, David and Jenny! Yes, that might work. Come to think of it, David did quiz me once or twice about her."

"So, I don't think David will be too concerned about you seeking to move away, but I definitely will."

"Will you? Really? But I thought…" and her voice trailed away as she realised that she had started to say too much about how she felt about him.

"Throughout March, Sue, we never seemed to be able to spend time together and I began to wonder if I should try to forget about you. Then the holiday offer came along and I thought this could be a test of my feelings. Not only was the holiday a disaster because of the weather and the accident, but also because I missed you terribly. I did try to phone you on my mobile on several occasions, but could never get a signal. Then for the last three days I have been watching the clock waiting for today. And you were here all the time thinking I was away."

"Does that mean that you really do have feelings for me?"

"My darling, I love you. That is the good thing about the last week. I know now that I don't want to let you out of my sight… ever. Please say that it is the same for you."

"Oh, this is the happiest day of my life. It was when I thought I might have to see you with another that I realised that I love you. Oh, yes, it is the same for me."

Again they were in each other's arms, but this was a much more passionate embrace than the rather cold affair when Dan arrived. When they parted, Dan asked, "Does this mean that if I ask you to marry me, you will say yes, because that is what I want to hear more than anything else."

"Oh yes, an unreserved yes."

[Dear Reader, we can leave out the next few minutes as their embrace continued and their speech became rather repetitive… I'm sure you can supply the script yourself.]

After further embraces, Dan asked, "Perhaps we can start to make plans now. Have you got anything booked for the rest of today?" Seeing her shake her head, he continued, "How about we go into town, find somewhere to have some lunch and then go shopping for an engagement ring?"

"Yes, please, but what an impetuous young man you are!"

"Maybe I'm not always so decisive, but I don't want you to have the chance to get involved with any more 'lame ducks' unless it's me. Seriously though, I shall have to ask your father for his permission to marry his daughter. I suppose we shall have to wait until half-term now before we shall have a chance to have a face-to-face meeting."

Sue disagreed, "We can go and see my parents before that, because there is a long weekend coming up for the early May bank-holiday. I think I must have spoken about you so many times when I was with Mum, that she asked, 'When am I going to meet your Dan?'"

"See if that weekend would be convenient for your folk. Perhaps we could have a summer wedding in August. Then you could make a short flight from this

Cedar tree to Lapwing Close and continue, for the time being at the same school, but under a new name."

"I'll ring home this evening. I think my dad should be back from his business trip. What are you grinning about?"

I have just realised what answer we shall have to give when we are asked how we met. We shall be able to say, "Our life together began in a graveyard!"

"You can't say that, but I suppose it's true, isn't it!"

Phantom Island Refuge

To: Reverend John Pinkerton-Small

Dear Pinky

I would have sent an email, but I think that what I have to write might be too much to send that way.

What I am about to share with you is the most extraordinary experience I have ever encountered. When you share this account with your wife, as I am sure you will, she will say that I must have dreamt the whole story and I would be inclined to agree with her except for the very real and happy ending. (Now please, Pinky, don't go to the end until you have read the rest.)

You will remember that living near to the Thames at Henley and holidaying in the Isles of Scilly provided many opportunities for my brother Sebastian, younger sister Stella and myself to spend much of our spare time rowing on the river or at sea. When Stella, at the age of 22, came home after completing her degree, she announced that, with three other girls from the university rowing club, she was making plans to row across the Atlantic. The project was already almost completely organised. They had a boat specially made for them, they had sponsors, the boat was equipped with the latest navigational gadgetry and technology and they were currently sourcing all the supplies they would need. They planned to row from Madeira in the Canaries to Bermuda.

The announcement took our parents by surprise. Although they had always encouraged us to be adventurous, they tried hard not to express openly their anxiety about the scheme. I understood their concern as our brother was away exploring, we believed, in South America, except that we had not heard from him for eighteen months. The last we knew was that he was in Ecuador and was thinking of trekking north to somewhere, unknown to us, where he thought the geology suggested it may be possible to locate diamonds. I am sure our parents would have been happier about Stella's planned exploit if they had known if Seb was still alive.

An ongoing priority for Stella's preparation was training to get her body in peak condition and she asked me to train with her. As I had decided to take a sabbatical from my medical research for a few weeks, that suited me fine. I even agreed to accompany her to Madeira and see her row out of Funchal.

We left England at the beginning of July and waited in Funchal for three days for a favourable weather forecast. Unfortunately, in that time, one of the girls slipped and fell and broke a bone in her leg and badly bruised her arm. The remaining three considered whether they would need to call off the whole expedition, but it only took them about two minutes to find a solution. That solution was me. I was available, with no commitments that could not be set aside. I had trained. I had experience of rowing at sea and I was the same size as the poor injured team member.

We set out on a beautiful morning cheered on by a good crowd of well-wishers and for a week we had calm seas and made very good progress. We even started talking about the possibility of achieving a record time. Then one night, a strong wind blew up without warning, the sea boiled and we were tossed about by gigantic waves like a cork on the edge of a waterfall. We fastened everything down, donned lifebelts, tied ourselves to the boat and prayed.

As dawn approached, the wind eased, the mountainous waves gradually subsided and by the time it was light, there was a gentle swell. We checked ourselves, our supplies and the boat and discovered, to our surprise and great delight, that we had suffered no damage. Or so we thought until we tried to get a bearing to find our position. None of our instruments would work. We could make no contact with our base and we were unable even to determine the direction of north.

We prepared to start rowing. The sea was now calm, the wind had dropped completely and we were becalmed. The sky was an opaque white with no breaks so that we could not even get a sight of the sun to give us a clue in which direction we should try to proceed. Looking around in all directions, we spotted what looked like an island. We checked our charts but were unable to identify any land. Was this some unrecorded atoll, something raised from the seafloor by an underwater volcano or earthquake or a lump of rock arrived from space, such as a meteorite? While we were debating this phenomenon, one of our number realised the island had got closer, or were we drifting towards it? Was there some strange magnetic force at work over which we had no control?

As the distance between ourselves and the island reduced, we noticed what appeared like a creek between the rocks. There was no beach and the rocks, a reddish-brown colour, seemed to be precipitous, but only about three metres high. We were so stunned by the way we were being sucked towards the island that not one of us thought to suggest that we try to row away from it. In fact, we were so absorbed by what was happening that we were dumbfounded. (I am sure that you cannot imagine that, Pinky; four girls speechless—for that to happen, you must accept that it was indeed a strange phenomenon.)

Our craft glided gently into the creek and neatly came to rest beside a short flight of steps. As we looked at the steps, a door opened in the rock at the top of the steps. Next a large screen appeared in the doorway with writing on it. We could not make anything of the top scrawl, but one of our number later suggested that it might have said *Arabic,* but below it we could read *Deutsch, English, Français,* and several other languages. I suddenly had an idea. Perhaps there were people on the island and they wanted to know how to communicate with us. So, I shouted *ENGLISH* and immediately a strange computer-type voice called, "Welcome, English people. We are delighted that you have come to visit us. Please disembark and come up the steps and through the door. Your craft and its belongings will be quite safe until you are ready to depart. A warning—we are not as tall as you."

I turned to the other girls and, because I thought the voice, although robot-like, seemed friendly, I said, "Shall we?" They all replied positively and got behind me. (Talk about 'the last one left standing'). So, I led the way. Up the steps, through the door, along a short passage and then up a staircase and out into the open on a sort of plateau area. And there to meet us was a group of the strangest beings I have ever seen. They were about a metre tall; they were dressed partly in green and their bodies were green. I didn't notice all this at first glance, but I soon realised that their heads were cubic with smiling mouths and four eyes, two facing forwards and two on the tops of their heads looking up. As they were only a metre tall, I thought having upward facing eyes was a jolly good idea. They stood upright on two feet, but they had four arms and four hands, each with five fingers and a thumb.

Their leader came forward and addressed me, "My apologies, Captain, for disturbing your progress during the dark. We thought there was no boating, no,

I should say shipping, in the area. This is the first time we have made a mistake, but somehow our systems, I think you call it radar, didn't notify us of your presence until we were touching down on your planet. Our retro thrust engines did rather make the water boil, enough to make many cups of tea." This last remark was followed by strange noises that came from different directions. And then I realised they were laughing at the leader's joke.

Realising that some response was needed from me I replied, "Thank you for your welcome, we are pleased to meet you, although you certainly gave us a scare when you arrived, but we came to no harm, except that none of our instruments will function properly."

"Oh yes, that will be the magnetic field round our vehicle that will be interfering with yours. The field extends about ten stadia which I think is about three of your miles. When we leave, we will move far enough away from you before we turn on our thrusters so that you will not be affected."

I then became bolder and asked, using a rather trite formula, "Do you come here often?"

"We have been coming at this season of the sun whenever we need to replenish our stocks of salt, that is about every five years according to earth time measurement. We normally operate in a different time frame, but we have to switch to earth measure when we land, or should I say, when we water or sea. When we dwell in our time, you would not see us, for whereas your world is three dimensional, ours is four dimensional, the fourth dimension being time. But may we offer you some refreshment? Please come this way."

We followed the green beings into a covered area where there were stools, or perhaps they were tables. They pulled out some smaller stools on which they sat and they invited us to sit on the tables. Beakers containing a yellow liquid were offered to us and also some square biscuits. Guessing our doubt about the drinks and biscuits, they explained that although we may not have tasted anything of the nature before, they believed they were quite digestible for humans. They had undertaken considerable research into the habits, interests and food of humans and they had no intention to hurt us in any way.

As my colleagues seemed to have elected me as their leader, I decided that I had better be the first to try the refreshments. I found the liquid very pleasant, although like nothing I had tasted previously. It was a sort of fruity wine, but with flavours I could not identify. Not only did I find it soothing for the throat but it also made me feel that I was in a safe place and removed my apprehensions.

The biscuits also were delicious, my taste buds responded positively and I was convinced that they were a complete meal in themselves. Although I felt as though I had eaten a full meal, I did not feel tired. Rather I felt much more alert and not missing the rest I did not get during the stormy night.

The leader perceived that I had two questions that I wanted to ask, so he provided the answers without me having to voice them. He, if he be correct, offered to show us the salt extraction process. He stressed that it did not interfere with any of earth's sea creatures. He also informed us that after we had been shown the vats accumulating salt, he and his colleagues would talk to us about the research they had been undertaking in order to try to understand humans. Before we set off, he turned to the other green beings and gave them some instructions. Well, I presume that was what he did, because the air was filled with a series of clicks, hoots and whistles, which we assumed was their usual language.

First, he led us across the island, or was it a spaceship, which did not seem as large as we first thought when we spotted it from our boat. At a point fairly close to the centre, he led us down a flight of steps. He warned us to duck our heads, but soon we realised that the ceiling was lifting up to accommodate our extra height. At the bottom of the steps, we came to a platform. As our eyes adjusted to the green lighting, we could see that the platform was in fact a circle. Inside this circle, there was a collection of wires or tubes criss-crossing the space and from these tubes, at junctions where tubes intersected, there were others that were immersed in the sea. Also, at these junctions, there were platforms, manned (that's probably not the right word) by the green beings who had accessed them by traversing the tubes from the outer circle. I hadn't noticed, until they moved, that their feet had two big toes and four smaller ones which enabled them to grip the tubes. The operators on these small platforms dipped wand-like rods into the sea which seemed to stimulate some form of electrolysis. Our leader then drew back part of the surrounding wall, behind which were chambers that were being filled with salt that had been sucked up the vertical tubes and sent along the horizontal ones. If I had understood the process more clearly, I would write here that the leader explained how it all worked. My poor grasp of the science involved only allows me to suggest that the power source for the operation came from batteries which were fuelled by energy extracted from rocks on their planet LUNERA. I assume that this energy had some sort of magnetic properties that had interfered with the equipment on our boat.

We were then invited to return to the covered area where they would explain the research they were engaged in relating to human activity on our planet. I asked, "Can you all speak English or other human languages?"

"No, only some of us," the leader replied. "Only those of us that have been fitted with the human languages module, or chip I think you would call it. We don't think in your language, but in our own, but when you shouted English it switched on the translation feature in my module so that we could communicate."

"So, if I had shouted one of the other languages it would have switched to that and you would be able to understand us?"

"That is what we intend, but as you are the first earth beings we have met, we have not been able to try it before and I am delighted it works."

"How were you able to learn our languages, if you had never met any of us?"

"Oh, that's not difficult. We have methods of listening in to conversations on earth. In fact, much of our knowledge of humans is discovered by that method. Let me show you."

After some more whistles and clicks, four of the green beings appeared with what looked like laptops or tablets in three of their hands and a device like an aerial clasped to their heads. It was then that I noticed that the leader had a cuboid about the size of a matchbox on the side of his head whereas his four colleagues didn't have one. I assumed that little box was his human language translator.

We were invited to sit on the stools again and we each had one of the four assigned to us. One of the receptors (I don't know any other name for them) each of the beings held had a screen that we were invited to watch. The other receptors were panels with buttons or keys on them. Using their fourth hands, the operators pressed keys on each of their other sets and also moved their aerials into different positions. After a period of adjustment, the screen came to life and on it, I was able to see a map of the south-west of England. My operator showed me some arrow keys on one of his other panels and when I indicated the one pointing right, he moved it and we moved across the map, until I indicated he go north. In this way, we located the Thames somewhere near Henley. He looked at me and I pointed down. So, he went to his other panel and we zoomed in until I could see roads and houses. By minute adjustments, we focussed down on to the river and boat house. He then flicked another switch and we could hear people talking and a coach giving instructions to a foursome rowing on the river. I said this is where we did some of our training. The leader heard what I said and gave some instructions to my companion and he did something that started to scroll back the picture. I was asked how far back and I suggested four weeks or 28 days. Another button was pressed and we were back to the time Stella and I were training. And there we were on screen and I could hear what we were saying.

The leader explained that by studying human activity and listening to what was said, they had been able to interpret our language. They could also learn about our society and the way it functioned. He said that there was so much information they could collect that they had to select the most relevant to their understanding and they could do this by manipulating radio waves, light waves and even time.

When he had explained how sophisticated their operations were, I had an idea that I might be able to obtain information for my own purpose. I explained how we had no knowledge of my brother's whereabouts. I was asked whether there was a particular point where we might be able to locate him. I suggested his arrival at the airport for Quito in Ecuador about two years ago. The information was relayed to my operator and he immediately started pressing buttons, adjusting aerial and twiddling dials. His dexterity was amazing and in less than a minute I could see a plane touching down at Quito. Next, I saw passengers getting off and then I spotted Seb. The screen was frozen and I pointed out Seb. Then more zooming and Seb filled most of the screen.

I called Stella over and she looked over my shoulder. "That's Seb," she exclaimed, "where is he?"

I told her that was when he had just arrived in Quito. I turned to the leader and asked, "Is it possible to find out where he went and where he is now?"

"Certainly," came the reply. "Now we can look at the big screen" and he pointed to the wall, where Seb appeared almost life-size. With the help of the skill of the operator, we were able to watch Seb, who was highlighted in blue, as he met other people and visited various places. As the picture was speeded up, we were able to follow Seb into the country, to see him examining specimens, and talking to other explorers. In a few minutes, we covered several months. Although the operator lost him a couple of times, he was able to backtrack and relocate the blue highlighted figure of Seb. Twice the picture was slowed to real time pace and we could hear Seb speaking on his phone. The third time, he was speaking to our parents telling them of his plans to try somewhere different. This was our last communication with him and I told the leader as much. "Now we can trace where he went," was the reply.

We watched with growing apprehension as Seb and another explorer set out alone. Although the film (I don't think that's the right word again) was speeded up to many times the original speed, the operator never lost him and I began to realise that not only was Seb highlighted for us to see, but the operator somehow had him tagged. I don't know how many months had passed when we saw them go into a cave and the picture slowed so that we could hear them speaking.

I heard Seb say, "This face looks promising, perhaps we should try here in this seam." After what must have been several minutes, we saw them come out of the cave and stand well away. Then we heard an explosion and dust started pouring out of the cave. Seb and his friend, no I'll change that, his colleague, went back in. Our operator fast forwarded the picture often pausing, when each time we heard hammering. On one occasion, our operator zoomed out and showed us the surrounding country. We could see a forested or jungle area that started about two miles away and spread over many square miles. Fairly near the edge of this jungle, we spotted some indigenous people that looked like a hunting party.

On another occasion, Seb came out of the cave on his own with something in his hand that he clearly wanted to examine in the light. We zoomed in to inspect the object and one of our party exclaimed, "A massive diamond!" Perhaps a day later, the other explorer came out with his bags and equipment. I assumed they might need supplies and he was going to fetch some. He disappeared, didn't come back, there was no more hammering and no sign of Seb.

It must have been two days later that a few of the tribesmen climbed the hill above the cave. It was probably a good vantage point. Two of their number came to the mouth of the cave and then went in. Shortly after, one came running out and called to the others above him, wildly gesticulating. His fellows joined him and together they went into the cave. (If you hadn't realised, Pinky, we could not see into the cave, although the operator managed to show us the entrance.) Some of the party re-emerged, and in haste, returned to the jungle from which they came back with a crude form of stretcher. By this time, you will guess I was fearful for Seb and what would be brought out on the stretcher. After a while, the stretcher bearers came out with a body lying on the stretcher. Stella and I both gasped, even though we already had an idea what we would see. We zoomed in and we were able to see our badly injured brother, who had obviously sustained a horrible blow to his head. We thought he must be dead, but the leader of the green beings said, "He lives, see he is still blue," and it was so, although a much paler blue.

By watching further footage, we saw that the tribesmen took Seb to their village, where they cleaned and dressed his wound and cared for him. We were able to watch him gradually getting better, until he started to take part in some of their activities. I noticed that some of his movements were not properly coordinated and I wondered if he had suffered some brain damage. I also noticed that his blue colouring was much stronger and then the leader informed us that we were now observing real time pictures. So, Seb was still with the tribe. I asked if it was possible to obtain earth coordinates for the village and they were supplied almost instantly. Another surprise followed as I was presented with a sort of parchment, rather like rice paper, with the references printed on it.

I hadn't noticed that one or the beings had moved away. When he returned, he had something else to show us. He had managed to discover a way of looking into the cave. He told the leader something with some whistles and hoots which the leader translated. "We have found how your brother sustained his injury and we can show you, but you must be ready to see something shocking." He was right. While Seb's back was turned, the other explorer lifted his pick and struck Seb a resounding blow on the back of his head. He was knocked out and while he was lying there senseless, he was hit two or three times more with a hammer. The other man then rifled through Seb's belongings until he found the large diamond, then collected his belongings and left. That was when we saw him leaving the cave.

Seeing that all we girls were distressed the leader brought us each another of the drinks we had tried earlier. Those drinks must contain some healing herbs, because we all felt better for drinking them. I then noticed that the green beings also had drinks because they had also been upset by what they had witnessed. The leader explained that they knew from their previous research that some humans could be violent and this was an attribute that they could not understand as they were peace-loving beings.

As we tried to digest the astonishing things we had seen, the leader came to me and formerly wished us farewell. He said, "It is time for us to part as we need to return to LUNERA. In your boat, one of your empty bottles has been filled with liquid you have drunk while you have been with us. When you find your brother give him some, just a little on several occasions. He will sleep deeply each time, but he will gradually regain his former self and his brain should be healed. I don't know whether you will wish to be able to tell others what happened to your brother, but this memory stick, that can be plugged into your computer, has all the data stored on it showing the assault on your brother."

I replied, "That is so kind of you and it has been a delight to meet you and to learn so much about you. I think you are a lovely, generous and peaceful people. We shall never forget your hospitality, even though we shall find it difficult after we have left to believe that our meeting with you ever happened."

He had one more thing to tell us, "It is unlikely we shall ever meet again, but we may be able to see and hear you. If you feel that we are watching, hold this disk in front of you and you may be able to see us. When you get into your boat, you will gradually drift away from us. Don't start rowing for 30 minutes in your time. Your instruments will start functioning correctly and you will discover that four earth days have passed since you met us and that your position is nearer your destination than you expected. Also, when you arrive, you will have difficulty in convincing your people that you have rowed through a part of the sea that other vessels have found themselves deflected away from. Some may even talk about a phenomenon they call 'The Bermuda Triangle'."

Well, Pinky, it was exactly as he said. We reached Bermuda without mishap and close to record time. No one could understand how we had consumed so few of our rations yet looked so healthy.

When we returned to England, I set about organising a relief party to find Seb. It wasn't easy and I had to knock on a lot of doors, but we managed to find him and to bring him home. When we first found him, because of course I went with two others to find him, he didn't know who he was or what had happened to him. I gave him some of the drink and he slept, but woke up with some knowledge, recognising me and remembering some English words. After he had had more small doses, he began to piece things together. During his time with the tribe who rescued him, he had learned to speak in their language, so he was able to express my thanks to their chief for the way they had cared for him.

We now have him back with us and I have shown him what happened to him in the cave. We are now considering whether we can take any action against his attacker. I am not sure a court of law will find my evidence from such a strange source admissible.

With my very best wishes,
Your friend, Sophie Strangeway

[Dear Reader, Please note that in order to protect the lovely beings that we met on our adventure, I have given the name of their planet in anagram form. SS]

Similitude

Part1 – Past Unknown

"I don't think you've heard a word I was saying, Alistair. Have you got something on your mind? Is it girlfriend trouble?"

"Sorry, Moira. Did you say something?"

"I have been talking to you and you haven't taken a blind bit of notice. If you hadn't answered when you did, Brother, I was going to throw something at you. Is something worrying you? If not, perhaps you will come and have a look at these statistics with me."

"Certainly, I will, but I was thinking about something Dad said to me today. I'd better help you while I can, because it seems I may not be around here much longer."

"What do you mean, Al? He's not chucking you out, is he?"

"No, it's more like a promotion, but it could mean a massive upheaval to my life, just as I was feeling that I am getting back some stability after four years of university study."

"You'd better tell me what's going on."

"Well, it seems he is pleased with my performance with the business. He said that he had had good feedback from the tours I led, and he has decided to expand the travel agency and he wants me to be a partner."

"That's good, Al, isn't it? What are you agonising about?"

"That's only part of the story. Dad has seen premises in Oldbury, near Birmingham, and he wants me to head-up a branch there. Apparently, there is a flat above for me to live in. I shall have to recruit and train staff, find a manager and set up the whole kaboodle. He also wants me to train tour guides to accompany parties on European holidays and undertake some trips myself to secure new holidays."

"But that's marvellous, you really deserve it. Aren't you pleased?"

"Yes, Moira, but can I do it? It's really daunting. I'm not sure where I shall start. Dad said he would help, but he is expecting me to take the lead."

"You know you have the ability to analyse and solve problems and you already know how the business operates both home and abroad. I'm sure it is your personal skills and your wide knowledge of languages that made you so successful with the overseas trips. You speak French, German and Spanish fluently and have a fair knowledge of other languages, including Italian. Do you know any Asian languages, because you may have customers who want to visit India, Pakistan, Sri Lanka and more exotic places?"

"But what sort of life shall I have shut away in a flat during the evenings and not knowing anyone?"

"Your interpersonal skills will soon enable you to find some friends. Remember, you knew no one when you went to university and you won't be that far from home. Oldbury is not so far from Stoke; you can either use M5 and M6 or go through Wolverhampton to Cannock and pick up the M6 there. And, when I am back at college in Worcester next term, you will be nearer me; only about five junctions on the M5."

Alistair, 24, and Moira, 22, were the children of Gordon and Jeanne Scott, and although they had spent many nights in student accommodation in the last three years, they still regarded the family house in Stoke-on-Trent, or more precisely, Newcastle-under-Lyme, as home. After spending four years studying modern languages at university, including a year in France, Alistair had worked for nine months in his father's travel agency during which time he led several parties of tourists on European holidays. His skill in languages stemmed from his mother's frequent use of French, her mother tongue, and Italian around the house as her children grew up.

Moira had one term left of her degree course, after which she would take up a teaching post at a secondary school in Bromsgrove where she had spent several weeks during her course on 'teaching practice'. She had been fortunate in securing the post when a vacancy to teach history and geography became available. She would take up the post at the start of term in September.

*

By October, the new branch had been established, a manager and part-time staff had been recruited and the agency had begun taking bookings for individual holidays and package tours, including river and sea cruises, to Europe and beyond. Alistair had appointed three potential tour leaders who he was training and had plans to take each on a tour with him before he invited them to lead on their own. After a hectic period when he seemed to spend every waking hour, and some sleeping hours as well when his brain would not rest, on the business, he felt he needed to widen his interests. He discovered that the library in West Bromwich was holding a series of historical lectures, so he set aside a Thursday evening each week to attend them.

On the third evening as the lecture was about to begin, a young lady arrived out of breath and sat on the vacant chair beside him. Three-quarters of an hour later, after a fascinating talk about the pyramids of Giza, the young lady turned to Alistair and remarked, "How wonderful, I should love to visit the pyramids, but I don't suppose I ever will."

"Why is that? What would stop you?"

"Well, I don't know how I would go about it. Who would I go with, because I don't think I could go alone? I'm sure it would be far too costly, even if there were package holidays available."

With his travel agency manner readily available, Alistair replied, "It might not cost as much as you think. I have recently opened a new travel agency locally and I have been thinking of establishing just such a tour as you envisage. If you would like to give me your name and a contact address or telephone number, I could send you details when we announce it."

So began a conversation, which developed initially into a regular weekly meeting, and before the series of lectures had finished, a post-lecture drink together. Alistair soon realised that Julie Summers surname described the atmosphere he felt while they were together even as autumn was making way for winter. He was exercising his mind to think of a way to extend their friendship beyond the end of the lecture series when Julie surprised him by suggesting that he could talk about the places he had visited as a tour guide. "After all," she said, "the organisers have been asking for volunteers to lead a series of lectures. Why don't you offer as next week is the last until after Christmas?"

"Well, I don't know, Julie. I'm not sure that I would have enough material and I'm certain people won't want to hear about me having to rescue tour members when they leave a camera on a train or forget to exchange currency. But I have been to some very beautiful and historically interesting places and have many photographs—many more than ever find their way into our brochures."

"Alistair!" she exclaimed. "I have a brilliant idea. If you can spare an extra evening each week, you could come home with me to Great Barr for a meal and then you could practise your lecture on me and my parents. I'm sure Mum and Dad would love it as they don't go out much since Mum had her slight stroke last January. They are always complaining there is nothing interesting on television and even the travel programmes are more about the presenter's escapades and the food they have helped to prepare than the history of the places they rush through."

Alistair wasn't sure about giving the lectures, but the thought of getting to know Julie better, and hopefully being accepted by her parents, was beguiling. He would need to undertake some research, but an afternoon trip into Birmingham, to spend time in museums and the more extensive library than that offered in West Brom, could be managed now the agency was functioning well. His fortnightly meetings with Moira in Bromsgrove would be opportunities to learn from her vast store of knowledge. He had already told his sister about Julie and she was waiting eagerly for Alistair to arrange for the two ladies to meet.

It needed only a tentative agreement to think about it for Julie to take action and volunteer his services to the organiser. At the last Thursday meeting before Christmas, it was announced that Alistair would lead a lecture series on historical holiday destinations starting in the middle of January, every week except for two dates when he would not be available as he would be leading tours to Rome and Vienna.

There was still one Thursday left of Moira's school term after the lectures had finished when her school would be giving a Christmas concert. Having received an invitation to attend the concert, Alistair suggested to Julie that she might like to join him and was delighted when she accepted. Having no role to play in the concert, Moira indulged herself in carefully observing the dynamics of the developing relationship between her brother and his lady friend.

On the evening of the next day, Alistair again drove to Bromsgrove to collect Moira so that she could stay with him in his two-bedroom flat for three nights before they returned to their family home on Christmas Eve. During the week between Christmas and New Year, the travel agency in Oldbury remained closed, although Alistair kept the online booking service operating from his parents' home. Nevertheless, there was time for family discussions and opportunities to meet friends whom neither sibling had seen for four months. Moira also made sure she had time to question Alistair about Julie.

Moira wanted to know how the pair had met, how long they had known each other and whether they had any joint future plans. She also asked, "In addition to attending lectures, what is Julie's occupation?"

"Julie works in the Town Hall in West Bromwich as assistant programme manager. She has responsibility with her boss for taking bookings from organisations wishing to use the hall and ensuring all functions, meetings or concerts proceed smoothly. I met her at the third lecture I attended when she rushed in, having worked late checking that all was set up for an event, and sat beside me."

"Is she the one for you and do you feel about her in the same way she feels about you?"

"I certainly enjoy her company. We have some good discussions and I am looking forward to getting to know her better. But what do you mean about the way she feels about me: you have hardly met her?"

"True, but I saw the way she looked at you. I think, to use a rather crude expression, she is quite willing to set her cap at you. Whose idea was it that you should give the lectures next term and… trying them out on her parents…?"

"I understand what you are implying, but we don't really know much about each other."

"You may not know much about her, but is she as ignorant about you? I hope you can get to know her better, because I like her."

*

By the time the date for his first lecture had arrived, Alistair had done sufficient research to feel fairly confident that he had enough material for his first three lectures. He had used the period at home with his sister to check historical and geographical facts and three Tuesday afternoons researching in Birmingham had proved most productive. At Julie's invitation, or was it her insistence, he had given a potted version of his talk to her parents.

Meeting Julie's parents and talking to them about places they had visited caused him to wonder about Julie's childhood. He estimated that they had probably been married for more than 40 years. It was when her father divulged the year when their foreign holidays were put on hold for a few years after the arrival of Julie that he was able to calculate that she was now probably about 23. He thought it strange that her father used the phrase 'the arrival of Julie' rather than saying 'when Julie was born'. He didn't like to look too closely, but he could not determine any physical resemblance between Julie and her parents, either in facial features or colouring. It made him remember Moira's query about how much he knew about Julie. He realised that he didn't know how old she was, her birthday, whether she had any siblings or whether she had always lived in Great Barr.

Alistair spent several hours until his next meeting with Julie, thinking how he should try to learn more about his friend. As he knew about her job, he decided to start there. At the end of his lecture, he accepted her congratulations and then commented, "You were in good time tonight. I assume you were not detained at the Town Hall." When she agreed that nothing had delayed her, he continued, "Did you go straight to that job when you left school?"

"Almost, after A levels, I joined a business studies course at Sandwell College. It was only a short course and as it was nearing the end one of the lecturers told me of the vacancy at the Town Hall."

"And the rest is history, as they say. Your father told me that one of his jobs sometimes required him to visit clients in Europe. Do you ever wish you had a job that took you abroad?"

"Not really. I have enjoyed foreign holidays, but I don't have the same interests or skills as Dad. That may not be surprising because he isn't my birth father." Seeing the surprise on Alistair's face, she explained, "I was adopted when I was a few days old. Mum and Dad had tried unsuccessfully for years to have children. Although they were quite old when I arrived, as they describe my adoption, they have been my wonderful parents for nearly 24 years. Before you ask, I don't know anything about my birth parents. I am a foundling, left in a carrier bag in a hospital corridor in Birmingham on the first of July; hence my name."

"I find that incredible, not that you were adopted, although that's something special, but that you will be 24 the day before I am 25."

"My adoption has been special. I don't think I could have been found by more caring people. Do you believe in fate or that some things are somehow predetermined?"

"Go on."

"Well, I nearly didn't attend that lecture when we met because I was late, but it was as though that chair next to you was waiting for me."

"Perhaps it was, because someone else was sitting there until two minutes before you came and then she spotted a friend and moved to another seat. If you hadn't been late, it would not have been vacant."

"I knew it; it feels as though I have been found again. I have had other boyfriends, but none that I can talk with like we talk and I never really felt comfortable with them. I didn't wait with eagerness for the next meeting with any of them as I do with you. Perhaps I shouldn't have said that; it sounds a bit forward of me."

"Let me put your mind at rest on that last point, as the feeling is mutual."

Feeling encouraged by the conversation Alistair resolved that he need have no qualms about letting the relationship develop. In fact, he began to think of ways to encourage its growth.

As he had a business appointment in his diary on the next Tuesday, he decided to make his weekly visit to Birmingham on the Monday. As his train from Sandwell and Dudley station was pulling into New Street, Birmingham, he saw Julie on another platform with a strange man who had his arm round her. She was facing him and the winter sun was full on her face. She was wearing a green anorak that she usually wore when she attended the lectures and although he could not see her hair, as she was wearing a cap, he felt sure it was her.

Leaving the train, he hurried up the staircase, across the bridge and descended to the neighbouring platform before he stopped to think what he was going to do or say. As he walked more slowly along the platform, a train arrived from the opposite direction to that of the one he had just left. He was quickly immersed in the movement of passengers alighting and embarking. By the time he was clear of the crowd, there was no sign of Julie.

Mystified and unsure of what he had seen, he made his way to the library, but found he had difficulty concentrating. Questions were going round in his head: *Was it Julie he had seen? If so, what was she doing in Birmingham and who was the man with her?*

When he saw Julie on Wednesday evening, he told her that he had done his research on Monday afternoon and asked her if she ever went to Birmingham. She replied that she didn't care for Brum and hadn't been there for at least six months. He didn't say anything about the girl he had seen, but decided to make his weekly trip to Brum again on Monday the next week.

A week later, as his train pulled into the station, he scanned the passengers waiting on the opposite platform. Yes, she was there again in the green coat, but this time alone. When he left his train, he had a good view of the girl in the green coat so, instead of rushing up the stairs, he got out his mobile and phoned Julie's number. When his call was answered, he realised the girl did not have a phone in her hand, but was still looking up the platform for her train.

It was a moment or two before Alistair realised that his phone had been answered and Julie was speaking. What was he to say? He had not told Julie about her 'double', although he realised now that the girl on the platform was not Julie. Thinking quickly he explained, "I have just had a strange experience and I think I need to talk to you about it. I am at New Street Station, having just arrived to spend a couple of hours in the library. What time do you finish work today and can I meet you when you leave?" They arranged to meet outside the Town Hall and go to a local coffee shop in the town centre, before Julie caught a later bus home.

"Now, Alistair, what was this strange experience you had that you needed to phone me about?" Julie asked as soon as they met.

"I'll tell you when we sit down with some refreshment, but you can answer me one thing. Have you a sister you haven't told me about?"

"No, but I must know why you ask."

When they had their drinks, Alistair explained. "I phoned you because I thought I saw you on a different station platform when my train reached Birmingham, but you didn't answer. Or at least the person I thought was you didn't answer. I saw her last week and I was sure it was you as she was wearing your green coat. I saw her last Monday, but I haven't seen her on Tuesdays. She looks so like you that I wondered if she was just your double or whether the two of you could be related as you don't know anything about your birth parents."

"Surely not! But how can we find out? We don't know who she is or where she lives or works and just because you think you have seen her twice doesn't mean she will be there again. And even if we do look alike it doesn't mean we are related."

"I know all that, but at least I know that she isn't you. That's why I phoned you to find out. I wonder if it was just coincidence that she was on that platform two Mondays in succession or if she regularly catches a train at that time. Perhaps I could catch an earlier train next week."

"What will you do if she is there? Stop her and say, 'Excuse me, who are you and do you know who your parents are?' You can hardly do that to a perfect stranger."

"No, I can't accost her like that. I shall have to think of something."

On the Friday following the above discussion, Julie's boss was surprised when she responded positively for someone to visit a firm in Birmingham City centre on the following Monday morning to discuss a possible booking of West Bromwich Town Hall. When Julie told Alistair that she would be visiting Brum on Monday, they arranged to meet in the concourse at New Street for a drink and a sandwich at midday while they looked out for the Julie replica.

About fifteen minutes before Alistair's usual train was due to arrive, he spotted the girl strolling towards her normal platform. Telling Julie to remain where she was sitting, he went purposefully towards the girl, who seeing him coming, smiled with the sort of smile that said, "I'm not sure whether I know you or not, but I had better smile in case we have met before." Taking the smile as a welcome sign, Alistair gave her his best travel agent's, 'Can I help you' type of greeting, saying, "Excuse me; I apologise for speaking to you as a complete stranger, but this is the third week I have seen you and I have been amazed at how much you resemble my girlfriend. She is just over there and I wonder if you would meet her and see if you get the impression that you are looking in a mirror, especially as she is wearing the same colour coat?"

"This sounds intriguing and as I have a few minutes spare, I'll play your game." They walked to where Julie was sitting. When the girl saw Julie, she gasped, as did Julie.

"You look just like me," said the girl. "Who are you?"

"I am Julie, but I do not know who my parents are as I was adopted almost at birth after I had been abandoned in a Waitrose carrier bag in a corridor of a hospital in Sutton Coldfield. What about you?"

"This is incredible. I think I had better sit down on something solid. I am June and I am also a foundling."

As the two girls were looking at each other with their mouths open like goldfish in a bowl, Alistair addressed June. "Could it be that you will be 24 on the next 30th of June and were you abandoned when a few hours old at a Birmingham hospital?"

"How did you know that?… Yes, wrapped in a blanket on a doorstep of Selly Oak hospital… Just a moment… Will you be 24, Julie, on the first of July?"

Both girls raised hands to their faces and exclaimed together, "We must be twin sisters!" Julie continued, "And we must have been born a few minutes apart, but one before midnight and the other after and given our names from the months in which we were born."

Alistair again interposed saying, "It seems a distinct possibility, but it will be necessary to make some investigations and perhaps take DNA tests. The first thing is to make sure you exchange addresses and telephone numbers as June has a train to catch."

"Oh, I had forgotten that. I'll catch the next one in an hour. Perhaps my boyfriend will be early and we can travel together."

Alistair looked around at other people on the station concourse and was pleased to see that the excitement of the two girls seemed not to have attracted attention. Perhaps, as stations are places where people often meet with a show of affection, the little scene enacted in front of him did not merit the interest of strangers.

Alistair continued, "If we have a few minutes together, perhaps we can start to make some plans to find out whether you truly are related. There may be some records at the hospitals where you were left and, although unlikely, there may be some help from your adoption papers. Which brings us on to telling your parents."

"Oh, yes," gasped Julie, "I don't know how they will take it. Being elderly now and Mum not well, I hope it will not be too much of a shock."

"I agree," responded June, "I hope my parents won't feel guilty thinking they should have made more enquiries about me when they adopted me. If they had, they may have discovered that another baby had been left at a different hospital at the same time."

"What we need to avoid is your parents finding out through the press, and newspaper and TV reporters turning up on the doorstep looking for a story."

"Oh, yes. Oh gosh!" exclaimed June. "Grant, my boyfriend, will be here shortly, and he is a reporter with the *Birmingham Mail*."

"Right," announced Alistair decidedly, "This calls for action. We can't keep this from him, but he must be silenced or rather sworn to secrecy for the time being. June, keep your eyes open; when you see him, point him out to me. What's his surname?"

"Bracewell; what shall we say?"

"Leave the introduction to me."

Alistair was thinking what he would say to Grant, whom he thought he had probably seen previously on the opposite station platform, when June saw him coming.

Alistair stepped out into the stream of commuters, thankfully not too busy or hurried, and accosted one of them, saying, "Excuse me, but I believe you are Grant Bracewell. My name is Alistair. Your friend June pointed you out to me. She did not catch the earlier train because she has had a bit of a shock and is being looked after by my girlfriend. If you will come with me; I must warn you that you may also have a shock."

Alistair took Grant to where the girls were sitting. When Grant saw them together, he stood still for several seconds looking first at one and then the other. Eventually, he turned to one of them and said hesitantly, "June, is there something wrong with my eyes? Am I really seeing double? Is this a trick and that is why you are both wearing identical coats? May I sit down?"

"This is no trick, Grant," replied June. "Thank you for recognising me. This is Julie, but Alistair will explain."

Alistair then told Grant how he had spotted him and June two weeks earlier on the platform and initially thought his own girlfriend had been two-timing him. He explained that the two girls were both foundlings, found in different hospitals a couple of hours apart. "Now, Grant, June has told us what your occupation is and you are probably already thinking there could be a great story for you to write, but we three are agreed that nothing can be disclosed until parents have been informed and further investigations undertaken, including DNA testing. So, we want you to swear to keep this discovery secret until it is confirmed that these two are long-lost identical twins. Then, when we say, you can have the exclusive story. Before you answer, just consider that your future relationship with June may depend on it."

Grant had continued to look at the two ladies while he listened to Alistair and after a pause, replied, "This is mind-blowing, who would have thought it? You have found each other without a search, which you would never have undertaken because you didn't know the other existed. Yes, I agree whole-heartedly, but to protect the exclusivity of the story, will you ensure secrecy will be kept by everyone else who will be involved in the investigation, including parents? And wouldn't it be advisable that you two are not seen together in public in case someone recognises one of you?"

Alistair suggested they find a table and over a cup of tea determine how they should make enquiries about the girls' births and parentage.

Part 2 – Past Uncovered

Two weeks later, all four were present when they were given the results of the DNA tests they had taken as early as they could after the meeting at New Street Station. They were told that there was a perfect match and that the ladies were indeed identical twins. Although they had suspected the outcome, they nevertheless needed a few minutes to absorb the news and to start thinking about the implications of such a discovery. They had not fully recovered their equilibrium before they were given further information. An additional match had been found; almost certainly an uncle. With the unusual name of Desmond Frobisher, they considered that it might be possible to trace him.

Grant turned investigative journalist and discovered Desmond, a pharmacist with his own independent chemist's shop, living in Solihull. Then he phoned Mr Frobisher, who was both surprised and delighted to learn that two nieces living in Birmingham were looking for him. Grant and Alistair visited him before they told June and Julie that he had been found. From him, they learned the story of the girls' births and abandonment. Having ascertained there was nothing unpleasant or sinister in the story, they arranged a meeting for the twins and their adopted parents so that Desmond could explain what happened on that night of June 30 and July 1.

After introductions had been made and Desmond had embraced each of the twins, he told his story. "I am the eldest of three siblings. I had two sisters, both sadly no longer with us, and we grew up with our parents in Hampshire. Our mother's parents lived in the Acocks Green area of Birmingham. When I was 19, I gained a place at Birmingham University and my grandparents welcomed me into their home while I pursued my studies in chemistry. Two years later, Edith, the elder of my sisters gained a place to train as a nurse at Queen Elizabeth's Hospital in Birmingham, where amongst other studies she trained in midwifery. After a visit home in February for our mother's birthday, Edith returned with news that May, my other sister, aged 18, was pregnant. The boyfriend had joined the Navy and disappeared before she knew her condition."

"She was distraught and didn't dare tell our parents and couldn't keep the pregnancy secret much longer. Could we find her a place to live in Brum? Then we had a bit of luck. Our grandfather was due to retire at the beginning of March and he and grandmother had decided to take a six-month round-the-world cruise while they were still young enough to enjoy it and while relatives were staying in their house. May had just completed a cookery course and had seen a post for a sous-chef in Edgbaston. With our parents' blessing, she also came to live in our grandparents' house to act as housekeeper for us."

"We went over and over the options for the baby and decided we would have to abandon it somewhere safe. We decided on hospitals and I was sent, as I had a car, to find a suitable location to leave the baby. When the baby arrived, with Edith assisting the birth, at about 11.30 pm, we wrapped her in a blanket and I took her to Selly Oak Hospital and left her on the doorstep. When I returned to Acocks Green, I was shocked to find that a second baby girl had just been born. I had to go out again, we didn't have another blanket, but we wrapped her in a towel and put her in a carrier bag. This time, I went to Good Hope Hospital in Sutton Coldfield where a door opened automatically, and I was able to leave the child in a corridor. If that's where you were found, then you are my nieces."

As soon as Desmond had finished, he was bombarded with questions. "What happened to our mother?" from June. "Did you ever enquire about us afterwards?" from Julie. "Are your parents still alive and do they know about the girls and where do they live?" from Julie's adopted parents. "Do you know anything about the girls' father?" Alistair asked.

Desmond held up his hand before replying, "I can answer some of your questions. Firstly, May died when on holiday with her fiancée, Norman. She was drowned when she was swimming in the sea and got caught in a riptide. Although Norman managed to recover her, she did not survive. She was 25. Second question: Yes, Edith took the opportunity several months later to ask some general questions when she heard of an abandoned baby boy being brought into the hospital where she was working. She did not wish to reveal her own involvement, but she did learn of two babies being abandoned in different hospitals on the same night and both had very quickly been adopted. She couldn't learn any more, but we often wondered what had become of you. Sadly, Edith died of an aggressive cancer when she was 31. Third question: Yes, my parents, your grandparents, are still alive and still living in Hampshire a few miles from Winchester. When Norman asked May to marry him, she shared her secret before she accepted and also told her parents when she informed them of the engagement. I think they will be delighted you have been found and be pleased to have two more grandchildren in addition to my kids. Your last question is the one I cannot give you information about other than to tell you that May only knew him for a very short time, before he started his Navy training. He was gone from her life with no forwarding address before she knew that she was pregnant."

Alistair thanked Desmond for providing so much information, and continued, "I am sure there will be many more questions and many more conversations, but…" here he paused and looked at everyone before saying, "I wonder if you would like Grant and myself to see if the Navy have any DNA records that might help us to trace the girls' father. Think carefully before you commission us to do so."

June and Julie looked at each other. After a pause, almost as though they were sharing their thoughts without speaking, June spoke for both of them. "It sounds as though he may not know we exist. Even if he can be traced, it will probably come as a shock to him that he has fathered twin girls. Will he remember our mother and how will he react when he discovers she is dead? Even if he accepts his fatherhood, will he want to meet us, and if he has a wife and family, will he want them to know of our existence?"

"Those concerns are exactly the reason why I asked you to think carefully," responded Alistair. "There is a risk. If we find him, he may be delighted to know about you both and wish to meet you, but, on the other hand, are you prepared to cope with another rejection?"

Julie turned to Desmond. "I assume you never met him. Did you know his name and did our mother ever talk about him? Do you think they might really have cared for each other, or did they just let things get out of hand?"

Desmond thought for a moment, then replied, "I never heard his name and I don't know whether Edith or my parents knew it. May did talk about him and I think that she regretted that she had not been able to tell him about her pregnancy. She often wondered if you had good lives and had been adopted by loving families. I remember an occasion when she was feeling rather low. She told me she wished she could have kept you and considered that your father would have been a good father. She also said that she was glad that he didn't know about you, because he would have felt that he would have had to give up the idea of a career in the Navy on which he had set his heart. I believe he joined up soon after he graduated from Oxford."

June and Julie looked at each other again, then both nodded, before June said, "I think we would like to meet him." Both then turned to their adopted parents and discovered that they were all smiling. Before they asked the question, Julie's dad said, "If you don't go ahead with this investigation, you will always wonder if you have missed something desirable. I say, 'Go for it.'"

The remaining parents together said, "Agreed, see what you can find out."

Part 3 – Past Revealed

After many phone calls, letters and interviews, Grant obtained information about a possible link to the twins. He was told, by a senior administrator, that there was an officer who had just retired whose DNA partially matched the sample from the girls. The administrator agreed to contact the officer and tell him that an enquirer with a DNA closely matching his would like to contact him. If the officer agreed to meet Grant to learn more a meeting could be arranged.

Two weeks later, Grant received an email from a Commander Robert Nelson (retired) saying that he would be interested to find out what information Grant had for him. An exchange of emails and phone calls resulted in the commander agreeing to drive up from the bungalow, to which he and his wife had retired on the banks of the River Severn at Bewdley, to a meeting in a hotel in the Hagley Road in Birmingham. During the discussions about the meeting, Grant had discovered that Robert Nelson had had a distinguished career and he asked if he could interview him for a newspaper article.

Alistair accompanied Grant to the meeting and after introductions, Alistair asked Robert, "To explain what this is all about, can I ask you if the name May Frobisher means anything to you?"

"May Frobisher?… Yes! I remember. She was a girl I was rather friendly with before I joined the Navy. Yet I was so keen on starting in the Navy that I neglected to write to her and time passed and I thought I could hardly contact her a year after I had last seen her. I assumed she would have another boyfriend by then. Do you know something about her and there has been mention of DNA? Where is this going?"

"This must come as a shock to you after so many years, but after you left, May discovered she was pregnant. She was desperate and didn't dare tell her parents. She was only 18. But her brother and older sister came to her rescue and arranged for her to join them in Birmingham where they were both students. At the time of the birth, she produced identical twin girls who her siblings abandoned in local hospitals. Both were adopted and have stayed in Birmingham with their adopted parents totally unaware of the existence of the other.”

“I think I can see where this is going. Their DNAs matched and mine also matches, making me their father. Yes, we did have one night together, just one. This is extraordinary. Am I right so far?”

“You are indeed. We can tell you how they found each other later, but we have sadly to tell you that their mother died in an accident when she was 25 and the mother’s sister is also dead. But the twins’ uncle, Desmond Frobisher, is alive and it was he who told us of the Navy connection that allowed us to find you.”

“This is marvellous news and could not have come at a better time. I am sure my wife, April, will be delighted. We have not been able to have any children and that did not matter while I was in the Navy as we could not have provided a stable home life. But as I have had to retire early, I’m not yet 48, we have to build a new life for ourselves. Having two daughters will give us a new focus. Can you tell me their names and how you are connected to them?”

“Before I tell you their names, sir, may ask if your retirement was occasioned by ill health? Please tell me you do not have a heart condition, because you have had one shock today already.”

“No, my ticker’s working well, thank you. I have some mobility difficulties and some balance problems with deafness in one ear. You’re not much good on board ship if you can’t stand up properly.”

“Ok, you will have to get used to having four females in your life whose names are April, May, June and Julie. June and Julie were named by hospital staff as June arrived just before midnight on the last day of June and Julie a few minutes after midnight. Grant is June’s boyfriend and my girl is Julie. Grant and I met on the day that the girls discovered each other on New Street Station in Birmingham.”

“Well, how about that! That’s amazing! I shall have to call them my calendar girls! How long ago did they meet?”

“We’ve been lucky. It’s taken us just under three months to find Desmond and trace you.”

“Three months! And you have been able to keep this out of the press. But Grant, you said you are a reporter.”

“That’s true, but I was sworn to secrecy on the understanding that I could have exclusive access to the facts to publish when allowed. June would not have it any other way as she did not want her parents to be upset or besieged by press or TV. I think that now we have found you and discovered that you are positive about acknowledging your relationship we could go ahead to a revealing. Would you be prepared to come back here with April in a couple of weeks to meet with your newly acquired family members?"

On Saturday, 2 July, the private function room of the same hotel in the Hagley Road had been booked for a gathering to celebrate two engagements. The couples getting engaged were Alistair Scott to Julie Summers and Grant Bracewell to June Martindale. Also present were Mr and Mrs Summers, Julie's adopted parents and Mr and Mrs Martindale who had brought up June. Other guests invited were Mr and Mrs Desmond Frobisher and their two sons who were accompanied by their girlfriends. Moira Scott and Trent Bracewell, siblings of the engaged young men were also present, as were Alistair's parents, but Grant's parents, who now lived in Australia, were unable to be there.

While refreshments were being brought in and guests were admiring the engagement rings, which were not identical, Desmond slipped out of the room. Only Alistair and Grant knew the reason for his departure. Guests continued to mingle, and Moira found herself next to Trent. They had just entered into conversation that might have been interesting to both, having never met before, when Desmond returned accompanied by a tall, handsome gentleman in full naval uniform and his beautiful wife. Desmond called for silence and then addressed the gathering.

"Ladies and Gentlemen, as the uncle of two delightful and identical young ladies here, I have the honour of introducing two further guests. I would like you to welcome Commander Robert Nelson and his wife April. Twenty-four years and two days ago, Robert became the father of twin daughters, but he only learned of their existence two weeks ago. June and Julie, you asked Alistair and Grant to search for your father. Well, as you may already have realised, they were successful. Robert and his wife are delighted that their marriage of more than twenty years is no longer childless. Come and meet them."

June and Julie needed no second invitation to detach themselves from their fiancés and greet the man who until that moment had been a mystery and of whose existence they had no knowledge.

After much chatter and more introductions, during which several people were heard to be working out who was related to whom, Robert asked if he could say a few words to the assembly. "I won't begin by saying, 'Ladies and Gentlemen', but rather address you as, 'family and friends'." Before he could continue, there was laughter and applause. "I think it was in a Gilbert and Sullivan Opera that one of the characters refers to a set of curious circumstances. It seems that this gathering would never have occurred, but for Alistair being suspicious that his girlfriend was playing him false when he thought he saw her with another man at a railway station. For my part and my wife's, we are most grateful that Alistair and Grant decided to embark on some detective work, which would not have been successful without DNA. I only knew my daughters' mother for a few weeks during which we indulged in a single one-night stand, when her parents were away for a night. Then my entry into the Navy separated us, and to my shame, I never contacted May again. Although I visited my parents occasionally, they had moved to another county shortly after I joined the Navy. About two years after leaving May, I met April, sort of turning the calendar back. Unfortunately, we have never been able to have children, but it seems now that I should turn the calendar forward. I recently retired from the Navy and April and I have been considering what should be our focus for the years to come. We rather think that focus will be family, if you will accept us. We already have a new occupation as Alistair has signed us up to help with the holiday tours he organises. Before I stop rambling on, I should like to say a public thank you to four people I have just met. From the bottom of my heart, I wish to thank Mr and Mrs Martindale and Mr and Mrs Summers for taking on the responsibility that should have been mine, of rearing June and Julie and making such a splendid job of it."

Two days later, the Monday edition of the *Birmingham Mail* carried the following front-page headline accompanied by a photograph of four happy smiling people.

TWIN GIRLS MEET FOR FIRST TIME TWENTY-THREE YEARS
AFTER THEIR BIRTH.

FATHER AND UNCLE ALSO TRACED.

Exclusive account by our reporter Grant Bracewell.

If you have turned to the end before reading the beginning, you will need to translate the code below to discover the newspaper headline with which the story concludes:

SGIRY IRVSG IVGUZ HIYZB VVISG-BGMVDG VNRG GHIRU ILU
GVVN HOIRT MRDG WVXZIG LHOZ VOXMF WMZ IFBGZU

For those who have difficulty solving simple codes, replace A with Z, B with
Y, C with X etc, throughout the alphabet and then read the result backwards.

The Mists of Time

Patrick Bolton yawned and realised that he had been driving for nearly six hours without more than a five-minute break. He had still more than 100 miles to travel, which according to his satnav would take well over another two hours. It was already after 6 p.m. and he had nowhere booked to stay the night. Perhaps he should look out for a B&B. He had intended to leave earlier, but the repair to the clutch on his car had been delayed.

Patrick had offered to make a delivery for his father who was an antiquarian bookseller. No, that could be misconstrued. His father, Arthur Bolton, was a dealer and seller of antique and rare books. A customer had ordered three sixteenth-century first editions and Patrick was taking the books to the client, intending to stay overnight in a local hostelry before returning the following day. Although this was the longest day of the year, the cloud level had increased and Patrick felt he should make a stop as soon as he could.

The road he was on was close to the coast here, but it would soon turn inland. The surrounding area was quite desolate with an occasional dwelling. He had just passed through a small hamlet when he spotted what looked like an old coaching inn. He slowed, spotted a parking area opposite and pulled up. The inn was prosaically named 'The Mists of Time' and there was a notice by the door offering bed and breakfast. He got out of the car, stretched and looked about him and saw that a mist was already beginning to roll in from the sea.

Inside the inn door, he found himself in a comfortable old-worldly environment and a welcoming innkeeper. Patrick asked if there was a vacancy for the night and was a little surprised by the reply.

"You wish to stay for one night. Have we a vacancy? Well, yes and no. You see, we has two rooms, but they be both booked. It be a longstanding booking, always for twenty-first June. However, if ye be interested, we has the tower room, we calls it, but 'tis said to be haunted, especially when the mist rolls in.

But that probably wouldn't bother a strong young man like you. Would ye like to see it?"

"Yes, please. It sounds intriguing." The landlord led the way, up one staircase, along a landing and then straight up a narrow wooden flight of stairs to a door at the top. The door gave access to a small cosy room with a very small bathroom attached. There was one window that looked out towards the sea. There was also a tree just outside the left end of the window.

Patrick asked the price and whether it was possible to get a meal anywhere. "I specks I can rustle you up a meal. I has a cottage pie with pays and carrots or I has some sausages with chips and pays."

"The cottage pie sounds great. I'd like to book the room for tonight, so I'll just fetch my bag from the car." Patrick also decided not to leave the package of books in the car.

When he entered the bar area, the landlord was ready to serve him a drink. "I'll just have a half of shandy to start with to clear my head after a long drive. It's very quiet here."

"Oh aye, it be early yet. Most folks round here work on the land and it be hay harvest now. Ah, that'll be Ted," as a tractor drove past. "He'll be here in half-hour with a dry throat. Others won't be far behind."

Patrick's meal, when it came, was very good and he enjoyed two glasses of wine with it. The inn began to fill as single men and men with their wives appeared to lubricate their throats after working outdoors most of the day. Amongst them was a big man with strong looking muscles. Patrick learned that he was the local blacksmith and he overheard a conversation between the blacksmith and the man the landlord had named Ted. Ted complained that he had been cutting the hay all day and had had to sharpen his scythe so many times that the blade was worn thin. The blacksmith agreed to make him a replacement on the following day. Many of the locals included Patrick in their conversations until he decided it was time to retire, but just before he left the gathering, the landlord offered him a liqueur on the house.

When he ascended to his room, he discovered that it was still not dark, although it had become very misty outside. His door closed quietly behind him and with his precious parcel in mind, he reached up to the bolt near the top of the door. He slid the bolt in place and went into his bathroom. When he came out, the door to his room looked different and then he realised there was no handle on the door. He was sure there had been one when he came in. He sat on the bed to try to work out how he would be able to leave the room. As he sat down the bed squeaked as though it said, "ouch." He got up, then sat down and it said, "ouch" again, so without thinking he said, "Sorry, did that hurt." He got a shock when the bed replied, "Yes, don't sit on the edge."

He stood up again and moved to the window and got another shock because the tree outside seemed to be moving. Or was it? Perhaps it was the effect of the liqueur affecting his sight. Perhaps he should wash his face so he went into the bathroom and ran some cold water into the basin. Finding it colder than he expected he ran the hot tap, but that ran cold. Thinking they were both cold, he said aloud, "Is there no hot water here?" And tried the first one again and it supplied hot water. But it was rather too hot, so he ran the second again and that also produced very hot water. Disconcerted, he exclaimed, "Either too cold or too hot; I just want a nice mix of the two." He tried one of the taps again and found the water just as he wished.

After he had washed, he went back to the window and received another shock. The tree definitely had moved; it was now in the centre of the window. Again he exclaimed aloud, "How did it get there? Is it moving or is the room moving?" No sooner had he uttered the thought that the room might be moving than there was a whirring sound and the room began to rotate. Soon the tree disappeared from view and after less than a minute, it appeared again in its original position and gradually passed across his line of sight disappearing again. The movement of the room began to make him feel dizzy. He shouted "Stop." Immediately, the whirring sound ceased and the room slowed until the tree was at rest where he had first seen it.

Wondering what further strange occurrences he might experience, he looked at the room more closely. As he gazed at the long wall against which the bed was placed, a dark mark appeared on it and then began to move leaving a trail behind it. Perhaps it was a form of writing but none that he had experienced. From where it began, it moved to the left, then dropped down before coming back below the first line. He was reminded of the writing that had appeared in Belshazzar's Feast. When it seemed to have finished, he turned to look behind him and realised there was a mirror on the opposite wall. In the mirror, it was easy to read the writing. He read, '*Welcome visitor. Greetings from your room. We hopes you will sleep well. You will be quite safe. Don't worry about our mystery games. We always has fun on summer solstice.*' He wasn't sure if the message reassured him or whether he should expect more surprises.

He read the message aloud and followed up with, "I wonder what further surprises there will be." His remark was answered by a host of laughing noises that seemed to come from many different parts of the room. He could hear noises coming from the bathroom, so he went to investigate. He was greeted with spurts of water being directed at him by the taps in the basin. He grabbed for a towel, but found that he wasn't wet. He had never experienced dry water before. Together with the chatter and laughter coming from all parts of the room, came some tapping on the window. He turned to look and saw that there was a host of bats seeming to fly in and out of somewhere just above his room. Facing the mirror again, he noticed a door next to it that he had not seen before. Could it be that it wasn't there previously? As there was a handle on it he went to try to open it, but was stopped by a voice that said, "No exit, beware sheer drop."

Thinking that he would never get any sleep in this room, his thoughts were answered by a commanding voice that seemed to come from above him, "Bedtime approaches, lights out in ten minutes." Without thinking, he responded, "But no lights are on." Again he got an immediate response with a brilliant flash of light from above him. He covered his eyes, but the intensity of the light gradually diminished and then started flickering. When he looked for the source of the light, he noticed that the ceiling was much lower that it had been a few minutes before and seemed to be getting lower. He was wondering how much lower it would descend when the voice spoke again, "Five minutes until blackout." He hastily prepared for the night and clambered into bed, taking care not to sit on the edge and was rewarded with a "Thank you for remembering."

Once in bed, which felt very comfortable, he began to review his predicament and realising that he received answers if he spoke aloud he called out, "How shall I open the door in the morning?" It worked; the door, he assumed it was the door, said, "Press the light switch." He hadn't noticed a light switch, but he saw there was one in the wall next to the door. It was just about within reach, but as he stretched his hand towards it, it disappeared and the light started flashing and flickering as though it was laughing at a great joke. Now the ceiling took centre stage calling, "Blackout starting." As he looked at the ceiling, he saw that a section near the window started to slide down in front of the window. As soon as the window was covered, the light switched itself off, everywhere became black and several voices whispered, "Good night, sweet dreams."

Patrick closed his eyes and almost immediately fell asleep. He slept very well and might have slept longer had not a voice somewhere said, "Good morning, you didn't tell us when you wished to start your day, but breakfast is being prepared." He felt quite refreshed and then remembered the communications of the previous evening, so he replied, "Thank you for the call and for yesterday evening's entertainment."

The reply came back, "Thank you, and hope you enjoyed it. We did, but now we shall have to wait another three years when the next summer solstice arrives in a year where the sum of the digits of the year is divisible by three."

No jokes were played on him when he went into the bathroom. When he was ready to leave, he realised that there was still no handle on the door. He looked for the light switch, again nothing. He scratched his head while he considered. He pulled back the bolt on the door, then spoke aloud, "One more joke? Mr Light, please reveal your switch."

"Certainly, sir," the light switch appeared where it showed itself briefly the previous evening. Patrick touched the switch and the door handle revealed itself. He put his hand on the handle, turned it, opened the door, stood in the doorway facing the room and with as much solemnity as he could muster addressed the bed, "Mr Bed, thank you for the most restful night I have had in many years. Goodbye everyone." He then bowed and went down to his breakfast and fancied he heard gentle clapping behind him.

He followed his nose to find a splendid breakfast awaiting him and the landlord ready to greet him. "Congratulations on your timing, sir. Your breakfast is just ready. I hope you slept well. You didn't have any difficulty opening your door this morning? I only ask, because we has to rescue most of our guests who use that room."

"None at all, I had a most comfortable night's sleep and shall enjoy telling my friends and relatives about my sojourn in your fine establishment."

"Ah, I be right glad about that. I had a feeling when ye arrived that you was special somehow. Before ye go, would you kindly sign our visitors' book?"

"I shall be delighted." He signed the book and then added, "Thank you for the most exceptional summer solstice experience."

Patrick returned to his car with his overnight bag and his precious cargo and continued his journey, reflecting as he went on the extraordinary happenings of the previous night. Was it the effect of that liqueur or was that place enchanted?

He found his father's client without difficulty, delivered the package, checked that the books met with approval and had a pleasant half an hour's chat with the recipient. He then started on his return journey.

It was just before 1 p.m. that Patrick realised that he was approaching the inn called 'The Mists of Time', but fortunately, there was no mist at this time of day. Should he stop for refreshment? He arrived at what he thought was the place, but there was no inn, only a convenience store. He stopped the car and got out to look around. Hearing another vehicle approaching, he turned to see a tractor, which pulled in and stopped behind his car. He recognised the driver as Ted with whom he had chatted the day before. Ted nodded and commented on the weather. "I nearly forgot I was told to collect some items on my way home. Are you going into the shop? It's not normally busy at this time of day and Sid usually has a pie or some sandwiches available. He might even have a take-away cottage pie; he makes the best in these parts just like his dad and granddad before him."

By the time he had finished his speech, they had both reached the door. Sid greeted Ted with "Had a good morning, Ted?"

"Aye, I cut the ten acre field today. To think it used to take my great granddad Ted three days to do that with his scythe and he were a quick worker, but he didn't half get though his blades."

He was soon served and then Sid turned to Patrick. "Now, can I help you, sir?"

"Well, yes, I thought there was an inn around these parts called 'The Mists of Time'."

"Aye, there was, but time caught up with it. It was sorely missed by the folks around here when it was pulled down, but that was after part of it collapsed. It was the tower room what came down. That room was supposed to be haunted. I've got a picture of it here if ye'd like to see it."

"I certainly would. When did it collapse?"

"Interesting you should ask that. It were twenty-first of June 1956. Some say there was something significant about the date. Here's the picture and that's my dad and his dad standing outside it in about 1930."

"Oh yes, just as I expected. I feel almost as though I have visited it before. The date; summer solstice, date divisible by three and the digits add up to 21. Was it misty by any chance that day?"

"Well, how would you know that? It was a terrible mist that night, a ship ran aground up the coast from here. You looking at that counter? It's used for the post office now, but it used to be the bar of the inn."

"Ted told me on the way in that you do a take-away cottage pie and he recommended it as being the best in the area."

"Almost ready, can you wait? Would you like a coffee?"

"Thank you, that would be most welcome. I still have about six hours of driving ahead of me and some refreshment would prepare me well for the journey. Do you have any further information about the inn?"

"There is a rumour that on the summer solstice, strange occurrences take place and they seem to be most prevalent on misty evenings in years in which the date is divisible by three."

"Like last night?"

"Why, yes. Very few folks round here will have ventured out yesterday evening. I think your pie should be ready now."

He returned a few minutes later with the pie and also a small bottle. "There you are, sir. May I offer you this bottle of liqueur which is made to an old family recipe, with my compliments? And would you also do me the honour of signing our visitors' book?"

Patrick felt he could hardly refuse to sign the book even though he was feeling more and more confused by the events of the past twenty hours. When he took the book, it looked identical to the one he had signed earlier in the day. However, it was not the same as his signature was not in it, although the first entry was in the year 2000. He signed, wrote in the date 22 June 2019 and passed the book back and watched as a strange expression came over the face of the shopkeeper, who reached under the counter and pulled out an ancient visitors' book. He turned over the pages of the book which appeared the same as the one Patrick had just signed but older.

The shopkeeper exclaimed, "It's uncanny. Look at this entry of 1902 and look at the comment my ancestor wrote beside it."

Patrick looked at the entry he had made that morning. Beside it, the landlord had written, "The only one to survive the tower room curse!" The two men looked at each other and seeing the glint in Sid's eye, Patrick felt there was some understanding shared by them, but he could not immediately define what it was.

As he returned to his car, he met Ted coming back to the shop. "Forget my own head one of these days. You bought some cottage pie, I see. Oh, is that some of Sid's liqueur? Take my advice; don't drink any of that unless you have nothing to do for twenty-four hours. It be mighty strong."

"Thanks for the warning."

Patrick sat in his car for a moment, hoping the coffee would not be as potent as the liqueur. He looked behind him at the back seat and noticed that his briefcase had slipped onto the floor. He then put on his seat belt, started the engine and a sound very similar to one he had heard recently seemed to say, "Very comfortable this back seat, just like a bed. Please drive carefully."

Dear Reader, I hope you have enjoyed this story. Please don't try to find explanations for the strange events Patrick encountered. He returned home safely, but could never understand what had happened to him on that summer solstice, but realised that it would forever remain a mist... ery.

The Parcel

Armed with knives and scissors, retired Colonel Monty (christened Montgomery) Edwards and his wife Margaret (usually called Maggie) sat opposite each other at the kitchen table. Between them was a pile of half oranges from which the juice, pith and pips had been removed. These were Seville oranges which the pair was preparing for their annual marmalade making. They were part way through cutting the peal into small pieces.

The only sounds were the clack of their scissors and quiet music coming from their radio. They worked quietly until Monty spoke, "You know, we have done this task so many times, yet there is a newness this year. The first day of a new month, the second month of a new year and the first time in this house. I know you have lived here for six months, but as I had to complete a tour of duty in Cyprus before I could join you in the middle of December, everything seems new. I still have much to discover about the area in which we now live."

Maggie responded, "That's right. It could be quite exciting; I have started a list of places we might explore and one or two people have suggested pubs that are worth visiting where the meals are good." She broke off for a moment, then said, "Was that the doorbell or the radio?"

"I don't know, I didn't hear the bell, but I'll go and have a look."

Monty came back carrying a parcel. "This must have been left by a courier. It was on the doorstep and there was a van driving off down the road. It is addressed to you. Is it a late item you ordered for Christmas?"

"I don't know," replied Maggie. "I am not expecting anything, and I've not done any online shopping recently. Let me see... It certainly seems to be addressed to me. The address is correct—Mrs M Edwards, 27 St Margaret's Road. Yes, well I suppose we had better see what is in it."

"Let us see first if we can learn anything from the outside," suggested Monty. "Has it got any indication where it came from or what it might contain?"

"Nothing, as far as I can see," responded Maggie, turning it over and looking on all six sides. "It's quite a neat cuboid and firm, as though it might contain a tin or a large book. The only clue on the outside is the label with the name of the courier and with my name and address. Perhaps we should open it very carefully. Nobody would want to send you anything nasty and tried to fool us by putting Mrs as the recipient, would they?"

"You are right. I can't think of anyone who knows where I have retired to and would wish me ill. The send-off I had gave me the impression that I was well regarded and everyone wished me a happy future. Nevertheless, although it is probably harmless and legit, it may be wise for us to take care."

The orange-peel snipping had been forgotten as they examined the parcel and decided where to start opening it. They unwrapped one layer successfully and discovered a bulky brown A5 envelope above another layer of wrapping.

"Perhaps we should look at the envelope before we go any further," suggested Monty. He picked it up carefully and examined it. "There is nothing written on it, other than Mary." He then put it to his nose. "I can't smell anything like explosive. It has been sealed, but with a clean warm knife we may be able to ease it open." While Maggie went to fetch a knife, Monty mused, "Why Mary? Has this parcel been mis-delivered or has the sender got the address wrong? What was the name of the people who used to live here?"

Before using the knife, he paused to try to remember the name of the previous occupants of the house who had been gone eight months. Maggie reminded him. "It was John and… erm… Rosalie Cook."

"No Mary there, so here goes. Gently and carefully, Monty! We could do with a forensic scientist to do this, but it is working. Here we are—open. Let's see what's inside." He was about to pull out the contents but stopped. "Maggie, could you pass me one of those Covid masks and put one on yourself, in case whatever is inside is contaminated with something that reacts with air to create poisonous fumes."

As Maggie passed him a mask, she commented, "I can tell you have served in war zones recently and haven't lost your suspicious mind."

Equipped with mask and disposable gloves that Maggie had also produced, Monty gradually withdrew a paper and bank notes. Retaining the gloves, he counted the bank notes. "There is £500 here in a mix of £50, £20, £10 and £5 notes. Whatever must be in the main package? Perhaps we had better look at the paper next." He carefully opened the paper on which was typed a letter.

Together they read:

31A Riverside, S-by-S
Dear Mary,

I realise that it is more than two years since I last contacted you. I thought I had lost your address, but found it on a scrap of paper I was about to throw out before leaving here for a spell overseas. It is because I shall be leaving the country within a few days that I am making bold to ask for your assistance. It is better that I don't mention my date of departure or my destination. The parcel with this letter needs to go to Duncan Kingsley at the Red Lion in Portsmouth. Unfortunately, he will not arrive until 14 February, by which time I shall no longer be in the country, and I do not know his movements until that date. Accordingly, the favour I am asking is that you despatch the parcel to the Red Lion on the 12th. I enclose sufficient to cover the courier's cost and a fee as usual to reward you for your trouble. As on previous occasions I am sending the money in used bank notes rather than a cheque which might be traceable. I am sure you understand. Many thanks for your help. Roger Black.

Monty and Maggie looked at each other after they had read the letter and both asked at the same time, "What do you make of that?"

"On one hand, it seems genuine in that he is in a bit of a fix, but on the other, it also sounds a bit fishy," said Maggie.

"I agree," responded Monty. "It seems a very large reward for what she has been asked to do, and why used bank notes and not a cheque or even a bank transfer? It also sounds as though she has assisted in some way previously although not recently. It makes me even more curious as to what is in the parcel."

"Also, Monty, how did he get hold of our name and address? I wonder if he has part of the address wrong."

"That's a good thought, Maggie. Do we have a telephone directory of the area?"

"Yes, we do. I'll fetch it." When she returned, Maggie was already turning over the pages until she reached the residential properties on the 'E' page. She found Edwards and scanned down until she found 'Edwards, C M 127 St. Margaret's Road'. "Look at this, Monty," exclaimed Maggie excitedly. "I bet this is where the parcel should have gone. What do we do now, having opened it?"

"What options do we have, Maggie? We can try to put everything back together and take it to No 127. Do we just leave it on the doorstep or enquire if Mary Edwards lives there? No, we can't do that because it would show that we had opened it as 'Mary' was only on the envelope inside and in the letter. Do we contact the courier and say the parcel does not belong to us and suggest they return it to the sender? Unless they have some code on the label or some other record, they would need to open it and discover what we did. How would they interpret the letter and its enclosure and what would happen to the money? In that we have both thought there is something fishy about the matter, do we seek advice elsewhere, such as the police or security services? Have we accidentally stumbled on a crime being committed or are we dramatizing something that is quite innocent?"

"I'm not sure, but I would be much happier taking it to No. 127 if I knew that it was all quite innocent. Do you know anyone who might advise us amongst the contacts you have made during your service career? We do have a few days as the package doesn't have to be forwarded until the twelfth, in eleven days' time. Naughty thought! We could forward it ourselves and keep the money."

"I suppose we could, but if there is some criminal activity involved, in addition to ours, those responsible will get away with it, whatever it is. But you make a good point about the time factor. Hey! Just a moment, what was the address on the letter from Roger Black? Notice everything was typed, no best wishes, no signature. Here we are: 31A Riverside, S-by-S. Where is S-by-S?"

"S-by-S. Where could that be? I know I'm normally pretty good on place names, in crosswords or quizzes. Let's think… I think I've got it; how about Shoreham-by-Sea, Monty?"

"That sounds possible. Perhaps we should look at 'street map' on the internet. Could you do that while I get a roadmap?"

A few minutes search and Monty had located Shoreham-by-Sea. "It is between Brighton and Worthing; tomorrow I have to visit an army base west of Brighton. I shall only be a few minutes away from Shoreham. Have you found anything, Maggie?"

"I can't find a Riverside, but there is a River Close. I can't get any house numbers on here?"

"Let me see. Ah yes, that should be quite easy to locate. Can you find a postcode?"

"Yes, here it is. I'll write it down."

"I have a feeling that 31A does not exist and if Duncan Kingsley does exist it may not be his true name."

Still pondering where the parcel left on the doorstep could have come from and what they should do with it, Monty and Maggie returned to their marmalade making.

The following morning, they were still undecided about what course of action they should take. They had discussed the situation, wondered if they should open the package inside the parcel, considered what it might contain but had come to no conclusion. They examined the package, turned it around, felt it, shook it but still their curiosity was not satisfied. They debated whether to mention it to their next-door neighbour with whom they were on very good terms. Miss Bryant was a single lady, having never married after her fiancé had died following a mountaineering accident. They thought she might know who the C M Edwards at number 127 was, but if she didn't they would whet her curiosity and being by nature inquisitive she might seek information they didn't at this stage wish to divulge. Did the M of C M Edwards stand for Mary or was C M a husband or partner? They decided to wait until Monty had made his visit to Brighton and Shoreham-by-Sea.

When Monty returned, he did have some news to impart. As he had made good time on his outward journey, he went first to Shoreham. He found River Close, but as he had suspected, no number 31A. He noticed a man working in his garden, so he stopped to talk to him. The man had lived in the area for more than twenty years, had never heard of Riverside and knew no one answering to the name of Roger Black. He did mention that some of the homes in Shoreham were second homes which were occasionally sublet for short periods.

Monty told Maggie that he then made his way to the army base, where after he had discharged the business that was the purpose of his visit, he had been fortunate to encounter a member of the Military Police. "I told him about the parcel and how we were suspicious about it, especially now that I had been unable to locate the address from which it was supposed to have been sent. Major Cowans invited me to have coffee with him and contacted his superior to join us. When they had heard the story and our concerns and dilemma as to how to proceed, they advised that we should not open the package until we had a police officer and perhaps a lawyer present. When the superior officer, whose name I didn't catch, learned where we lived, he realised that he had a good contact in the Hastings police. He left Major Cowans and myself to finish our coffee while he went to get the contact's details. When he returned, he said he had contacted Superintendent Hemmings who had agreed to visit us. The Super now has our telephone number and will call us to make an appointment to visit us."

"Well done, Monty," enthused Maggie, "it could get quite exciting now. If there is a crime in progress, I wonder if we shall hear all the details and know if we have helped to solve it."

"Don't get too excited, dear, it may all be quite harmless and above board, although I can't believe there is nothing unusual about the parcel. If the police think the matter is suspicious, they will have more resources and time to investigate than we could ever muster. We now have to wait for Superintendent Hemmings, or someone he assigns to the case, to get in touch."

Monty and Maggie had just settled down to an afternoon cup of tea when the phone rang. Monty answered the call and heard, "Is that Colonel Edwards? This is Detective Inspector Frost from East Sussex police. I have been asked to contact you about a suspicious parcel you have received. Is it convenient to call on you in about 30 minute's time? I shall have DC Cousins with me." When Monty had confirmed he was happy with the arrangement, he warned Maggie of the visitors they could expect shortly.

When 35 minutes later, the doorbell rang, Monty admitted the two police officers who both showed their ID cards. He noticed with satisfaction that they had arrived in an unmarked police car; he also spotted the blue lights fitted behind the front grill of the Range Rover on the drive. When introductions had been exchanged and cups of tea offered and accepted, DI Frost began the conversation. "I understand that you have received a parcel that you were not expecting and which you believe was sent here in error. I believe it was only after you started to examine it that you became convinced that you were not the intended recipients. Correct?" Seeing both of the householders nodding, he continued, "Could you tell me why you thought it had been left at the wrong house and what made you sufficiently suspicious to refer it to the police."

Monty, supported with comments from Maggie, explained how the parcel arrived and how they removed the outer covering, trying not to leave fingerprints, before discovering the letter and cash, which he showed to DI Frost. He also explained that after reading the letter, they decided not to open the accompanying package. Monty described his attempt to find the address from which the letter appeared to have been sent.

"I think we may need to open the package but we shall not do that here. That is a task for the forensic department." Turning to his companion, he asked if he had a large enough evidence bag to take the package, the letter, cash and outer covering. He then told the couple that he would give them an official receipt for the items.

The next comment from DI Frost took Monty and Maggie by surprise. "You have told us about the theories you have explored, but it seems to me, there is one you have not considered. You have assumed that the parcel was left at the wrong address although the name on the label was correct. Have you considered that it was left at the intended address and the error was in the name? Was it addressed to Mrs Edwards to deflect thinking from the fact that the intended recipient was Colonel Edwards? It could be that the sender believed, Mrs Edwards, that your name is Mary and had not realised that three other names begin MAR, namely Martha, Margaret and Marjorie or Margery."

Monty just managed to contain himself, but nevertheless in barely controlled anger responded, "Are you suggesting, Inspector, that we are involved in some criminal activity?"

"No, I am not suggesting that. But we do need to consider that someone else may wish us to believe that you are intermediaries to some criminal enterprise. Of course, we do not yet know what the package contains. What might be in it? Stolen goods such as jewellery, rare stamps, coins or books? Or drugs or perhaps explosives or poison?"

"Oh, I see," interjected Maggie. "You think it possible someone may wish to harm us. I did ask Monty if he knew anyone who might have a grudge against him, but he didn't think so."

"Maybe we could explore that thought a little. Colonel, did you have occasion to discipline anyone or even be involved in a court martial while you were in the service?"

"Well, yes, several times I have needed to reprimand private soldiers and occasionally, I have spoken to junior officers about their conduct. And, yes, I was a member of a court martial about, let me see, seven or eight years ago."

"Can you explain the nature of that trial, such as offence, evidence, sentence and even name of the offender?"

"The name I shall have difficulty with, but the Army will have the record. The offence I do remember; it was to do with the theft of armaments and ammunition from the stores. We didn't get to the end of the trail, but I believe the offender was being paid quite handsomely by gangsters operating in Nigeria or Angola or even possibly Sudan. He was dismissed from the Force. He was not the only culprit, but we were not able to build a case against anyone else, so he was the only one convicted. He had also previously been the subject of discipline over thefts from the stores and from other personnel. Thinking back, I believe his name was Lance-Corporal Rogers, but I cannot recall his first name."

"Thank you for that, Colonel. I think we will investigate that lead. If we were to be in a position to prosecute you for, say, receiving stolen goods, or if you suffered an injury ex-Lance-Corporal Rogers may view your misfortune with some satisfaction and view it as revenge for having his name blackened by you. I can imagine he would like you to know that he had taken his revenge and to make sure he signed himself Roger Black."

"Do you really think that is what this is about?"

"No, but it is one line of investigation for us to pursue. I need to keep an open mind. No case is complete until we have all the facts supported by appropriate evidence. We shall have other lines of enquiry to consider when the package is open."

"What about Duncan Kingsley and the Red Lion in Portsmouth?" Maggie asked. "Presumably, he will expect to collect a parcel in a few days' time."

"That's quite correct, Mrs Edwards. We shall be making some discreet enquiries about that establishment and its guests. Also, I haven't forgotten about the other Edwards in this road. On that last point, I am sure you will be interested to know if there is a Mary Edwards living in your road. Now, we shall take the parcel and its contents with us and ask the forensic boffins to see what they can discover."

Maggie asked, "Will you be able to let us know what is in the package?"

"Possibly, if it is harmless; if we cannot trace any other intended recipient, I assume it will be returned to you, including the £500. However, if the contents are deemed sensitive and may be important evidence in a criminal investigation we may not be able to divulge what they are, probably not until the investigation has been completed."

DI Frost and his companion took all the elements of the parcel with them when they left, with the assurance that they would keep in touch, and tell them as much as they could. On the way back to their base, the two policemen planned their next moves. DC Cousins was given the task of checking on C M Edwards while his senior colleague lost very little time in taking the parcel to the forensic lab. He watched as the package was delicately opened to reveal what at first sight appeared to be a leather-bound book.

DI Frost initially thought that it might be a rare and valuable first edition, but then one of the scientists indicated that the book opened, unusually, down the spine. Inside there was a cavity. From this recess, a scientist carefully withdrew just a new pair of socks. She then discovered a further sock, but this was not new and was not empty. Inside it were two packets. Then the companion to the old sock was revealed—this also contained a packet. Finally, another new pair of socks was drawn out.

When the packets were opened, the reason for the concealment became clear. The hoard consisted of seven rings with large solitaire diamonds, a very fine natural pearl necklace, several gemstones, eight early gold sovereigns and a rolled up small painting. DI Frost realised that this hoard may have come from one or more thefts and he immediately arranged for enquiries to be made into recent break-ins of jewellers, large houses and art collections. He was pondering aloud about the planned destination of the hoard and what the contact, who was to collect it from the Red Lion, was required to do with it. The young lady scientist, with small enough hands to be able to reach into the cavity in the book, heard him and volunteered another discovery. "Sir, I believe the answer to that question might be here." She had continued examining the book and noticed that what appeared to be a decoration in the cover was a small switch. When twisted slightly, a flap in the cover could be opened. Inside was a piece of paper. She handed this to the inspector saying as she did so, "I found this switch by accident, I don't know if the paper provides any clues."

"Thank you, show me the switch." When he had seen it, he continued. "It's very neat, isn't it; you did well to spot that. Now, let's see what the paper tells us." He examined the paper, reading the message on it, then commented, "This is most revealing. I think we are onto something big. I need to report to the Super and he may decide to set up an operation which will require careful planning: timing will be important."

When DI Frost returned to base, he arrived a couple of minutes after DC Cousins, who reported that he had made some discoveries. "I checked electoral rolls and the last two census returns. Mrs C M Edwards is a widow and the C M stands for Colleen Mary. Her husband died just over two years ago, about eighteen months after she married for the second time. I think he was an early Covid victim. Previously she was Mrs Black. Go back ten years and there was a

Mr Black and an adopted son who seems to have taken the surname Black with a first name of Roger. I have checked with funeral directors and one says they cremated a Stanley Black nine years ago. I have also begun searching press reports and crime data. I found reference to a Roger Black who has recently been released from prison where he spent four years of an eight-year sentence for his part in supplying arms to a rebel organisation in Nigeria."

"Well done, I remember that case, maybe he has put his hand to the same plough as before. That seems to put the colonel and his wife completely in the clear. I have a meeting with the Super in five minutes. You had better come with me and then I can tell both of you what I have discovered."

In Superintendent Hemmings' office, DI Frost explained all the information that had been assembled then revealed what had been typed on the paper inside the phoney book. He read from the paper: *D, follow these instructions to the letter. Take the contents of the hiding place in the book. Place all the socks plus contents in your luggage. Don't remove anything from the socks. When you have read all these instructions memorise them and destroy this paper. Parcel up the empty book securely and send it to Major Webster at 31A—you know the real address. Tomorrow 15th February, go to Southampton airport where a seat on the 10.30 flight to Belfast has been booked for you as Jonathan Green—make sure you have your ID in that name. When you arrive in Belfast, you must make you way to Dublin during which time you will become Connor O'Dowd. You will make your way to our contact in West Dublin where you will meet Dr Kelly and hand over the consignment you are carrying. Return immediately to Belfast, find a B&B for the night and phone Steph to report your location and get further instruction. R.*

The Super listened carefully then asked, "Do we know where the contents of those socks came from?"

DI Frost responded by saying that he had asked DC Cousins to arrange for checks of recent thefts of similar items and if information was found to report to this room. DI Frost was then asked if he had formulated any suggestions for proceeding. DI Frost replied, "Yes, sir, may I suggest that the package be returned to its original condition with replacement items in the socks. I think we could reduce the cash to £100. The package can then be sent, via Mrs C M Edwards, to this Duncan Kingsley at The Red Lion. We need to put the Red Lion under constant observation in the hope of identifying this courier who presumably will have booked a room at the hostelry. If we miss him, we have a second chance at the airport, where we shall have another officer waiting to board the same flight. I suggest, sir, that we put two tails on him and inform our Irish colleagues with whom I understand, notwithstanding Brexit, we have very good relations. I imagine the Irish police will be pleased to know of Dr Kelly's whereabouts and his activities if they do not already know him."

"That sounds a very good plan, get it organised. Now, what do you plan to do about Connor O'Dowd? Let the Irish pick him up?"

"No, sir, I think we should continue to tail him. Let him return to Northern Ireland. Then will come the tricky part of the exercise. We shall need to watch him like hawks as the time to detain him is when he is ready to return the empty phoney book which should by then have the correct address for 31A. As soon as we have that, we can lay siege to the instigator in this country. However, we do not yet know where the stolen items came from or how?"

He had barely finished speaking when the Super's telephone rang. Everyone kept still while the Super answered the call. He listened for a few seconds and then said, "Please send her in immediately." He then addressed the meeting saying, "This may answer your questions."

A young police constable entered with information. "I have found details of two recent thefts related to the items that Stuart, sorry, sir, DC Cousins asked me to investigate. One theft was of a large quantity of jewellery from a substantial property near Norwich and the other was from a National Trust Property in Essex where a collection of sovereigns of significant dates was stolen and a small painting was taken from its frame. I understand that the painting is highly prized and valuable as it was a small preparatory sketch of a landscape by John Constable. The Norfolk and Essex forces are certain that the two thefts were the work of the same small gang. One of the gang members has been identified and apprehended. He is on police bail, but hasn't yet revealed the names of his accomplices. His movements are being monitored in the hope that he will lead us to the mastermind behind this activity."

Having heard her report, the Super asked her to stay in case there were further tasks she might be able to perform. He then turned to DI Frost. "Having heard that report, do you have any further thoughts?"

"Yes, sir. We may have recovered the stolen goods, but I would not like that knowledge to leak out. The houses concerned will need to believe their valuables are still missing. Had they not accidentally fallen into our hands I think the jewellery items would have been broken up in the next few days. I would like to know where this Roger Black is. Is he still in this country or has he gone abroad? I doubt, even if we find the true location of 31A, he will be found there. Would this Steph, possibly wife, housekeeper or secretary know where he is? I have a sneaky suspicion that he might be not far from Dr Kelly in West Dublin. It may also be that Roger Black uses other names, one of which could be Major Webster."

"Good thinking. Now, constable, you wanted to say something?"

"Yes, sir, if I may. It may not be relevant, but the mention of Ireland reminded me of something. When DC Cousins asked me to help with the investigation of Mary Edwards, I looked at the prison reports of Roger Black. I viewed one document he had been required to sign. It was signed Roger Black, but something else has been written previously and heavily crossed out. I took the paper to the light and turned it over and although I could not read it clearly, I think it had said Brendan Rogers."

DI Frost exclaimed, "Lance-corporal Rogers, the man whose trial was witnessed by Colonel Edwards! The colonel couldn't remember the man's first name. I think we begin to see the complete picture. It looks as though we have intercepted a fund-raising exercise to raise money for arms, either to support insurgents in an African state, or heaven forbid, to re-arm a remnant of the Real IRA."

"Are you ready now to lay plans to give these malefactors a nasty surprise?" Superintendent Hemmings asked. Seeing nods of heads, he continued. "Right, put them into action, consult where you need to, particularly with the Irish, and good luck. Keep me fully informed."

The investigation began well. Duncan Kingsley led his 'tail' to Dr Kelly who was arrested the following day by the Irish police. By then Duncan Kingsley had been apprehended as he was making arrangements to send the 'book' to the address represented by 31A. When the police arrived at the Major Webster address, they found the place empty. They entered the building through a kitchen window and found sufficient evidence to suggest that the property had been vacated in a hurry. The occupants in their haste left the police with two pieces of useful information. The first was a telephone message that had not been deleted. It simply said, *Hi Steph, Connor here, mission accomplished, posting parcel shortly. I may have been followed. I saw a guy at Southampton airport and I think I saw him again in Belfast. If I don't phone again in half-an hour, you may need to leave quickly.*

The other piece of information was a notebook with some foreign addresses in it. The police informed colleagues in France, Spain and Italy and asked for the addresses to be checked. Most of the addresses produced nothing of help, but the search continued. Then the Italian police thought they might be on to something and asked if their English colleagues had any photographs. A rather poor quality prison photo of Roger Black was wired through to Rome, but it was sufficient to move the hunt forward.

Early in April, three people were lazing by the pool of a small rented villa in southern Italy enjoying the late afternoon sunshine. In the centre, lying on his back, was a man wearing just bathing trunks. He was in his late thirties with hair that had been very short, but had recently been allowed to grow. He was caressing the shoulder of a lady on his left who was wearing a two-piece swimsuit. The lady was a similar age and may have been his wife. However, on his other side was another lady, probably in her early 20s, wearing the scantiest of flesh-coloured bikinis. She rolled over towards the man, whispered something in his ear and placed her hand on his stomach.

If the man was contemplating his enjoyment of the forthcoming evening, those thoughts were suddenly interrupted by shouts from behind him. Roger Black aka Brendon Rogers aka Major Webster sat up and turned round to discover four armed policemen, no more than a cricket pitch length away, approaching at speed.

It was in the middle of April, just after Easter, that Monty Edwards took a telephone call from the police. It was DI Frost who asked if it was convenient for him to call on them. This time he came alone. "It may seem a long time since we last met, but we have been very busy. The parcel that came here by accident has enabled us to crack down on a terrorist activity in its infancy. In a little over two hours, identical statements will be issued to the press in London and Dublin. Those statements will inform the public that a conspiracy to arm insurgents to start a bombing and shooting campaign has been foiled and several arrests have been made. A simple mistake in addressing a parcel and a suspicious recipient enabled us to break up this gang before their plans had sufficiently advanced to create mayhem and death or injury to the public. You will be interested to know that the mastermind behind their organisation, a certain Roger Black, was an Irishman who for years had also operated under the name Brendon Rogers. The parcel contained valuable jewellery and other stolen goods that were going to be converted into arms. Mrs Mary Edwards is the mother by adoption of Roger

Black. She has helped the police with information, and although she will be charged with receiving stolen goods, will probably escape a custodial sentence. The remainder, especially as all have previously spent time behind bars, are likely to be required to spend a substantial number of years at His Majesty's Pleasure."

When One Door Closes

"Are all women perverse; is it in their nature to imply one thing and mean another?" Andrew Latham asked himself as he walked along Guernsey's Coast path. He had expected not to be walking alone but with his girlfriend of a year. He had arranged this long late Spring Bank holiday weekend trip for them to cement their relationship. They had been going steady for the last twelve months with visits to shows and the cinema, meals out and trips into the country. They had enjoyed mealtimes with both sets of parents.

When Andrew had been offered the post of deputy head at a middle school in the same town in which he was already teaching, he had put his name down to buy one of the new houses being built in a select cul-de-sac a few minutes' walk from his new school. He had consulted his girlfriend about fittings and colours, and she had suggested ideas for the layout of the garden. This holiday he had planned to take her to a beauty spot on the island and propose marriage and if she accepted, they would visit one of the jewellers in St Peter Port to choose a ring. But two days before they were due to leave England, she had told him that she had decided to spend the weekend with a girlfriend visiting Cornwall.

He felt he had been led up the garden path, only for her to bolt over the hedge at the bottom of the garden and send him back indoors. He felt he wanted to have nothing more to do with the female of his species. His mood was as black as the section of the path on which he was walking with trees in full leaf blotting out the sun. As he was approaching a bend on the path that led from Fermain Bay to St Peter Port he expected shortly to be able to view the sea at Soldiers' Bay. His reverie was broken by a crash and a cry.

Hurrying round the bend, he first saw a small dog by the side of the path. The dog was whimpering and seemed to be trapped. Reaching the dog where he could see down to the beach through the trees he heard a cry for help and spotted a young woman lying against a tree part way down the slope. "What's happened here?" He cried.

"Oh, please help," the woman responded. "My dog must have seen a rabbit or something and chased after it but has got caught in some netting. I was trying to release her, but the tuft of grass I was standing on suddenly gave way and I fell. I think I have hurt my foot."

"Are you securely wedged against that tree?"

"I think so, I don't think I can move."

"Well, don't try to move until I can help you. If you can wait, I'll try to release your dog. I can see the lead up here that you must have dropped when you fell. What is the dog's name?"

"It's Topsy."

"Ok, have courage, I'll be with you shortly."

Andrew then turned his attention to Topsy. "Now, Topsy, let's see what we can do for you. I'm Andy and I am going to help you get out of there. That's a good dog, just be quiet and try not to struggle. Oh, I can see where this wire goes, it's a pity I haven't any wire clippers but I think we can manage—it's so rusty in places I may be able break it. We'll do this together. I'll move this bit and bend that one and see if we can ease your leg through that loop. Yes, it's coming; just a little more bending and here we go and out comes your leg. Now let me help you out. There, my friend, you are free. Now, we will put your lead on again and tie you to this tree while I go and help your mistress. I'll just check your leg for abrasions. It looks alright. Good girl—oh, thank you, that was a lovely kiss." The last comment was in response to the dog licking his face as he bent to inspect the leg.

Next, Andrew turned his attention to rescuing the dog's mistress. She had fallen about five metres down the sloping hillside that was nearly vertical at the top. He could see some saplings and exposed tree roots that could give him hand holds as he descended to her position. Having reached her, he assessed how he could help her up the bank. But first he asked her name. "It is the same as yours, but Andrea."

"I think this is going to be rather tricky and we may need to get much more personal than would normally be the case on a first meeting. I shall need my hands to pull us up the hill, so if I hold on this tree root with one hand I can assist you with the other to climb on my back if you can hold me round my shoulders." After a few minutes of manoeuvring, they managed to get into a position to enable Andrew to start climbing back up grabbing hold of projecting roots and rocks.

When he regained the path, Andrea rolled off his back and tried to stand up, only to yell and collapse again. "I can't stand on my left foot, it's so painful."

"Let me assist you to that tree stump there. Now, sit down and let me have a look. Can you move your foot from side to side or backwards and forwards? No, I think you may have sprained it. I hope you haven't broken anything, but there are so many little bones in the foot. How far away do you live?"

"About half a mile from here, near Fort George; fortunately, it's not as far as town."

"Ok, Andrea, I am going to have to carry you on my back or else assist you to hop all the way home. But you will also have to hold Topsy's lead. Fortunately, you are not heavily built and I should be able to carry you, so we'll try that to start with you."

With Andrea on his back, with her holding Topsy's lead, they started the walk to her home. When they came to a point where the coast path met the end of a residential road, there was a bench. Carefully placing her on the bench, Andrew took a rest. Andrea fished in her pocket and found her mobile phone and found that she had a signal. "I'll call home and see if anyone can come and assist us."

Her mother answered and when she explained that she had hurt her foot and could not walk, her mother called Andrea's younger brother who offered to fetch her by car.

As Andrea sat on the bench, Andrew made sure that her left leg and foot were as comfortable as possible. Andrea assured him that the pain was easier and then asked, "Do you live on the island or are you just visiting?"

"I am here just for the weekend. I arrived on the early ferry this morning and I go back to Poole on the 6 p.m. on Monday. I left my car at the hotel at Fermain and decided to walk into town for coffee, with the intention of returning to the hotel later to book in. I shall be interested to see what has changed since I was last here about ten years ago. I used to come every other year for two weeks, but since my dad had an illness that made it difficult for him to travel any distance our Guernsey holidays ceased. I assume you are a local."

"Yes, born here, but I spent three years teacher training in Exeter which I completed last June, so even I found some changes when I returned."

"So, you are a teacher, in a school on the island? I am glad you are not a librarian."

"The primary school at St Martin, with just one half-term until I complete my first year. What do you do Andy and what have got against librarians?"

"I also teach, in a middle school in Wiltshire. I have just this coming half-term before I move to a deputy headship in another school three miles from my present one. As for librarians or at least one in that category…"

At that point, a car arrived, and the young driver joined them. Andrea introduced her brother Silas to Andrew who shook his hand and explained, "Your sister fell down the cliff, but fortunately, her fall was arrested by a tree. I am not sure how she did it, but she has hurt her foot and can't stand on it for the pain."

"You look as though you have been mud-sliding. Did you get dirty rescuing her?"

Andrea explained how they managed to claw their way back up to the path and also where Topsy was at the time. She pointed out that Andy had spotless white shorts and shirt when she first saw him as were hers before she fell down the cliff.

Silas asked Andrea, "Can you walk to the car?"

Andrew replied, "I'll carry her if you can open the passenger door as wide as you can."

When Andrea was in the car and Topsy had jumped into the back, indicating no problems with her leg, Andrew was ready to resume his walk, but had what he thought was a last word with Andrea. "I hope your foot recovers quickly and that you are fully fit for when school opens again, goodbye."

She called him back, "Please don't go, why don't you return to the house with us and have coffee there."

Silas also invited him to join them saying, "I am sure our mother will want to thank you for saving my sister. And you may get some funny looks in town wearing those dirty clothes."

"Well, thank you very much. I hadn't thought about my appearance." And at Silas's invitation, he joined Topsy on the back seat.

On arrival at the house, Andrea spotted her father in the front garden talking to a neighbour. "Look there's Dad and he is talking to Jenny from next door. She is a doctor at the hospital and works in the orthopaedic department."

Silas stopped the car and jumped out to speak to the pair in the garden, interrupting their conversation. Meanwhile, Andrew got out to help Andrea. By the time he had helped her to swivel round in the seat so that both legs were out of the car, Jenny the doctor was coming to meet them.

"Can we get her out of the car and then I can examine her?"

Andrew called Silas, "Do you know about a fireman's lift?" Seeing Silas looking blank, he put out both of his hands with one hand clasping the wrist of the other. "Now, you do the same and then grasp my free wrist and I do the same to you. Now, we have a seat for the patient. Fortunately, we are a good match in height."

They soon had Andrea out of the car and sitting on a bench in her parents' front garden. Jenny examined the foot carefully and gently and then pronounced, "I don't think anything is broken, there is no swelling, but I can't tell definitely without an X-ray. I think it is a sprain and there may be some bruising. I will bandage the foot to give it some support, you can also have some pain killers. Give it as much rest as you can."

Next Silas and Andrew helped the casualty round the side of the house to the back garden where they met Andrea's mother with coffee ready for them. Andrew was then properly introduced to Andrea's parents. Andrew apologised for his scruffy appearance, but when they looked at him more closely, they realised that it could not have been an easy rescue. Her father, Gerald Sim, suggested that he would take a walk to see where his daughter had fallen which prompted Andrew to remark that when he had released Topsy, he had intended to check why there was wire lying around, but that having rescued Andrea all he could think of was to get her home.

Mrs Sim turned to Silas. "You and Andrew are about the same height and build; do you have a spare pair of shorts and a shirt you could loan Andrew? I could then wash the sand and mud out of what he is wearing." She then offered Andrew the opportunity to have a shower and invited him to stay for lunch saying, "We usually have a ploughman's lunch on a Saturday because we never know if we will all be together at the same time. I believe Silas has a friend calling for him soon after 1 o'clock to play in a cricket match."

Andrew looked Silas up and down, "A fast bowler?" Seeing Silas nod, he continued, "An important match today?"

"Yes, it is Guernsey versus Hampshire Colts, but the visitors may have one or two in the team who have played for Hants first team. Do you play?" Andrew replied that he usually opened the batting for his village team.

The cricket conversation was left in abeyance while Andrew made himself look respectable. Andrea also managed to clean herself up, so that when Andrew returned, he had to do a double-take when he looked at her and realised that she was a very handsome young woman. He guessed she could not be more than 24 and although he avoided staring at her he mentally described her as a hazel-eyed brunette. He also noticed some dimples in her cheeks that he thought were probably accentuated when she laughed. He wondered if he dared tease her to see what effect it had upon her features.

They had their ploughman's lunch in the garden soon after noon and 30 minutes later, Silas decided he needed to make sure he had everything ready for when his friend called for him. It was then that Andrea remembered something and called to him, "O, Silas, I'm sorry, I said I would come and watch you today, but I don't know how I can."

Andrew, hearing what she said, offered, "I could take you, but I shall have to go back to the hotel to fetch my car. I wouldn't mind watching a bit of cricket. I haven't planned anything else for this afternoon."

"Will you? Really! I'd be ever so grateful, but I don't want to impose upon you anymore. I can see this foot is going to present me with some problems. Dad, I have just remembered I am on the rota to read the first lesson in tomorrow's morning service."

Andrew grinned and said, "Would you like me to carry you to the lectern in the way I carried you this morning? The pain might be easier by the morning, as long as you don't go dancing this evening. If I don't carry you, I could assist you to walk if you would like help." He was rewarded by a laughing grin that lit up Andrea's face in which her eyes sparkled.

Mrs Sim displayed her practical nature by saying, "Now, Andrea, you can pile the plates and remnants on to a tray and if Andrew would be kind enough to carry some through to the kitchen for me I will wash up and perhaps, Gerald, you could take our guest to reclaim his car. If you wish to join us in church tomorrow morning, Andrew, we would be delighted to welcome you and perhaps you would come to Sunday lunch."

"I would be very happy to join you tomorrow. Which church do you attend?"

"It's the town church, you can't miss it."

"I know it, but I don't think I have ever been inside. When we used to holiday here, if we went to a service it was usually the church in St Martin with 'La Grandmére' at the gate checking us all in."

"Is that what you thought La Grandmére du Chimquiêre did, Andy?" Andrea laughed.

"Well, as a small boy, I wondered what else she would do standing at the gate even if she was carved out of stone."

As Gerald gave Andrew a lift to Fermain, he asked, "Are you here on holiday on your own?"

"Unfortunately, I am. I had booked two nights for two of us but my companion pulled out on Thursday. The hotel was very understanding and has reduced my bill slightly and the ferry booking was for a standard car plus two occupants. Thank you for the lift. I think I could book in and put my bag in my room and return for Andrea. She did not seem to be in so much pain by the time we left."

He booked into the hotel, checked mealtimes and drove back to the Sim's house. On the way, he asked himself, *What do you think you are doing, Andrew? I thought you had decided not to get mixed up with another woman!*

Andrew and Andrea spent the afternoon together at the cricket match. The route Andrea chose avoided St Peter Port, but Andrew was surprised that as they passed the butterfly centre at Le Friquet, that he remembered, he noticed that it had been replaced by quite an extensive garden centre selling a wide range of goods. Before they left the car, Andrew asked, "Is anyone likely to quiz you about your companion? If you need to avoid an embarrassing situation, you could introduce me as a cousin on holiday from England."

"I could say that, although there is one character I would quite happily inform that you are my new boyfriend."

"I guess this is someone whose attention is not welcome to you, in which case I give you permission."

Their conversation during the match was quite wide ranging and they explored Andrew's memory of the island, exchanged experiences of teaching, hobbies and places they had visited on holidays. Eventually, Andrea plucked up courage to ask the question that had been on her mind for much of the day. "Do you usually go on holiday on your own, Andy?"

Andrew had wondered when that question would be asked and he had already decided that he would not prevaricate. "No, this is a first time for me to travel alone and it wasn't my intention. My companion pulled out two days before we were due to depart."

"Would it be indelicate to ask whether your companion was male or female?"

"I'll tell you plainly, but I'm not looking for sympathy. My girlfriend of more than a year was due to accompany me on what I hoped would be a rather special weekend, but she had other ideas as she told me that instead of coming with me, she had planned to spend some time with a girlfriend as they had decided to get married."

"What a rotten thing to do to you. I am surprised you were willing to spend any time with another girl."

"Actually, I had determined not to have anything more to do with women and I don't know why I got myself into this situation. But I do think this day has turned out much better than I had hoped, although for you, I am sure it wasn't how you had planned to enjoy yourself."

"Well, I was just thinking that I have been very lucky to have an escort to protect me from unwanted attention."

"Perhaps I can be indelicate now and ask if you have a steady boyfriend."

"No, I haven't. I spent time with a couple of boys when I was at college, but neither friendship developed into a relationship. When I started teaching, I determined not to encourage any attention from boys until I have finished my first year."

"Is that individual over by the scoreboard who has been watching us almost from the moment we arrived, one from whom you wish protection?"

"That's the one. Silas has warned me about him. He likes to boast about his conquests and it is believed that he has fathered more than one illegitimate child."

When the visiting team's innings closed after their 20 overs on 147 for 9 with Silas having taken 4 for 25, Andrew began to feel weary. Andrea noticed him trying to stifle a yawn and he had to admit that his early start to the day, that saw him rise before 4 a.m., was catching up on him. She suggested that they should go home while he was sufficiently awake to drive.

"Now, your admirer is still watching, so try to walk normally, but hang onto my hand for support and we will walk to the car hand-in-hand for his benefit."

Andrea was quick to respond and played her part by smiling as she looked at Andrew, so that he bent to say something in her ear. "He is taking it all in and doesn't look happy." Andrea laughed aloud, again smiling up at Andrew. In this manner, they reached the car.

On Sunday, Andrew joined the rest of the Sim family for the service in the town church at 10.30 and supported Andrea when she went forward to the lectern for her reading. When the service ended, he was introduced to some other members of the congregation as Andrea's rescuer as questions were asked about her injury. After the service, the two Andys had time to take a drive to Jerbourg Point to gaze out to sea where Sark was clearly visible and a dim outline of Jersey could also be identified. On the road back towards St Martin, Andrew noticed a house on the left and remarked that he remembered when it had been a restaurant or tea room.

Over a roast lunch, Andrea was complimented on her reading, which caused her to comment on the quality of Andrew's singing. Her father agreed, "I could hear him and I also heard some bass harmonies at times."

Andrew admitted that he could only remember some of the bass parts and then took the opportunity to change the subject by turning to Silas and asking, "How did the match finish yesterday? I'm sorry we didn't stay to the end but after my early start to the day my body was telling me that I needed to close my eyes for a few minutes."

"I'm sure you would have enjoyed it and the last over was really tense and full of drama. With six balls left, we needed four runs and had four wickets left. A run out on the first ball, which meant it was my turn to bat, but I was at the non-striker's end. Two runs were scored from the second ball, none from the third and then our number four, who had held the innings together, was bowled. If another wicket had fallen our opening bat, who had retired injured, would have been required to face the last ball. However, our number eleven snicked the penultimate ball of the match through the slips and we managed to run two. That gave us a win by two wickets with a ball to spare."

"So, you were left not out without facing a ball. I thought you bowled very well and took wickets at crucial times."

"Thank you, I thought you did well to protect my sister from the attentions of a somewhat dubious character."

"We were aware of him observing us, so we made sure that he saw us holding hands as we walked back to the car."

"Who was that, Silas?" Gerald asked.

"He is now referred to by some of the lads as Willy Fletcher the lecher. I guess he is looking for a new girlfriend. It seems he has dispensed with Jess Craig; I saw her in town the other day and from the look of her, I thought she must have been eating big meals with lots of carbohydrates or else she is shortly to add to the island's population. Willy asked me before the match if my sister would be coming. I didn't tell him she would be accompanied. He was clearly miffed when he saw Andy and wanted to know who he was, so I was a little inventive in my reply and said that she was with her boyfriend who was visiting from England. I then added, for good measure, that I thought they were quite serious."

When everyone had finished laughing, Silas addressed Andy, "How long will you be staying? I ask because we have a match on Wednesday evening, St Martin v. St Sampson, and we need to find a replacement opening bat. Do you fancy joining us as a guest?"

Andrew replied, "I would have loved to play but apart from having no kit and not having a reservation at the hotel, I must return tomorrow evening. My mother contacted me early this morning to say that my dad has been admitted to hospital and will be having open heart surgery on Tuesday. I feel I should be there to support Mother."

Mrs Sim, Joan, immediately responded to the news, "I am so sorry to hear that, I hope the surgery will be successful. We shall be thinking of you all. It is a pity you cannot stay on; I am sure kit could have been found for you and you would have been welcome to stay with us as we have a spare room."

The meal being over and everyone had helped with washing up, Andrea asked, "Have you any plans for this afternoon?"

"I had thought of visiting some of the places I remember, starting with Pleinmont, then L'Erée before following the coast road up to L'Ancresse or Chouet. Do you fancy a ride and do you know where there used to be orchids somewhere near Fort Grey?"

"I do know the orchid fields and I would love to come."

The Andys spent the afternoon together on their sight-seeing trip, finishing sitting on a bench overlooking the beaches at Grande Havre eating ice creams.

By the time Andrew had taken Andrea home, they had arranged to meet again the next day. On account of her injury, which seemed to be getting easier, Andrew ruled out shopping in St Peter Port, considering High Street and Le Pollet too steep, so they agreed to visit the Gold and Silversmiths near the end of the airport runway and then the complex at Le Friquet for lunch.

When Andrew arrived at the Sim's house at 10.30, he had already been to the Freesia Centre and presented both Andrea and Joan with bunches of the flowers. He said that rather than buying any to take home to his mother he had arranged for them to be sent by post.

The two spent an enjoyable day together and when they looked at the cosmetic jewellery on a stall, Andrew noticed that Andrea was attracted to a particular ring. He didn't say anything, but while waiting for their lunch order to arrive and with Andrea sitting down to rest her foot, Andrew revisited the stall and bought the ring.

Taking Andrea home, Andrew had sufficient time, before he booked in for his return ferry, to park the car for a final chat. They both agreed that they had thoroughly enjoyed the time they had spent together and promised to keep in touch exchanging the necessary details to be able to do so. Andrea told him that her mother had said that if he ever visited on his own again he was invited to stay at their house. Andrew then withdrew from his pocket the ring he had bought earlier and turning in his seat he said quite simply, "Andrea, I bought you a little present, partly as a keepsake to show my appreciation of your company these three days and partly for you to put on whichever finger you prefer if you wish to repel unwanted admirers."

She turned to him and replied, "Oh, thank you, Andy, its lovely and the one I would have chosen."

While she was looking at him, he said, "I shall have to take you home shortly and then go to the ferry, but I am not going to say goodbye, but wish you Au Revoir in this manner," and then gently pulled her to him for them to enjoy their first kiss.

Anyone who had observed them since they met on Saturday morning would be forgiven for believing that it may have been their first kiss, but it surely wouldn't be their last.

Sitting on the ferry, Andrew reflected on his short holiday and said to himself, "Maybe I was wrong and not all women are perverse after all."

Which Way to Die?

Detective Inspector Josh Carter was examining an evidence bag containing items that had been dumped behind the bushes in a layby on a B road in the county, when DC Julie Perrin entered his room. "What have you got there?" his colleague inquired.

"I'm not sure. Well, that's to say, I'm not sure what they would have been used for. Have a look and see if you have any ideas. They were found by an eleven-year-old boy when his family stopped in a layby and he got out for a pee. These tubes were dumped alongside some used syringes. The boy told his father who decided to call the police. While he was in the process of doing so, he spotted a patrol car and flagged it down. The officer collected the evidence. His report and the evidence bags have landed on my desk."

"They are rather small for the test tubes you would get in a chemistry lab, but I have seen some before. My sister-in-law is of a rather nervous disposition and she has consulted a homoeopath who prescribed some Bach flower remedies which are effective in treating emotional conditions such as bereavement, anxiety, anger and others. The remedies are little pills and they come in little glass tubes with screw tops like you have there. She also has a small homoeopathic first aid kit with remedies like arnica and hypericum that she carries in her handbag. I suppose the kit contains 20 or 30 of these little tubes, all carefully labelled."

"I don't think any of these have labels. Although, just a moment. Are those the screw tops you mentioned at the bottom of the bag?"

"Yes, that's right. Is anything written on the tops?"

"Let's see. I have a glove here so I can get some out. Here we are; now, what have we got? How well do you know homoeopathic remedies?"

"There are hundreds of them but I know some of the common ones. Ca: that could be calendula or cantharis, or could it be cannabis? He: there is a remedy called hepar sulph, but it could also stand for heroin. What's that one? Co: there is a remedy called colocynth, but what about cocaine? It looks as though there is some sort of residue in some of the tubes: it would be worth asking the lab to take a look. This one just has E. I can't think of a remedy beginning with E although I am pretty certain one of the Bach flower remedies is elm. But E could also be ecstasy."

"Are these tubes easy to obtain?"

"I am sure there are suppliers, but it might be worth checking homoeopaths or complementary health therapists to see if anyone has lost any."

"Good idea: can you get on to it? In the meantime…"

At that moment, the DI's phone rang. He listened for a few seconds and then asked questions and gave instructions. "Where is this? How long ago? Don't let anyone touch anything. Get the police body expert there. I'm on my way but update me if there is any more news." Turning to his colleague, he commanded, "You had better come with me. A woman has been found hanging in a barn. Don't know whether it is murder or suicide, discovered by sixteen year-old son."

When they reached the farm, a police patrol car and an ambulance were already there. The constable in attendance had done a good job in keeping everyone clear of the scene and was talking to the son who had discovered the body of his mother hanging from a beam in the barn. DI Carter immediately took control by questioning the lad, Clark Mercer. "I understand that you raised the alarm. Tell me when and how you made the discovery."

"Yes, sir. My dad and elder brother Gary went to the market early this morning to look at rams. Mum, my younger brother Giles and I had breakfast together and then I cycled into the nearby village to see a mate and returned about 11.30. When I found no one in the house, but the back door open, I called but receiving no answer I went looking. When I came to the barn, I saw Mum hanging there. I didn't know what to do so I phoned the police. I have since phoned Dad but could only leave a message on his answerphone. I don't know where Giles is, which is worrying as he is a bit simple and can't talk much and isn't good at looking after himself. Although he is twelve, he has a mental age of about four."

"Ok, lad, you have obviously had a nasty shock. Did you see anyone else around? And do you have people working on the farm?"

"I saw nobody, sir, and the two men that help us were not working at the farm today as it is market day."

"Thank you, Clark. I may want to ask you further questions later, but in the meantime, go with the constable here to the ambulance crew who will check you out for shock."

With the arrival of the police pathologist, the action moved inside the barn, as DI Carter, DC Perrin and Dr Foote examined the scene. They were shortly joined by the Scenes of Crime team, although at that stage it was not known if a crime had been committed. DI Carter stated, "I have doubts about this being a suicide; we won't know if she was suicidal until we have questioned her husband. I don't believe she could have jumped off that stool that is lying there conveniently, possibly to mislead us? It surely isn't tall enough. Have you boys seen all you need, and can we get her down?"

"Just before we do," interrupted DC Perrin. "What do you make of that barrel over there? The victim could not have stood on it, it is too far away, but could someone else have used it to put her up there?"

"Let's investigate that theory."

One of the team went to examine it and called back, "There are two muddy footprints on it, sir."

"Right, bring the body down carefully and then Dr Foote can examine her."

Before any action was taken, there was a commotion outside the barn and the constable appeared to say a very agitated farmer had just arrived.

DI Carter called for him to be brought in and went to meet him. When Farmer Mercer saw his wife hanging from the beam, he almost collapsed and would have fallen had not the inspector caught him. He then cried, "Surely, she didn't kill herself. I know she was dying, but I never thought she would do that."

DI Carter, still holding him, said quietly, "I don't think she did, but what do you mean that she was dying?"

Steadying himself the farmer replied, "She was diagnosed with a virulent form of cancer several months ago and she was told last week that she probably had less than two months to live."

DC Perrin came forward and quietly, sympathetically and efficiently guided Mr Mercer out of the barn and to the ambulance crew.

The body was returned to ground level and it did not take many minutes for Dr Foote to suggest the cause of death as strangling as there was bruising on her throat. "So, it seems we now have a murder investigation on our hands," commented DI Carter.

Leaving the SOC team to continue their investigation in the barn, DI Carter went outside to look around. As he emerged from the barn, he was met by Clark Mercer who asked to speak to him. "What is it, Clark?"

"Sir, I was worried about Giles, so I went searching for him and found him hiding behind a tractor in another barn. I asked him why he was hiding. He managed to reply saying, 'Nasty man, shouting, I frightened so I hided. Man came in car. I show you.' And let me take you to what he showed me."

The two of them walked round the side of the tractor shed where Clark showed the inspector some scratchings in the dust. Upon careful scrutiny, they were able to distinguish letters and figures which the inspector was able to recognise as a vehicle registration number.

"Well done, Giles!" exclaimed DI Carter. "Now, I wonder if this is where the car was parked. Look, he must have stepped out just there as he left a footprint and what's this?" As he spoke, he bent down and picked up a plastic bag with some little glass tubes in it. "This could have fallen out when he opened the door."

Later in the day, DI Carter called a team meeting with DC Perrin and two other DCs to review progress and to initiate further investigation. He reported that Mr Mercer had told him that three days earlier his wife had received a phone call from her estranged brother. She had not heard from her brother for at least five years when he accused her, bitterly and unjustly, of receiving more than her fair share of their father's estate. The brother was asking for a gift or a loan of a four-figure sum urgently. The evening before her death her eldest son overheard her on the phone. He heard her say, "I can't possibly lay my hands on £5000 cash and why is there such urgency?" and then he heard, "What do you mean; you're a dead man if you don't come up with the goods?"

DI Carter continued, "There are four lines of inquiry I want pursued. I want to speak to that brother, his name is Sean Robins, and I want to know if he visited the farm today. Secondly, I want the car traced—you already have the number and it has been circulated, but we may have to try to trace it by checking the DVLA database that could give us owner and make of vehicle. The son who gave us the number may be mentally retarded, but he may have given us our best clue. Thirdly, I want to know if a particular boot or shoe made that distinctive footprint. And I want to know more about these glass tubes—Julie is working on that."

Tasks were allocated to team members, but they were all told to keep aware of all the areas of investigation. "Finally," suggested DI Carter, "I will share one thought, which may turn out to be wide of the mark, but might be worth bearing in mind. Is Sean Robins mixed up with a drug distribution racket that has found a new way of marketing drugs? Does he want to get out, but is it going to cost him? Did he visit his sister to try to extract money from her, got angry with her and, possibly before he realised it, killed her and then hung her body up to make it look like suicide? Let me know if you discover anything. We meet again at this time tomorrow."

Late afternoon the following day, the team met again with the station sergeant also present. DC Perrin had sent a message to say that she was delayed but was on her way. DI Carter explained that he had asked Sergeant Coxon to be present as he may be able to make a contribution as he had extensive knowledge of local felons.

Josh Carter's first question was, "Have we any news on the car?"

"Yes, sir, I think so," replied one of the DCs. "We drew a blank initially on the DVLA database, but then we tried a 'D' instead of what we had thought was an 'O' and got a match. It belongs on a mini pick-up and is owned by a Sean Robins living in a village in the New Forest a few miles from Lymington. We only completed the search thirty minutes ago, so we haven't taken any action until you say go."

"Well done, Vishnu, that's a useful lead we can follow up tomorrow, perhaps pay an early morning call. Now, anything on the shoe?"

"Yes, sir, but not much help. It is a bog-standard trainer and there are many thousands of them and lots of outlets where they could be bought."

"Right, I think we can forget that unless Mr Robins' footwear, when we find him, contains traces of mud from the farm. Thanks for your effort, Ian."

"I don't think you'll get anywhere with that," commented Julie Perrin, who had just walked in. "My apologies for late arrival. I called at the hospital morgue to see Dr Foote. He wonders if sufficient pressure was exerted on Mrs Mercer to cause her death and whether shock in her weakened state was a contributory factor in extinguishing her life force. As I was about to leave, I was asked to examine a casualty that had just been brought in. He had been found close to drowning in Lymington Marina. He had been shot in the back, either before going into the water or after he was immersed. His name is Sean Robins. I waited until an officer arrived to keep a guard. The medics think he will live. But his shoes, trainers, had been washed clean."

"Thank you, Julie. I think things are moving forward and expanding. It seems that we may not be the only ones who have an interest in Mr Robins. It sounds as though he may be mixed up in something sinister. Have you had any luck on the glass tubes?"

"Yes, I have. I phoned my sister-in-law yesterday evening and she was able to give me the names of three homoeopaths in the area as well as a firm that supplies remedies. I struck lucky with the first one I phoned. She was delighted to help and was most surprised to learn that we knew she had lost some of her stock of new remedy tubes. She said that she orders them a hundred at a time, but doesn't use many as she has most common remedies already prepared or else gets very unusual ones from a central source. If she needs to prescribe a remedy she hasn't in stock, she can make it and then she will use one of her glass tubes. She needed to do this two days ago and was most surprised to find her stock of tubes depleted. I asked her if she could give me a list of clients, but she felt that to do so was unethical, so I asked if she had a client by the name of Sean Robins. That was a name she knew."

"It seems that Mr Robins is leaving quite a trail around the place. I wonder if he has some sort of machine that enables him to form pills from drugs supplied to him. Do we have the results of any analysis that has been made on the residues in those used tubes?"

Sergeant Coxon spoke up saying that he had received a call from the forensic lab that they hoped to be able to provide some results before the close of play. "Would you like me to phone them and see if they have any initial indications?"

"That would be most helpful," replied the boss. "It occurs to me that if Sean Robins told his masters that he wanted to stop playing their game, they may have decided that they would like to get their hands on his bat and ball. If they were involved in his shooting, they will know that he will not be returning home tonight, so this would be a suitable time to conduct a search. If we have an address, I think we should keep a watch on it overnight. Now, if someone comes into bat, do we wait until they have finished their innings and follow them back to the pavilion?"

Sergeant Coxon re-entered the room. "There are traces of cocaine, heroin and cannabis found so far and they are checking for amphetamine."

"Sir, may I make a suggestion?"

"Yes, what is it, Vishnu?"

"If Mr Robins met with his accident at Lymington Marina, is it possible the drugs come in that way by yacht or launch? Would it be worthwhile keeping a watch for the batsmen returning at the close of play?"

"Good thought. Sergeant, can we get warrants to search both Mr Robins' house, and if we have reason to need to do so, to examine a craft in the marina?"

By an hour after sunset, an unmarked police car was parked about sixty yards from Sean Robins' house with two officers in it. A similar disposition was arranged in sight of Lymington Marina. DI Carter was in mobile phone communication with both teams. Just before midnight he received a call from the car at the marina. "News, sir, it has been quite busy most of the evening, but it started to quieten down about half-an-hour ago. Nothing happened for a while, but we have just seen two men go to a hut or garage and have come out in a mini-pick-up. We think it could be the Robins car. Should we wait here or follow it?"

"Did these men carry anything with them?"

"Yes, sir, they walked under a streetlight and one was carrying a tool bag."

"Right, stay where you are. I'll alert our colleagues in the other car. That's quite clever, using his car to visit his house. Did they come from one of the craft moored in the marina?"

"We are pretty certain they did and we think it is one of three on the same slipway."

"Ok, keep watching and be ready for action when they return although I am not certain that is their plan. Also, see if you can identify their yacht."

DI Carter messaged the other crew to be watchful and to tell him if the mini arrived. Twenty minutes later, he received a call to say the mini had arrived and parked outside the house which had been in darkness from the time they arrived suggesting that it was unoccupied. Carter asked for a commentary on what was happening.

"They have gone round the side where there is a window obscured from the next building by a tree in full leaf… There's a light inside—I think it's a torch… They haven't thought to draw the curtains… I can see them at a cupboard and I think they are taking something out… One of them has gone further into the house as though he is still searching… Oh, he has come back—he has found what he wanted; some shopping bags. They obviously didn't come properly prepared… They are just coming out. Do you want us to arrest them for burglary?"

"No, not yet, Ian, but follow them as discretely as you can. I expect they will make for the marina. I'll meet you there, but keep in touch."

Ten minutes later, Ian's co-driver called his boss, "The mini has stopped, we think it may have broken down and Ian has gone to offer assistance. They have the bonnet up and the driver and Ian are looking at the engine."

DI Carter ascertained their location, and having given instructions to let him know if the pick-up started again, he set out to join them. Within two minutes, he received more intelligence when Vishnu called to say that he had spoken to a security guard at the marina. He had ascertained that the garage from which the mini emerged had been hired by the owners of the yacht 'The Firefly' and he had been shown the berth that was the current location of the yacht. Before he reached the last known position of the mini DI Carter decided to act on a hunch and asked for a recovery vehicle to be placed on stand-by.

On arrival at the stationary mini, he invited its occupants to get into his car, saying that he would place a Police Aware notice on the mini so that it could be recovered later. His 'guests' appeared decidedly uncomfortable when he stated that he would transfer their belongings into his car. Addressing them he remarked, "I am DI Carter. I can understand your nervousness about me identifying those items, because some are not yours, stolen from the house you broke into tonight and the others contain the tools you used to break in. We have it all on camera. I am placing you both under arrest and restraining you with handcuffs. You don't need to say anything until I formally charge you back at the station."

The officer who had accompanied Ian was about to transfer to DI Carter's car, when Ian suggested that he could bring the mini to the station. "How do you propose to do that?" Josh asked.

"I have a can of petrol in my car. We should be able to get it going once we have overcome its fuel starvation." After coughing and spluttering, the mini started when supplied with fuel.

Back at the police station, Sergeant Coxon welcomed the visitors who initially refused to give their names until the sergeant addressed one of them, "Well, Mr Freddie, 'fingers' Fisher! I haven't seen you for a couple of years. You were only in prison for a year this time, weren't you? What mischief brings you here today? And who is your friend?"

"I'm not telling you."

"No problem," said DI Carter. "But first, we'll charge you both with using a vehicle without permission, breaking into and entering a house and stealing items from it." He then read them their rights and continued, "And we shall probably be able to identify you when we search the yacht 'The Firefly'."

"We didn't take the car without permission—the owner leant it to us."

"Really? Having a bullet in the back and being left to drown is a most unusual way of granting someone permission to use their car, don't you think? Or were you using the car the previous day to visit a farm where a farmer's wife was later found hanging in a barn?"

"We don't know anything about a murder at a farm, honestly that wasn't us."

"Ok, we note what you have said, but you can be our guests in separate accommodation while we continue our investigations and consider whether either of you is to face a murder charge. Sergeant, please see they are made comfortable after they are searched and we'll return to interrogate them individually later. Oh, and invite them to undertake a drugs test; there was quite a pungent smell in the mini, which might also provide some fun for a sniffer dog."

When the men had been taken to the cells, Josh Carter dismissed his team to go to their beds, asking them to return for a meeting at 11.00 later in the morning. He then asked the duty sergeant if he had a patrol that could relieve Vishnu and his colleague so that a watch could be maintained on the yacht. Finally, before going home to his own bed he sent a message to Julie Perrin asking her to visit the hospital in the morning to see if she could obtain a statement from Sean Robins before joining the 11.00 meeting.

By the time the team met for their 11.00 meeting, search warrants had been issued for Sean Robins' house and the yacht 'The Firefly'. Search teams were organised, but before they set out Julie reported on her trip to the hospital. "Sean Robins was awake and fairly comfortable. The bullet has been recovered; it just missed his spine so he should be able to walk again. I have the bullet," she passed it across to Josh in an evidence bag, "so if we find a gun forensics should be able to tell if the gun fired it. Mr Robins struck me as being a rather pathetic little man, reminded me of a ferret. But he is not unintelligent, having been a chemical engineer, before he got himself mixed up with the drugs trade which he says he now regrets. We already know that he was estranged from his sister and two years ago his wife walked out on him."

"I asked him what he was doing at the Mercer's farm. He admitted that he went there to try to persuade his sister to give him £2000, but when she refused, he got angry. He grabbed her around her neck and shouted at her and intended to shake her, but she went limp in his hands. He let go of her and she fell to the ground. He expected her to get up and then he realised that she must be dead. Seeing a rope hanging from a beam gave him an idea. He was surprised how light she was when he picked her up. He then left as quickly as he could. The next morning, he went into Lymington—he was expected to supply some drugged pills or hand over money as an exit fee. He couldn't make the pills because he had lost the tubes to put them in and he didn't have any money. He told his masters on 'The Firefly' that he hadn't been able to borrow the money from his sister as she had died. He asked for more time and was told to get out. As he was leaving he felt a pain in his back and he fell into the sea. The next he knew he was in hospital."

"Do you believe him?"

"I think he is so frightened, both by the death of his sister—I don't think he knows of her illness—and the way the crooks treated him, that he wants to tell everything. I didn't ask him how he was recruited as he is clearly quite ill."

"Thank you, Julie. We will have him kept under observation and ask further questions later after we hear what our cage birds have to say. Now, let us undertake our searches."

The search of Sean Robins' house did not reveal much new information as useful evidence had already been removed during the night-time burglary and confiscated by DI Carter. 'The Firefly' on the other hand provided revelation of a sophisticated drugs racket, including lists of suppliers and vendors with locations and telephone numbers and a passport of the other detainee, a certain Ho Ching. In addition, a plainclothes officer on watch joined forces with a port security officer to question any visitors to the yacht, inviting them to leave their details 'for the owners to contact them when they return'. The two officers enjoyed observing the consternation and confusion that resulted from their invitation to provide identities.

When all the questioning had been completed, Freddie Fisher and Ho Ching were remanded in custody charged with taking a vehicle without permission, breaking and entering, theft and involvement in the procurement and supply of drugs. Ho Ching was also charged with attempted murder as a gun found on the yacht had his prints on it. Sean Robins was charged with attempting to extract money by intimidation, of involvement in the supply of drugs, theft from a homoeopath and, after discussion with the public prosecutor, the manslaughter of his sister.

As a result of the visitors' list compiled by the two officers at the marina, DI Carter's team spent a few happy hours detaining and questioning several drug vendors. 'The Firefly' was impounded awaiting clearance to send it to auction to raise finance for the 'Ill-Gotten Gains' Fund.